HOUSE-BOUND

Persephone Book N° 72
Published by Persephone Books Ltd 2007

First published October 1942 by Faber & Faber

Endpapers taken from a 1941 watercolour design by Eric Ravilious
(b. 1903, d. September 1942) for a textile commissioned
by the Cotton Board as a way of persuading cotton
manufacturers to produce economical fabrics in
wartime conditions.

Typeset in ITC Baskerville by Keystroke,
28 High Street, Tettenhall, Wolverhampton

Colour by Banbury Litho

Printed and bound by Biddles, King's Lynn

ISBN 978 1 903155 622

Persephone Books Ltd
59 Lamb's Conduit Street
London WC1N 3NB
020 7242 9292

www.persephonebooks.co.uk

HOUSE-BOUND

by

WINIFRED PECK

with a new afterword by the late

PENELOPE FITZGERALD

PERSEPHONE BOOKS
LONDON

'I must unlearn the pleasant ways I went'
Christina Rossetti

CONTENTS

HOUSE-BOUND

CHAPTER ONE
DOMESTIC EXODUS

And I was left alone,
She left me there alone.

A E Housman

It was as she stood in Mrs Loman's Registry Office for Domestic Servants that Rose Fairlaw suddenly realised what a useless and helpless woman she was. Up till that moment she had always assumed vaguely that she was a busy and useful member of society.

Mrs Loman, who cocked an appraising eye at Rose, even as she made acid efforts to stem the volubility of the stout lady who held her ear, had no such illusions. There, sitting against the wall on hard chairs were rows of ladies the very image of Mrs Fairlaw, waiting desperately for an interview. They all wore the same type of well-cut, well-worn tweeds, shoes, and gloves, and, beneath their well-bred self-restraint, the same hunted and hunting expression. For thirty years they had come to her office, as they wandered in the wilderness of domestic troubles, and most of them, in her eyes, deserved

the troubles they had and the half-crowns they paid her. They were, with their domestic ignorance, laxity, and tolerance of waste and impertinence, just as bad mistresses as their grandmothers had been with their severity and stinginess. Some of them, like this Mrs Fairlaw, had earned the reputation of a 'good place' by making few changes in their staff, but what was the good of imagining that this would secure them preferential treatment now, when in all her books Mrs Loman had but one candidate for the hundred vacant places, and she a daft old dirty body who would only go where there was a single gent!

'Well, I'll do the best I can for you, Mrs Lunga, that's all I can say!' Mrs Loman had barked out this conversational 'Amen' of registry offices four times already, in the hope that it would cut short the stout lady's voluble admonitions. Her patience was wearing as thin as the hairs of her pepper-and-salt fringe in the domestic crisis of this war. She had put up a brave fight for two years, but now, in the December of 1941, it looked as if she were going to be beaten at last.

'I should hope so, Mrs Loman!' The stout front of the distracted lady heaved beneath her lace jumper and loud check coat, and her voice fell into that Castleburgh intonation which she shunned so carefully in society. 'It's tomorrow forenoon my girls walk out on me, I hope you understand? Leaving me with no one, literally no one. You must send someone round tonight without fail! You'll not be expecting me to manage my house myself!'

'I don't know why not!' For the first time in her career Mrs Loman was stung, by the insolent tone of command, to lose her temper, and answer back a lady. 'Millions of women do just that, Mrs Lunga!'

'That's true, of course!' Rose succeeded the indignant Mrs Lunga to the counter opposite Mrs Loman. Her family had an amused tolerance for her habit of uttering her thoughts aloud, but Mrs Loman stared in surprise at this unusual greeting from Mrs Fairlaw. 'It's perfectly true that millions of women do, and I suppose we should imitate them, but then, of course, they haven't all got basements!'

'No, indeed, and what can I do for you, Mrs Fairlaw?' Mrs Loman ignored such generalisation, for, with a semi-royal memory, she was already reviewing Rose's history. A Miss Seriton of Seriton House, she'd been, who had married a sailor in the last war, and been left a widow with a baby girl. She had first come to Mrs Loman for under-servants for that big place, when she was trying to manage it for her invalid mother in the last war. Then her parents had died and she had married Mr Stuart Fairlaw, a widower with one little boy, and come to live in Castleburgh in that odd place of his called Laws House. 'Is that house of yours giving you trouble again? Rather unmanageable, isn't it?'

Rose winced a little at that phrase. How often her nurse had used it in the past, not so much with reference to the nurseries as to the odd assortment of children: her own dark, difficult Flora; Mickie, her charming, mocking stepson; and Tom her only child by her second marriage, who would certainly have been a peace-maker if he had not been a little young for the part in those days. And since then how many cooks, parlourmaids, and housemaids had not used that word as they gave notice!

'Part of it's old, of course, but it's all been modernised,' she pleaded. 'And before the war I had those three nice Mack sisters you got me from Inverness for five years. They only left to get married, and then you got me two delightful girls who were called up, if you remember? My husband thinks we should manage with two, as some of the rooms are shut now my family is away, you see.'

'And after that, surely, I suited you with two older women? Wasn't it that Highland cook, Catrine Smith, I got you, and she'll never see forty again. And that Jessie Mackay from Glasgow? I didn't know her, but she seemed a decent little house-tablemaid enough, and thirty-nine too!'

'Oh, yes! But she was so very, very Glasgow, you know!' Rose hoped that Mrs Loman realised the self-restraint she exercised in withholding the saga of Jessie's bad manners, self-assertion, and contempt for the costly simplicity of Rose's equipment, and uncrowded beautiful old furniture. 'She was always wanting lace tea-cloths, and small polished tables, and embroidered sheet slips – you know the sort of thing. But the real trouble is,' she added hastily, as Mrs Loman's fingers played indignantly with the vast volume before her at such inept complaints, 'that she's a socialist, a violent socialist, and she talks so bitterly about there being no more service after this war that she's persuaded Catrine to go into munitions with her. They say it's patriotism, and I hope it is, but I expect it's mostly nights out,' concluded Rose, in a muddled parlance which was perfectly intelligible to Mrs Loman. 'So I thought if you could just find me two maids till the spring –' All Rose's friends uttered this vague aspiration as hopefully as if there were any possible reason to believe that the coming of swallows and daffodils would solve the servant problem automatically.

'Two's hopeless, though I don't know if three's much better. I'm at my wits' end to supply all you ladies, as you know very well!' Mrs Loman began to flutter the leaves of the vast tome, which was believed to contain the names of all the maids who had ever passed through her hands, since she placed a scullery-maid at Balmoral in Queen Victoria's married life. 'When do you want them? You'll take three I suppose if I can get them? When do the others leave you?'

'They say they'll stay till after Christmas – I expect because of Christmas gifts and a day off,' replied Rose with weary cynicism, 'but that's only a week now.'

'Oh, well, then, we've a little time to look round!' Mrs Loman snapped her book shut with obvious relief. 'It's not as if you were alone yet, and I'm sure I'll do my best for you!' By that formula she still managed as a rule to convey a little hope to the hopeless, but Rose's mind was still under the spell of her sudden new illumination.

'But I don't think I can keep three maids again, Mrs Loman. We can't afford it, and there isn't really work enough to keep three women waiting on us in wartime. I shouldn't really feel it right. In fact I'm going home to think over what you said to that lady before me. If you can't get anyone I expect I had better try to manage for myself.'

'Oh, it's out of the question for you, Mrs Fairlaw!' Mrs

Loman might bristle up at a stout, jumped-up rich party from the suburbs, who'd probably done all her own work without any help before her husband made a fortune out of profiteering in the last war, but she had not moved so far with the times as to feel that ladies, real ladies, could be reduced to such straits. 'Why, you've not the experience, and if you'll pardon me you're not as young as you were.'

'Still, as you said, millions of women do!' Rose smiled as she quoted Mrs Loman's dictum. She looked young for her age, thought Mrs Loman, as she stood there in her blue tweeds, and pretty still with her wavy hair, and a white skin that still flushed becomingly as she talked. But why shouldn't people keep their looks when they had nothing to do but take care of themselves? But Mrs Fairlaw looked slim and frail too, for work at her age, and by rights Mrs Loman should have managed to get her some of those girls who liked to serve a lady of good family with pretty English ways. Only what hope was there with girls streaming away from service into the Services, and the Government doing nothing about the servant problem, and worse than nothing?

'Well I hope you won't be one of them, Mrs Fairlaw, and I'll do the best I can for you.' It was in Rose's favour that she recognised the 'Amen' at once this time, and resigned her place at the desk to the next lady in tweeds, who also obviously wanted new maids at once, as hers were called up.

'Millions of women!' murmured Rose to herself as she made her way down the dark stairs which smelt perpetually of cats and gas. 'What is there so special and sacred about any of us that we can't even try?'

'Rose dear! Are you talking to yourself? That's a very bad sign!' Rose awoke from her reverie to find a large shopping bag almost in her chest, and behind it, wearily climbing the stairs, her greatest friend, Linda Carr-Berwick. 'Are you interviewing an imaginary cook?'

'Very imaginary! Oh, Linda, don't go up there! There's a queue of almost thirty desperate employers, and though I've been waiting hours for my turn not one single maid came in, not even the old woman in blacks with a red nose who's cooked for all the gentry in Scotland!'

'Oh well, I won't!' Linda turned downward, with relief. 'I was only going up to ask for a kitchenmaid, so that I could tell my cook I'd tried. She knows, and I know, that there isn't a hope, but I always go if she looks like giving notice. I think this'll count, don't you? Rose, let's be rips and go and have coffee together somewhere! We never see each other often enough now!'

There is in northern cities a shining freshness of thin, crisp air on autumn mornings, and something of that characteristic is shared by their middle-aged inhabitants. Life is not lived at the pace of London in pre-war days; those whose first youth is past are mostly content to sit back and watch their children, so that they are free from the haunting spectre of Being Out of Things, Looking Your Age, or Losing Touch. If no one knows everyone, they all know about everyone, so that pretence or affectation, those foes of peace, have little scope.

Anyone glancing at the two women settling down with an air of almost schoolgirl content to the reviving drink, which neither would have dreamt of asking for or dared to suggest at home, could have placed them pretty accurately in the social and financial scale. Their husbands were partners in a famous old Castleburgh legal firm; both they and Linda and Rose had connections with half the county families and clans of Scotland. Each family had a big house near the west end of Castleburgh, and took shootings or went abroad every summer. All four, and all their children, had been at popular English schools. If they had had to practise economy in their early married lives, they had come to be as far from economy now as from extravagance. They had enough always to buy what they wanted, and the very best of its kind. They were all charitable in the sense that they wrote suitable cheques for deserving societies, handed on outworn garments to suitable cases, looked after their poor relations and dependants generously and tactfully, and often, though they knew it to be reprehensible, gave sixpences to beggars in the streets. They gave a reasonable amount of time to what they termed 'good works', and both women had devoted considerable thought and care, if with varying success, to the upbringing of their families. They were, in short, from a communist's point of view, typical members of the effete and worthless class of the high English bourgeoisie. But there, to any observant critic, the resemblance between the two women ceased.

For up to the August of 1938 Linda, plump, pretty, gentle, and lovable, had certainly believed that she and her Ian lived in a permanent world, designed happily for themselves and their friends. They were a genuinely social and friendly couple, and everyone loved them, and confided in them, and especially in Linda. The deep cream sofa in her gay drawing-room had had more secrets whispered over it, said her children, than any in Castleburgh. 'People throw the stories of their lives before her, as if she liked cats showing off their mice to her,' they grumbled. But beyond that sofa Linda's interests were a little circumscribed. No social questions troubled her, unless Rose had persuaded her to embark on some uncomfortable book, and, if she could do nothing about the problems they presented, it was best to leave them to others and forget them. The last war was a thing to be forgotten; 'abroad' a picturesque place made for the British to visit: pogroms or concentration camps were as unreal to her as the Spanish Inquisition. And now that the war had come and turned the world upside down, and already life had lost its old value for ever since her elder son went out to France, never to return, Linda, however, still unconsciously dreamt that some day some peace would come, and the old world be restored for her other children. Though it could never be the same for her without her Geordie, who had fallen at Calais, she made one sure, as her younger daughter Iona would say thankfully, that all these disgusting war works and rationing and economy wouldn't go on for ever, and that peace would come, and they would all be happy again. There is perhaps no more popular person than the convinced, if unreasoning, optimist in a war, and the corner of Linda's sofa was more frequently occupied than ever.

Rose had, to her shame, none of this unconscious gift of diffusing a sense of safety and happiness about her. She did her best to present a façade of equable calm to the world, but anyone could see that it was only stucco, and cracking at that, she admitted. Fear had entered into her life in the Great War, when as a mere girl of twenty-two she had married and lost her gallant sailor husband. It had stalked her in her difficult family relationships all her life. Although she and Stuart had plenty of friends and acquaintances, they were alike in a love of their own fireside, and a passion for solitary reading. Stuart Fairlaw's interests were confined mostly, indeed, to the *Scotsman* and *The Times*, which he read daily from cover to cover, and to the history of the Fairlaw family which he was compiling, with scrupulous accuracy and vast detail, from the papers left by a family who seemed for the last twenty generations to have had ten children apiece, every nine of whom had kept a voluminous diary. Rose was free, therefore, to read as she liked, when the children were away at school and college, and, like all intelligent people, as she followed the histories of the countries of Europe lived under the perpetual menacing fear of another war. ('And some day, perhaps,' she confided to Mickie, 'we shall find out why our statesmen didn't realise it as well!')

And now the fears of those years were realised, and she could only, like Linda, throw herself into war work, which was necessarily dull and unspectacular at her age, and struggle with the difficulties of housekeeping, rationing, economy, and the domestic problem. Only, even apart from her fears for Mickie, her darling Mickie, who was a Flight Lieutenant, and for Tom, who at nineteen was in the ranks, she had no hopes that her old world would ever return. Theoretically she knew she should not even hope for those bad old days when she had been so happy. But to herself she admitted that, whatever happened, there did not seem much to look forward to in any future.

'But even our dear Mamma doesn't impersonate Jeremiah all the time,' Mickie would say, when her family complained that yet another book on atrocities had come from the library; and today in the pleasure of meeting Linda for a chat, and the fun of breaking all the conventions of their Victorian youth by indulging in a middle-morning cup of coffee, her cheeks were glowing with colour and her pretty lips curved in smiles. Rose was tall and dark-haired while Linda was fair and plump and of medium height; Rose was one of those women whose charm consists rather in graceful movement and expression than in noticeable features. 'Her eyes are too big for her face, like a cat's,' said Tom once, 'and she doesn't smile with them, only with her lips. Now Aunt Linda beams all over!'

'Mother's like a delicately stepping stag, and Aunt Linda's like a friendly cow – all red and white,' Mickie had declared in a phase of R L Stevenson.

'Mother,' said Flora severely, 'is utterly morbid, and Aunt Linda utterly sugary.'

Rose and Linda had often laughed over those comparisons, and remembered how they ended, when little Iona, Linda's younger daughter, said hotly: 'They're both perfect and I love them both!'

'Have you any news of the boys, Rose?' The two women agreed that most of their friends never waited for an answer to this question, made so perfunctorily before they went on to their own affairs, but each of them had cared for the children of the other since nursery and schoolroom days, and they shared every family interest in common.

'Tom's been recommended for a commission, and may get into an OCTU any time now. Oh, Linda, it will be a relief not to think of him sleeping twenty in a room, and drinking tea out of the pail he uses to keep his metal polish in! But he'd be angry to know it!'

'I felt just like that about Ken,' agreed Linda. 'Just as I hate his being right away up in that desolate northern island in all this hateful, cold, damp weather. But of course I can only say that to you, Rose! I say to everyone how lucky I am that he's safely there. And you've such real ceaseless anxiety over Mickie that I am ashamed of myself.'

'Often I just daren't think of him at all,' agreed Rose. 'He's a darling about telling me that he'll probably be resting on certain days to cheer me up. And of course I always imagine when he does that there'll be some particularly frightful job that night, and he's double-crossing me. However, I think he must have some leave soon – and I do hope it will be before the maids go. It would be wonderful if he were home for Christmas! Now tell me about Wanda? Aren't we dreadfully Victorian the way we put our boys first!'

'Oh, well, they're in the front line!'

'So was Flora with her ambulance in the blitz at Eastminster and she did behave magnificently, you know!'

'Yes indeed! And Wanda seems to be a changed creature now she's married. Oh dear, Rose, what a lot of happy peace days we wasted over our difficult daughters, didn't we?'

'Wanda was only difficult because she was just a graceless

little flirt, and that sort always turns into model wives and mothers as far as I can see! Poor Flora's a harder case, because wherever she travels she'll have herself for company – that's Montaigne, dearest, and rather cultured!' Rose pulled herself up with a laugh. 'Let's put our worries to sleep and make pigs of ourselves. I've taken the largest cake, I'm afraid! Let me ask for another!'

'Oh no, I'll have two,' replied Linda with simple greed. 'To think that three years ago, when I could have had as many cakes as I wanted, I was slimming! How I grudge all the good food I didn't eat! Well, we won't talk children any more except to tell you how lovely it is to have Iona at home, I don't know why!'

'I do, it's because she's exactly like you and absolutely livable with. But I am bursting with great thoughts for you, Linda darling. Do you know I've made up my mind to give up trying to get maids – there aren't any! – and I'm going to try to manage my house myself.'

'You can't,' was Linda's plain and daunting verdict.

'Why not? Look at that nice Colonel Bay's wife, and lots of officers' wives who just manage with a batman.'

'They have batmen and they live in flats or small houses and they're mostly younger!' Linda's impressive refutation was a little blurred by cream and puff pastry.

'Millions of women do manage. That's what Mrs Loman said to a ghastly female who was throwing her weight about. It was like a flash of illumination to me! It's so absurdly, simply true!'

'Rose darling, they were brought up to it! They don't have big houses and area kitchens. They're younger.'

'If they are they've probably a swarm of children, and I'd rather make the experiment with a double basement, than even two babies!'

'Dearest, be practical. You've never done any housework in your life. You can't keep Laws House clean yourself.'

'But, Linda, it makes no difference to the war if our houses are clean and polished and shiny. Ought we to be house-proud in wartime, or isn't it more patriotic to be just reasonably dirty?'

'And who's going to cook for you – and Stuart? I know you can't, Rose, because think what a mess we made when we had to take it on at the canteen, the night Miss Ross broke her wrist.'

'One could learn. Think of the utter morons who are good plain cooks.'

'Poor Stuart!' said Linda sarcastically. 'How he'll enjoy the early experiments. No, Rose darling, have sense. If you really can't get anyone you'll just have to go to a hotel till you can.'

'But Stuart simply loathes hotels. We couldn't afford an expensive one just now – he's been pretty hard hit over some blitzed London property, you know. And he'd be so utterly miserable at one of those places with old hags at bamboo tables, catching you behind the aspidistras to tell you of their last operation. Linda, we've got to do something about it, and when you come to think of it were there ever a more utterly useless and helpless and – unproductive sort of women in the world than people like you or me?'

'Oh, but we're rather nice you know,' protested Linda,

smiling. 'And not as useless as all that. Think of the families we've had and brought up –'

'With the aid of nurses and governesses and baby schools and boarding schools, and every one of them doing their best to keep their mothers as far from the children as possible.'

'Darling Rose, you have gone Bolshie and no mistake. Think how we've been rocks and props to our husbands, and entertained their friends, and made a Home with a capital H.'

'Given lunch parties or dinners to people we like one day in the week, and gone out on the others – that's all that comes to, my dear hypocrite.'

'Well, think of all the committees we've both of us had to sit on in our time – it makes my tail ache only to speak of them.'

'I expect you've been very good on yours, Linda, but I'm not,' retorted Rose. 'If they were big I never said a word, like the Infirmary one, and if they were small I always agreed with other people so as to get home in time for lunch, and might just as well not have been there at all. You can't say we've justified our existence in the world by sitting on committees, or even by having a few babies as comfortably as possible.'

'And why did we ever have them?' asked Linda in a low bitter voice. And then hastily both women drew away from the narrow crust beneath which lay the volcano of pain and dread they must avoid if they were to keep their sanity.

'Of course you may say we've been doing war work!' Rose hastened to escape first, and drag Linda back after her, for so far she had only suffered the anticipation, and Linda the reality, of loss. 'Most of the women I know are doing work they may be proud of and are indispensable. I don't imagine any place could show a better record than Castleburgh for the service of its women. I should say that everyone we know between thirty and fifty was doing some essential job. And some of the over-fifties who are either born organisers or have trained themselves to be so.'

'Like Cousin Mary,' said Linda, 'and the Peels and Macans, oh, and hundreds more.'

'Just so. But I'm not one of them, Linda dear. That's my point. I'm getting on, and I'm not very strong, and my house keeps me from a full-time job. I can't flatter myself I was indispensable at canteens or work parties, for they went on quite well when I was ill. But I'm strong and well enough, I imagine, to keep a house going somehow, and leave any maids there may be to the people who are doing such marvellous work in the WVS or YWCA. or the police, let alone the Services. They've trained themselves for life and I haven't, so I must be contented with a very humble job. You may say it's not much of a war work to keep a home and husband going, but I suppose someone must do it, and Stuart's serving his country after all, in all sorts of part-time jobs, like Ian.'

'Rose, darling, do think of the details before you go all heroic. How could you possibly get up and light a range, and fill up coal buckets, and put out rubbish tins, and dust and sweep and cook all before breakfast? You know you don't begin to come to life till your tea's brought to you. Think of that time in Norway when we couldn't get it, and you looked like a draggled hen half the morning. A very nice hen, but definitely draggled.'

'Millions of women do,' repeated Rose, clinging to her text.

'Not at your age. Consider what a great girl you are, my love.'

'Excuse me, madam!' A voice from the table behind made both women start, and both their faces registered polite surprise and repression instead of schoolgirl amusement, as an officer in the uniform of an American army doctor crossed to their table, and stood upright with twinkling eyes before them. 'I felt I was eavesdropping on you two ladies, and I ought to tell you so, and then I realised that I had met you before, Mrs Carr-Berwick, on that hospital ambulance committee, so I've just ventured to butt in and re-introduce myself. Major Hosmer at your service – over here with an American field ambulance. May I have the pleasure of meeting your friend? Pleased to meet you, Mrs Fairlaw.'

'But I'm afraid I must be going,' smiled Rose, picking up her gloves with dignified embarrassment.

'Oh, don't you run away in disgust with me,' pleaded the newcomer. 'I know I've done an unconventional thing, but that conversation between you two ladies interested me so very, very much. You see, I come from a place, Cleveland, Ohio, where hired help is practically unobtainable, and every American-born woman, or any who come out from England, have had to look just your problem in the face. And it heartened me up considerably to hear the way you were looking at things, Mrs Fairlaw! For you ladies over here have so much influence that until you get down to fundamentals, and realise that your old world is as dead as a flayed horse, I don't see that you've much hope of winning this particular war.'

'What an extraordinary creature,' signalled Linda's gently raised eyebrows to Rose, and 'Oh, but he's rather a dear,' replied Rose's smiling eyes.

'I'm only converted in theory, you know, and only ten minutes ago,' she said. 'And I don't see that people like us have any influence in the world at all – it's purely a personal problem.'

'No, there I don't agree with you.' Major Hosmer took off his round horn-rimmed spectacles, ordered more cups of coffee without consulting his guests, and settled down to enjoy himself in his favourite pastime of conversation – 'And he stoppeth one of three': Rose recalled the Ancient Mariner in hypnotised helplessness – 'As I see this war on the home front it's just a truce in the class war which has to come in your country sooner or later, unless a pretty remarkable conversion takes place all round. And there'll always be some very rich people, because there'll always be some sort of governing class, whose wives will peacock around in glad rags and jewels, as they do in Italy and Germany and even in Russia. And there'll always be very poor, because there'll always be people who are cent-wise, dollar-foolish to the end of the world. But humanity likes those contrasts, and they don't hurt 'em. But what does make for social trouble is to have whole ranks of social parasites who depend for their existence on the attendance of others. It's not only pitiable in itself, it makes a false social ideal. Why, see here, in the boarding house where I reside there's one young girl, dressed up in cap and apron and all, who took my grip out of my hand and tried to carry it upstairs for me, and carries off my shoes to shine every morning. Well, I figure out that she does so just because the lady manager knows that's what servants do in the best families, and so she hasn't the guts to tell us all to go to hell (beg pardon, ladies) and carry our grips ourselves! All English domestic life seems to me just one long series of imitation and pretence, and until you, who set the standards, have the sense to shake yourselves free and start again from the beginning you'll have envy and hate from the classes below, and you'll find yourselves full of envy and malice, just because the world won't wait on you any more. And it's right there that *lanternes* and guillotines begin.'

'Oh dear, you do disapprove of us,' sighed Linda, thawing over her second cup of coffee. (After all, as she said to Rose later, it was quite creditable to be picked up in a teashop when you were over fifty, even if you could only claim half of the man to your credit.) 'Don't you think that it's rather nice to have just a few people with time to make their homes beautiful and leisurely, and even, yes, I'd even say of mine, fairly cultured, although two or three servants are needed to achieve it – and they have quite a comfy happy life in doing it?'

'But they're not needed if one's efficient, I expect,' put in Rose eagerly. 'I remember reading a story of a woman in America – Baltimore I think – which began describing how she left her home, all perfectly spick and span, with a radiant dinner in the icebox (isn't that the right term, Major?) and set out in white kid gloves to attend a lecture or study circle on Dante or psychology or something. And on the top of all that she even found time to murder her husband quite too cleverly!'

'Poor Stuart!' murmured Linda. 'I expect that'll be the result of your radiant dinners, dear.' She had not meant Major Hosmer to catch her words, and was not a little startled when he wagged his finger playfully, and addressed her as *advocatus diaboli*.

'For I can just size you up as one of the last ditch, Mrs Berwick,' he said, 'whereas your friend's thoughts run on far more progressive and constructive lines, though I'd leave out the last part of the programme, madam, if I were you! Believe me, Mrs Fairlaw is right, and the days of feudal domestic service are over. Now tell me, Mrs Fairlaw. How do you propose to reorganise your house? Has it a sunk area?'

'Oh yes, and – well I haven't thought about organising, let alone reorganising, yet.'

'Well, you must, you know. What's in your area?'

'Oh, the kitchen with rather an old-fashioned kitchen range, I fear. And scullery and servants' hall and the maids' bedrooms and bathroom.'

'They sleep down there? Mrs Fairlaw, you put me in mind of your poet Eliot, not your TS but Ebenezer, on the British workers: "We're low, we're low, we're very very low".'

'But they like a flat to themselves,' protested Linda and Rose simultaneously, in the manner of generations of British women. 'And it slopes to a little garden at the back, you know!'

'Still, you can't manage all that anyway, whatever I think of your base British feudalism. Now you listen to me. I've a friend, a Mrs K Burlen of Chelsea, London – perhaps you know her?' (Rose shook her head, while Linda's charming manner implied that, though she had not that pleasure, it was the merest chance that Mrs K Burlen of Chelsea was not her greatest friend.)

'Well, she came right up against your problem and asked my advice, and with her husband we went into the business thoroughly. You must do what she did, put in electric power, with a thermostat in your hot-water system.'

At this point Major Hosmer became so lyrically technical that Rose's thoughts wandered. Of course it would be heavenly to get hot water by merely switching on a tap, but would Stuart ever consent to anything so revolutionary?

'And one room upstairs you must convert to a kitchenette. Mrs Burlen had an odd little hole called a pantry.'

'Oh, so have I, next the dining-room, but it's tiny!'

'Too small for a gas stove? Take the measurements and apply to your gas company, and if it can't be done, and you say you've electric power, put in an electric stove. Mind you, you'll find it difficult after cooking on a range, just as Mrs Burlen did –'

'But I've never cooked on a range or anything, so I shan't mind the difference,' put in Rose.

'Never cooked at all?' Major Hosmer looked properly shocked. 'What on earth was your mother thinking about?'

'Oh well, there were lots of servants then.' Rose decided that she had better not shock her new friend by entering into details of the kitchen-maid, vegetable-maid, and scullery-maid who formed an unknown army of aides-de-camp in the spacious stone kitchen premises of her old country home. 'And our cook was with us for fifty years, so I expect my mother thought mine would be –' (not, she told herself, that

Lady Seriton, exquisitely secure over her petit-point in a world that was made for her, had ever conceivably given a thought to the matter).

'Well, well, you'll have a hard row to hoe, I guess, but it's worth it, little lady, it's worth it.' (Not, oh not if I'm to be called 'little lady' in the process, reflected Rose.) 'You take your stand on your new ideas right away. Show all your lazy friends the dignity and beauty of women's labour. What did your prophet Ruskin say was the meaning of your word "lady" – the loaf-giver? – the loaf-maker, too, I reckon.'

'I should keep to the baker if I were you, Rose,' said Linda, rising. If she meant to show her annoyance at being described as a lazy friend, her pleasant smile failed to demonstrate it. 'But if you really can't get any maids at all, and Stuart won't go to a hotel, I should certainly inquire about all those electric gadgets if I were you. At least they'd save your poor hands a little. Are you coming my way, darling?'

Rose got up reluctantly. She recognised, of course, that she could not spend the whole morning discussing her household arrangements with an unknown American officer, but she found herself inevitably compelled to ask Major Hosmer to come to see her house and offer practical advice, however disapproving Linda's back might try to look. 'And I'd like a word with your husband too, Mrs Fairlaw,' was his farewell in a hearty carrying voice. 'Gentlemen often run away with the idea that hard work may be bad for a woman who's not as young as she was, owing to the contraction of the muscles, but I can assure him that he's wrong.'

'Oh dear!' Rose had to stop and wipe her eyes when she

and Linda had at last made a safe getaway, and hurried uphill into Augusta Square, 'What shall I do if he does somehow contrive to meet Stuart, and begins to chat about my inside muscles?'

Linda's disapproval was forgotten now, in her helpless gurgles of amusement. 'But don't go putting in all these fearful gadgets really,' she begged. 'Stuart won't want to, they'll cost the earth, and the minute they're installed Mrs Loman will produce three perfect servants!'

'If I thought that,' said the new and unregenerate convert to the beauty of labour, 'I'd get the whole house and myself included electrocuted, but no such luck, Linda. I've got to face up to this at once and we'll all have to sooner or later. I'm sure he's right and that the day of domestic service is over and that a useless, unproductive leisured class like ours can't be tolerated much longer. Why should we?'

'But why go ahead to meet trouble?' protested Linda. 'Why not hang on to our dear old ways, however sinful you think them, as long as we possibly can?'

'Because I've always hated being the last at a party,' replied Rose energetically. 'Because I'm sick of lying awake worrying whether I'll get servants or not, and sick, simply sick of doing with people of the servants' mentality. Look at my Catrine, such a darling and so nice to me till she was influenced by my quite odious Jessie with her hateful Glasgow ways and socialist chat! Do you remember how Marie Antoinette said: "Nothing can hurt me now", when she knocked her head on the lintel on her way to the guillotine? Well I'd like to get to that point about domestics or the want of them. Besides, Linda' – she stopped dead on the hill, as they reached the beautiful old row of houses which had been the home of the Carr-Berwick family for three generations – 'you know, though we don't talk of it, that day and night we're in agony over the thoughts of our sons – yes – and daughters, in other ways. And you know that war work – where people say: "Oh, is your boy in Egypt? I quite envy him in that climate", or "How proud you must be of your pilot son, Mrs Fairlaw!" – only makes it worse. Wouldn't hard work be a comfort? Won't it be nice to think one will be tired enough to sleep? Won't it be nice not to be able to go out to meals any more – for I'll be far too tired and dirty – and hear people grumbling about food and petrol restriction when our sons, our sons are dying to keep them safe?'

'But, Rose dear, people aren't mostly like that!'

'Well if not, they're painfully brave and cheerful, and talk about morale and stiff upper lips (why upper? It's my lower that wobbles when I'm upset). Everyone says work is the best dope, and this will be real work, not sitting sewing or knitting or making up parcels of smelly old clothes for the bombed, who mayn't ever want them.'

'Rose darling, you may be saying all this to convert your-self but you won't convert me.' Linda shook her head as she fumbled for her latchkey. 'Never mind, I don't believe you really mean it all, and we've had great fun this morning anyway. I'm going to boast to Ian that I was picked up at MacVee's.'

'So shall I to Stuart. It's a pity we have to share one between us though. I like him, Linda. I think he is a Born Helper.'

CHAPTER TWO
HOUSES LIVE AND DIE

Houses live and die: there is a time for building
And a time for living and for generation
And a time for the wind to break the loosened pane.

T S Eliot

When Linda had vanished into her spacious beautiful hall
Rose walked briskly on, consulting a shopping list and filling
up her shopping bag with an effort at concentration. 'Five
minutes by tram' was an accurate description of her home,
but like most of her friends, Rose walked everywhere in
Castleburgh. Even in old days they had used their cars very
little for their errands in the city, with its wide spectacular
streets and gay convenient shops, and she agreed with Linda
that it was for this reason they and their countrywomen
probably retained their figures, without all the trouble over
slimming which their friends took in London. In most of
them was ingrained the habit of walking in the country
in their youth, where despotic old coachmen could not be
expected to exert themselves merely for the sake of the

daughters of the house, and they retained the habit to the amazement and surprise of their young people, who could, as her husband complained, manage thirty-six holes of golf in a morning, but could hardly drag themselves on foot to the corner of the road if a car was available.

It was odd, she thought, as she turned down a little unexpected lane from the tram-line, and opened a gay green gate in the old wall which bordered it, how many different things one house could represent to different people. To her husband Laws House represented that sense of property and family association without which no Scotsman is wholly content, even though Stuart, as a sensible Castleburgh lawyer, resented the ceaseless expenditure on repairs and modernisation. The Laws House, he would declare caustically, with its gas piping and electric wiring, was like nothing in the world but a rotten tooth held together by its filling, yet he would not have parted with it for the world. For after all it was a discovery and not an ordinary inheritance.

Long ago the family of Fairlaw had held most unjust and piratical sway over large tracts of the eastern Border marches of Scotland, and, having dotted castles on convenient hills all over Peeblesshire, added to them a little residence on the outskirts of Castleburgh in which dowager mothers could not only live in peace and dignity, but also provide a hiding-hole for their lawless clan in the troubled days of the Regent. One by one the border fortresses fell to rival families, or the fire of besieging forces, as the generations passed; the last of the Fairlaw Border property was confiscated when the head of the house went out in the '45; only the cadet branch of the family

survived, fallen on such evil days that they had to take to trade in Castleburgh. Even the little house of Laws passed out of their hands and fell into disrepute. In the great rebuilding of the eighteenth century no one wanted the little square tower with its round turret guarding one side, six-foot-thick walls and crowstep gables. After generations of cramped life in crowded flats towering to the sky in the Old Town, the citizens betook themselves to the spacious grey houses which spread in squares, crescents, and terraces, like smoke rising from a train engine, all over the New Town. The little tower on the hillside, outside those charmed circles, languished in neglect and suffered the last indignity of being let in tenements. It never occurred to Stuart's grandfather when he married a modest heiress, and bought a partnership in one of the most famous legal firms of the city, to tempt his wife from her vast west-end home, full of such modern conveniences as gas jets and one cavernous bathroom, out to the little derelict home of his ancestors. It was only when the city spread still further westwards that Stuart's father found himself negotiating for a client over the sale of the land on which it stood.

'Oh, the house must be pulled down, of course,' said the client contemptuously. 'It's hopelessly old-fashioned and inconvenient, forbye that it's in a shocking condition and beyond repair. Who wants a dreich old tower in these days?'

Stuart as a boy accompanied his father on an expedition to the forgotten little property, and though barely a word passed between them the two were agreed from the first. The property was purchased by the Fairlaws, the house stripped, pointed, and cleansed. To the winding turret, which contained the winding stone staircase, Stuart's father added a modern wing, and since then ever-changing improvements in plumbing, kitchen equipment, and lighting gave its owners infinite pleasure and unlimited expense. It was not just a house or even a home to Stuart. It was the realisation of his father's dream.

To Rose herself Laws had many different aspects. It was a dear house, a quaint house which she was proud to show to visitors, and a house, she insisted to her mocking family, with a kindly, welcoming atmosphere of its own. Sometimes it seemed to her too, in the strikingly incongruous combination of new and old, to represent the maladjustments and rubs of their family life. To Mickie, in a short phase of architectural ambitions, the solid Victorian wing with its bow windows was an eyesore, a blight only fit for destruction, but still he considered that Laws was a very decent little shakedown. 'If the bathroom were a bit bigger, and there was room for a billiard table, it would be perfect,' admitted Tom, in his lordly Eton days, while two years later he condemned it as a survival of the rotten feudal system. To Flora, her daughter, who found very little to approve of in the home circle at any time, it was a dismal, poky old building, and had better be exchanged for a modern luxury flat at once. And after all it was natural enough, Rose said in extenuation, that Flora, who was not a Fairlaw, should have no particular interest in the Laws House.

To the servants, in their frequent moods of discontent the house was a just awfu' inconvenient wee hole, and indeed there was some justice for their complaints. For Laws House was built on the steep slope of a hill, so that, though the lowest storey overlooked a pleasant drying-green at the back, the sunk windows in the front seldom saw the light of day. 'Must have been dungeons once,' Jessie complained, quite inaccurately. The main room was probably once the living-room of the old family, but Stuart's father had fitted it out for a kitchen, and made the room above into the dining-room. As no lift could conceivably be introduced into walls of such thickness every meal had to be carried up the narrow winding stone stairs, 'and the wear on the feet is just fierce,' said Jessie. The maids' bedrooms had been contrived out of a row of cupboard-like larders, wine-cellars, and store-rooms, and though Rose had squeezed in a tiny servants' hall and bathroom under the pantry, no one could say their quarters were luxurious. Rose's former staff had only complained occasionally, because they had, after all, a flat to themselves; from the kitchen and hall windows they had a fine open view over drying-green and the smoking chimneys of the houses below, of distant fields and the silver line of the Firth; and, above all, they were so well shut off from the outer world that no bells of 'followers', or overloud wireless, could be heard by their employers. But to Jessie it was a 'fair dreich little place, the like of which you'd never see in Glasgow', while Catrine moaned over imaginary ghosts and blackbeetles. Indeed, in the light of Major Hosmer's strictures it was rather dreadful to think that, during those years while the children were at school, she and Stuart had been free of nine or ten rooms in the upper earth, while three women shared the exiguous darkness of the basement.

It was with new eyes that she scanned her home now, wondering if she could subdue it to her own control, or if it would

get the better of her unmercifully. The front door opened straight into the low circular floor of the turret, a small and poky entrance, as Flora said contemptuously, but with its stone floor and rugs, and no furniture but a low oak chest, it would be easier to keep clean than Linda's spacious marble hall. Opposite the door was a cloakroom and the pantry: the latter would indeed be very small for a kitchen, thought Rose as she looked into it. There was a sink and a table, four big deep shelves in the thickness of the wall, and a big closed cupboard for glass and silver and china. There certainly wouldn't be room for a gas stove, though she supposed an electric stove could be squeezed in by the window. It would be easy enough to carry the meals into the dining-room, and that room in the old part of the house was, from her present point of view, mercifully small, though at moments in the past it had seemed tiresome never to be able to have more than eight for dinner. 'And that won't trouble me when I have to cook the dinner,' thought Rose, smiling.

The family held very strongly that the library on the ground floor of the new wing should be the dining-room, but Rose had never contemplated asking such a sacrifice of Stuart. She was very fond of the room, but she could see, now that she looked at it with new eyes, that there might be some grounds for Jessie's complaints that she had to get up before cock-crow to get it done. For not only was it lined with bookshelves but Stuart's books of reference round his big desk by the window overflowed perpetually on to the tables and floor around it. In old days it had been his alone, but the exigencies of fuel shortage and staff in the war obliged Rose and the family to sit there in the mornings when he was at the office. There was a sort of gentleman's agreement that his gypsy encampment of books by his vast desk, and the terrain round his huge comfortable red leather armchair on one side of the fireplace with its gas stove, should be sacred to him. So Rose pitched her tent, as it were, on the vast deep leather sofa opposite, or at her tiny writing bureau, and her knitting, her books, her papers, and her parcels spread themselves over the big mahogany table behind it, while everyone combined to drop in and throw down any portable possession they had with them and had not room for in the hall. In one corner were golf-bags, in another fishing-rods and gun-cases, removed to the owners' rooms at intervals only to reappear again almost immediately.

'Not an easy room to sweep or dust, I expect,' Rose murmured to herself with discouragement, 'and whatever anyone says I won't shut the drawing-room and live here altogether. I must have one pretty, comfortable room; besides Stuart would hate not to have it to himself in the evening!'

She was interrupted in her survey by a noise of clinking china and silver in the pantry, followed by the appearance of Jessie, her ugly shiny little face, with its wide nose, set in lines of passive disapproval. 'I knew she was like a pig when I engaged her, but I thought it was a nice pig,' Rose had mourned to Linda.

'Your lunch is set, 'm, and Lieutenant Fairlaw rang up to say he'd be coming on leave tonight for a week,' she said grudgingly, as if unwilling to give her mistress so much pleasure.

'No, really! Oh how wonderful!' Rose turned, glowing, expecting a glance of sympathy, but it was not forthcoming. 'Have you done his room, Jessie?'

'Not without instructions, 'm, and the silver's taken me half the morning. Will you be expecting me to do it after me dinner in my off-duty time, and does it mean there'll be company this evening – and that?'

'Of course it means that my son will dine here, strange as it may seem to you, Jessie,' retorted Rose, stung out of her usual propitiatory attitude to her hateful attendant. 'And I shall probably ring up and ask a friend to dinner to meet him too –'

'I'm sure I was hoping to get out tonight to see my sister about my overalls – and that,' grumbled Jessie, moving slowly towards the basement stairs.

'Well, you can't, that's all!' Never before in her life had Rose snapped at a servant so viciously. 'And go and ask Catrine to come and see me at once, as I must think of something special for dinner.'

'Catrine's busy dishing up our dinner, 'm,' protested Jessie, and received the shock of her life, for:

'If you speak like that to your foreman you'll get court-martialled and shot, I expect, and a very good thing too,' said Rose, as she ran lightly down to the basement calling: 'Catrine, Catrine, what shall we have for Mr Mickie?' For, after all, servant troubles and plans for the future, and the beauty of labour, were all forgotten at the thought that Mickie, her own Mickie, was coming home this afternoon.

Catrine, who was at the moment at loggerheads with Jessie, and regretting the loss of a comfortable place with a casual mistress who never noticed if a few odds and ends found their way to relatives, was far more sympathetic, and with all that re-arrangement and telephoning which wartime householders know so well, a good dinner was evolved before Rose sat down to the bit of rabbit which the maids had spared her from their own all-important dinner. As she faced it distastefully her mind was wholly preoccupied with the question of a girl for Mickie. His love affairs were so frequent and easily outlived that it was very easy to make a wrong choice. That Mylne girl – no, she was sure Mickie recently referred to her as a pie-face. She couldn't remember the name of that little major's wife. On the whole it would be safest to ring up Linda, she decided. For though true to tradition the boys and girls of the two intimate families viewed each other with bristling suspicion, both Mickie and Tom had remarked that Iona was a decent kid and not half as repulsive as Wanda.

'Isn't she too young?' asked Linda doubtfully, when she answered Rose's telephone call. 'You mustn't let your fascinating Mickie break her heart. Well, I'll ask her. Yes, she says it would be marvellous – everything is marvellous to her, bless her. How lovely to think you'll have him safe for a bit. I suppose you're cooking the dinner for them all, darling, after your grand decision this morning.'

It was only when all that was settled, and the pig-like Jessie safely on her way to Mickie's room, that Rose went to the telephone again and rang up her husband's office:

'Stuart, Mickie comes home on leave tonight! Isn't it wonderful?' She tried to sound completely natural, but even as she said it she recognised that most wives would have rung their husbands up with such news first of all.

'That boy seems very good at getting off duty,' was Stuart's dry comment. That had always been his tone about his son in old days, and he would revert to it automatically now, even though his former fits of annoyance and impatience over Mickie's refusal to take life seriously at school or college had disappeared when war began, and Mickie went into the Air Force. 'It's a bit of luck, too,' he added, evidently regretting his tone, 'for Tom's just sent a telegram here to me, to say he'll be home tonight on his way to his OCTU. They'll enjoy meeting each other again.'

'And Tom's really going to leave the ranks, and get into the cadet business at last! And coming tonight! Oh, Stuart, this is a lucky day!'

'It's a busy one for me,' said Stuart with meaning, and at that Rose controlled her raptures and rang off. Wouldn't any other wife have added, 'Be sure to come home early,' she considered penitently, and of course she did want Stuart back, only it was rather fun to have the boys to herself for a little. She must reorganise dinner again, anyhow, at the moment, instead of falling into abstractions – would one chicken go round with three hungry men – perhaps if she ran out and got sausages – there wasn't time to get hold of another girl anyway – and she must try to get to the library for some new detective stories for the boys. With such disjointed reflections she broke it to the outraged Jessie that two rooms must be got ready at the top of the house instead of one, and interviewed Catrine. Yet even as she ran about these duties, and stood in a queue for sweets and cigarettes for the great occasion, she found herself wondering uncomfortably exactly how mothers without servants managed when their sons came home on leave.

The thought must not spoil the boys' leave. Nothing could do that for the first few days and the few last were always so haunted by the prospect of farewells that nothing could make them worse. But today, especially when she was tired, she felt a little persistent nag of bewilderment in her mind. Would she really wake one morning to find no one with a tea-tray at her bedside, not even Jessie, pig-like as she most definitely looked in the morning? What would it feel like after her afternoon of shopping, though anyway Christmas shopping would be over, to come back to a dark empty house and cook the dinner? What would happen when visitors came to the door when you were in the bath? These were only a few of the spectres which haunted her already, and there were even less worthy moments when she caught sight of Catrine's rough swollen hands, and Jessie's dirty nails before she 'cleaned herself' at tea-time. Somewhere she had seen a line of Clough's put up as a motto: 'Labour, and labour alone, can add to the beauty of women.' Clough had probably only known hospital nurses, like his adored Florence Nightingale, whose nails were clean with disinfectants, she fancied! And then she rebuked herself and told herself that she was glad to do any work however humble, to free abler women for the War Services, only it would have been nicer to make a great act of renunciation than to be left, as she was, alone on an uncomfortable shelf. And when the boys arrived only the old life would seem real, and afterwards, when they went, what did anything matter?

CHAPTER THREE
HOMELY FEATURES

It is for homely features to keep home.
Milton

Rose had spoken of herself and her husband, Stuart Fairlaw, as commonplace types of their age and generation, but Linda had privately disagreed with her. Far more typical she considered was the way in which she and her Ian had grown up together, fallen in love, married, and remained in love while they brought up their family of four children. There had been no such unchequered happiness in Rose's life. There had been indeed many cross-currents of difficulties and misunderstandings, and these were not wholly dissipated even when the Fairlaw family met, happy and reconciled, round the dining-table gay with glass and candles and silver. Even the pictures which hung on the wall told something of that complicated story.

Rose Seriton was the only child of a family which had made its money two hundred years before at the time of the Union, and had, after the purchase of large estates and the

building of a great house, been losing it ever since. A sketch
of the Adam palace which had replaced the little old dark
Seriton House hung in a dark corner of the dining-room.
'Aunt Jane's effort should be hung better,' Mickie would say.
'No impressionist rubbish there! No doubt as to which are the
bathroom and lavatory windows!' There Rose had grown up
in security and luxury, and though her father would often
stride out of the pillared hall on to the wide terrace, declaring
he was ruined, and Lady Seriton, in hat, gloves, and veil, followed by her maid and Pekinese, would agree that it seemed
dreadful not to give their daughter a London season, Rose
accepted ease and safety as her inevitable lot, right up to the
very outbreak of the Great War. The long series of big reception
rooms had been filled and overflowed on to the terraces,
even in 1915, when she made a romantic and improvident
marriage to a naval lieutenant, and she still remembered the
sunshine and scents of lilies and white peonies when she
looked at the sketch: it was the last time that Seriton House
opened its arms to entertain its neighbours.

Rose's baby girl, Flora, had been born in the room above
the great drawing-room; in that room she had heard of her
husband's death in action. In the course of a few months the
bedroom with three sedate windows beyond was perpetually
occupied by Lady Seriton, who decided that an invalid's life
was infinitely preferable to struggling with the need for economy and domestic difficulties downstairs. In the library below
Sir Robert Seriton huddled in gloom over a meagre fire most
of the autumn and winter – for what was the use of going
round to the stables when there were no horses, looking into

the plantations when there were no pheasants any longer, or interviewing the factor with his long dismal tale of expenses and falling rents? Rose, with her aching heart, had felt too lonely and incompetent to attempt to help them till their party was augmented by the arrival of her second cousin and greatest friend, Lilias Fairlaw, for the duration of the war. It was only two years since the girls had come out together at one of the great balls of pre-war Castleburgh, and Lilias had dazzled their little world with her beauty. Everyone, including Rose herself, had been surprised when she married Stuart Fairlaw, that worthy, dry, Castleburgh lawyer, instead of any younger and more arresting admirer, but Lilias herself had no doubts. When he was sent out to France she could not endure her solitude, and found a warm welcome at Seriton. She supported Rose through her first heartbroken desolation: her baby boy, Mickie, shared little Flora's nursery. The two girl wives, for they were little more, helped to manage the house and amuse poor helpless, petulant Lady Seriton with her patiences and petit-point and endless complaints. They made gallant ineffective efforts to help Sir Robert to get his affairs into order; they worked in the garden under the direction of the head-gardener till they were too tired to think; and, above all, they read together and talked together, for, as they agreed, they really hadn't had any education to speak of, and they must know a lot of history and poetry and literature to hand on to their children. And then, just before Stuart returned home on leave, poor beautiful Lilias died suddenly of pneumonia, and Rose was left in charge of the two children in the nursery, of a mother who was rapidly becoming a permanent invalid, and a father who was sunk perennially now in his armchair over his fire, contemplating the ruin of his house.

It was during the next year, no doubt, that Rose developed a taste for solitude and a passion for reading, which, she felt sometimes, disqualified her a little for life in Castleburgh. It was not that she did not like people, and make easy friendships and a host of acquaintances later on. But out of the misery of her losses, and as a change from her passionate absorption in the nursery, she found her only happiness in her sunny panelled room by escaping into all the other worlds which lie between the vellum or cardboard covers of books. Her dear, dead Tim was with her as she read, and Lilias perhaps was even nearer still, for Tim as a matter of fact had not much use for any books but thrillers. She was ashamed sometimes to realise that, when the children were asleep, her mother settled comfortably for the night and her father, cheered by a hot toddy and her reassuring chat, safely on his way to bed, she shut herself up to read for half the night with a feeling strangely akin to happiness. She was too much accustomed to the illness and inertia of her parents to worry overmuch about them: her only piercing anxiety was the thought, which would obtrude itself at times, that some day Stuart Fairlaw must come home to face his lonely life as a widower, and take Mickie away from her. And though she would never have admitted it to herself, much as she loved her own robust, dark Flora who was so tall for her age and already, admittedly, a difficult child, it was Mickie, beautiful, adorable, adoring Mickie, who had no mother and needed all her love, to whom she gave the very keys of her heart.

Stuart did return at length, after a prolonged absence in the Army of Occupation, and all the gossips of Castleburgh agreed that his heart was in his wife's grave but that he must certainly marry again to provide a housekeeper for Laws House and a mother for Mickie. The gossips of the county were quick to observe that his visits to Seriton were very frequent, though apart from the presence of his son in the Seriton nursery, the fact that he was Sir Robert's legal adviser would have warranted almost a perpetual residence there.

However, in the end the gossips were right, for when Sir Robert and his wife followed each other to the grave in the autumn of 1919 Rose turned naturally to the lawyer for comfort and advice about the future.

'Of course Seriton must be sold, and of course I must move to a little house,' she said drearily, looking round the long desolate drawing-room, with the galaxy of chairs covered by her mother's embroidery, and the rose border below the terrace where only the faint pink autumn roses relieved the grey approach of a winter's dusk. 'Quite a small house will do, with two really good nurseries, and a few sitting-rooms and bedrooms,' added Rose, trying to sound efficient and practical.

'And, of course, I must relieve you of the care of Mickie,' said Stuart, a little nervously. 'It is really wrong of me to have trespassed on your kindness for so long, but, of course, it's difficult for me –'

'Take Mickie away from me?' Rose's anguish showed in her voice. 'Oh, I know! I know! You must have your son if you want him. But – but forgive me, do you really want Mickie?'

And at the naked misery in her voice Stuart was startled into utter candour as he replied: 'To tell you the truth he's so like her – so painfully like his mother, that I can hardly bear to look at him.'

If Rose had been older and wiser and less afraid, in her recent losses and solitude, of going out of Seriton alone into the world, she might have been warned of the difficulties ahead of her. But as it was she had only time to rebuke herself for hardly understanding a love so passionate and so unreasonable, when she found that Stuart was standing beside her, taut with nervousness, yet warm with compassion and friendliness as he said: 'Now you know that I've perhaps no right to ask you, and yet you're lonely and I'm lonely and we both know that the best part of life can never come again! Do you think that perhaps – perhaps we could comfort each other a little, and make a joint home for our children?' It was not at all surprising that Rose, who had the utmost confidence and respect for Stuart, and saw at last a happy ending to her fears of losing Mickie, should give an unqualified assent.

As Rose looked back she often reproached herself for not making a better job of her marriage. She was still very young, ignorant, and romantic, and though she was generously convinced that the shadow of anyone as radiant and exquisite as Lilias must always stand between herself and Stuart, she was not prepared for the masculine interpretation of this position. She was surprised that Stuart suggested a honeymoon at all, and still more surprised at the honeymoon itself. She had assumed that Stuart was dry, reserved, and undemonstrative because his heart was in his wife's grave, and she was contented to accept it, for were not her own memories entwined for ever with her dear boy husband? But Stuart's simple masculine attitudes about graves and beds were entirely different from her own, and though she accepted them dutifully they never seemed a prelude to closer confidence or intimacy in ordinary everyday life. Still, she was very pleased and proud and happy when a baby, Tom, was added to the family. As she looked at the pastel portraits of the three children which hung on the wall she would tell herself that they had all really enjoyed a normal, happy, family life in those first days at Laws House. And she and Stuart were certainly growing nearer to each other, when the shadow of illness and danger fell on their home.

Mickie was ill one day, sick and complaining of headache and pains, 'And I can't leave him,' said Rose. But Stuart, who thought her fussy, not without reason, had dragged her off to a shooting-party. Next day, they were summoned home by the dreadful verdict of infantile paralysis, and for the next two years, so it seemed to Stuart, Rose disappeared into Mickie's sickroom. She never turned upon her husband or reproached him for that enforced absence: she never neglected his home or his comforts: she just simply, as he told himself with a sense of legitimate grievance, was not there. By day and night she hovered round Mickie's sickroom in the crisis, and when it was over insisted on taking the role of day-nurse herself. When two years later she emerged with Mickie, saved triumphantly, and almost cured at last, it was to find that the whole disposition of the family was altered. Flora had become a changed being. She had always adored her mother fiercely and jealously: now the love had vanished apparently, and only the jealousy was left. She was rebellious to every authority, and to a passionate temper was added now a supreme capacity for sulking. Rose and the nurse were at their wits' end, and Rose had no adviser, for Stuart had crept back into his shell, and Rose could hardly wish him to emerge when he showed so obviously a healthy man's annoyance with a delicate child, and silent disapproval of the way Mickie absorbed his wife's time and thoughts to the neglect of her social duties. Only Tom remained the same, a fat, cheerful, imperturbable child who seemed equally pleased to share the society of any of his family, or to be left alone, sublimely happy, with his picture-books and toys. As both Stuart and Rose were reserved and well-bred people, they made no attempt to talk over the estrangement which had come about so naturally, or to remedy it. They remained on pleasant friendly terms, on the terms indeed which Rose had accepted in Stuart's suggestion of marriage. But in their dealings with their children they reached the absurd situation that if Flora cared for anyone or heeded anyone it was her stepfather, while Rose's attention and devotion were given to the delicate stepson who needed her.

Life was not always at cross-purposes, of course. The tension slackened naturally as the children grew older and went away to school. If Flora's difficult temperament and the troubles it created had been eliminated, all the association of those days would have been happy. And when the war took Mickie away to his training, and Flora to an ambulance unit in the south, the husband and wife could forget that Stuart

had always felt Rose a failure with her daughter, and Rose could ignore those words which had burnt themselves into her imagination – 'To tell you the truth, he's so painfully like his mother that I can hardly bear to look at him.' But the fact remained that the small house had been obliged to bind together in itself a good many warring elements in those years of peace, when as it seemed now to Rose, as to all other parents, every moment should have been flawlessly happy.

'Well, we only need Flora here to complete the party!' Stuart made that statement as they all sat down to dinner, and Rose found herself wondering whether it was due to a Borderer's loyalty to absent friends, or to a Scotsman's curious habit of accepting family solidarity as a matter of principle, even though his natural acuteness must make him aware that it did not exist. He was a tall, loosely built man, whose long face and lacklustre eyes beneath straight dark brows gave an impression of absent-minded tolerance in repose. When, however, he was moved to amusement or to wrath his eyebrows would bristle up, and he would jerk himself erect, until he looked, as Tom said, like a Border chief on a foray. These changes had made him rather alarming to his family in youth, though it was a joke with them now. But his eyebrows were bristling at this moment as he caught Mickie's wink at Tom, implying, as he knew, that the two boys felt home more peaceful without their turbulent sister.

'We haven't even seen her,' Rose hastened to intervene, 'since she did such splendid work at Eastminster in the blitz. Weren't you very proud when you read those letters from the Commandant saying what a heroine she was?'

'Oh, Flora's a great girl!' said Mickie easily. 'I always did tell you and Papa that if you went sick and mental she'd come the ministering angel – the fighting sort of angel, of course.'

'It would be marvellous to be like that,' said Iona wistfully. Linda's younger girl had inherited all her mother's prettiness and comfortable charm, and the gay pink crinoline frock, which she had worn as bridesmaid for her sister, made her exquisite skin, untroubled wide blue eyes, and plump cheeks and neck, seem the reincarnation of all Linda's sweetness and sympathy and serenity. 'Luscious,' Tom had said on her arrival, putting an imaginary monocle to his eye, 'or is appetising the word for her, Mickie?' But when both boys laughed at her for her longing to imitate Flora, whose dark, proud, repellent beauty looked down severely from her portrait on the wall , Rose wondered whether the child mightn't have as much heroism in enduring grief and pain if she were tried, as others showed in action and adventure.

'Don't you be such a mug,' said Mickie, 'a womanly woman, that's your line, and there'll be precious few of them after this ruddy war –'

'Doormats,' agreed Tom. 'It's the doormat we'll want to build a brave new world on. You qualify for that, Iona! You learn to wash up and cook and keep the home fires burning!'

'I'm going to,' put in Rose, fearing that Stuart might bristle up in Flora's praise. 'I settled it this morning. It's quite impossible to get any maids, so I'm just going to look after the house myself as my war work.' Like most wives she liked to introduce any innovation to her husband when there was an audience.

'My poor father!' Mickie bent his head over the table groaning. 'There will be another fatal casualty in this war not reported on the Roll of Honour, if Mummie really means to cook. And no easy death to die!'

'Not a bit of it, she'll be the first casualty herself,' said Tom. 'She'll set herself on fire at the range, and blow herself up on the gas stove the moment she begins to try! Leave it to the Huns, darling! A bomb would finish it far more neatly.'

'What's all this about?' demanded Stuart, his eyebrows almost touching the ceiling. He hardly listened at all to Rose's reiteration of the patriotism of her resolution, and cut her short by telling her to go to the registry office and engage some decent women the very next morning.

'But I have! I've been! And there isn't such a thing to be had! You must know that, Stuart! I'm sure all your country clients come and wail in your office about it.'

'Dearest Mamma, it would seem that it's necessity rather than patriotism!' said Tom. 'But look at it as you will, it's tougher on Papa!'

'What about her?' demanded Mickie. 'What about the basement stairs and washing up? Pale hands I loved, where are you now, or where will you be? No, Mummie darling, I insist on having a real lady, who's never done a hand's turn, for my mother.'

'But wait a minute, you haven't heard my plans. Did your mother tell you, Iona, about the marvellous American doctor we met this morning?'

'She told me you'd got off with a boyfriend,' replied Iona, 'or at least that you had to share one between you!'

'How many more shocks for you tonight, Papa?' asked Tom sadly. 'And at Mother's age too!'

'No, but listen,' said Rose with her prettiest flush. 'We only got off over household management. He's a wizard about it all, and he's going to come and show me how we can have the water electrocuted, and an electric stove in the pantry and never use the basement at all. Why this house will be almost a labour-saving bungalow by the time he's finished with it!'

'So this is the price of a woman's honour!' said Mickie happily, observing Jessie's horrified expression as she offered him the sweet. 'Women are all alike, diamonds for one, an apartment for another, an electric stove, it seems, for another, but –'

'Mickie, be quiet!' Iona bent forward laughing. 'I think Aunt Rose is marvellous –'

'That's nothing! You told me I was marvellous in my sapphire uniform, and you told Tom that it was marvellous he was going into an OCTU, though the poor boob would have a far better chance of keeping well out of danger in the ranks.'

'Not if he got a commission in a regiment that had lost all their equipment, like Ken,' said Iona. 'It'll be ages till they can be sent anywhere!'

'Not the voice of Kipling, sister,' rejoined Tom, 'but I see your point. Now just tell my father that he's marvellous too! He's the only one left out.'

'So he is, for having me here, and giving us champagne,' said Iona, turning prettily to her host. 'And Daddy says it would be marvellous if he could teach me grammar – it's my propositions or pronouns or whatever you call them that still go wrong. You know how you say "Do come out with Mickie and Tom and I –"'

'God forbid! I mean –' said Mickie.

'And then I try to do better and say – "Won't you come out, because Mummie and me are going into Castleburgh", and it's no better,' said Iona mournfully. 'So I've christened my new golden retriever Mimi to help me but I don't know if it will!'

It was so wonderful to have the children laughing and bickering round the table as usual that Rose spun dinner out as long as she could. It was Mickie who sprang up first, saying that they must be off, and would Tom kindly ring up some female to make a fourth, and see to it that she was as little repellent as possible. Then, of course, Tom claimed Iona as his partner, and the two united to urge Mickie to ring up one of his legion of former lovers, 'that gold-digger you sported at the Highland Ball one year', 'that officer's wife who let you in for paying for her meals at the Medici.' If, said Mickie, he could remember their names he would oblige, but he had only a vague idea that one of them, and he didn't know which, was called Lalage. 'Or that might just be memories of Horace in Upper School,' he concluded. 'Culture, my boy, culture! There's nothing like it for getting out of a tight corner.'

'Well, anyhow, let's get a move on. And as for you, Mummie –' Tom swung Rose round to one of those long, tarnished, eagle-crowned mirrors which are so flattering to those of riper years, 'just look at yourself in your black flounces and frills and all, and don't talk nonsense about turning into a charwoman. It's not your line!'

But Rose shook her head, as she looked at the glowing phantom of her prettiness. Was Tom, her brilliant, intellectual Tom, in his line in that battle-dress? Mickie was standing, balancing his heels on the fender beneath his mother's picture. Lilias had been so exquisite, so frail a thing, that it had seemed a justifiable extravagance for Stuart to employ the most fashionable painter of their period to portray her. And Merzow, who was so skilful in making plain women beautiful, accepted real authentic beauty with gratitude, and painted simply and sincerely. Out of a dark background Lilias, all gold and white, seemed perpetually to escape joyfully, one arm raised a little, a rose in her hand, the other stretched a little behind her, as if to brush the shadows away. What would Lilias have felt if she had known the clouds which threatened to blot out her son's life? Was the daily risk of a violent death Mickie's line? What would a little honest work on Rose's part be, compared with the monstrous current which was sweeping away all the old landmarks of her children's lives?

There was no need to answer Tom, for the taxi arrived and the usual hunt for change, gas-masks, and what Mickie called their whole lousy medieval equipment, began. But to her surprise Rose discovered that she had to defend herself again. Stuart had been listening to the conversation more closely than she supposed, and instead of retreating, according to invariable rule, to *The Times* and his papers in the library, asked her with bristling eyebrows to tell her what this absurd idea of hers implied.

Rose's arguments were by this time assuming a note of certainty through repetition, but they had not the least effect

on her husband. No reference to millions of working women made the faintest appeal to his feudal convictions. Like so many men of his generation he faced the war with sick disgust for the waste of the best years of his life twenty years ago. The war to end war had merely engendered it, and all his patriotism could offer now was the acceptance of unpleasant civilian jobs, and a life of impatient endurance instead of his youthful flame of service. His children must go – he couldn't help it, but to his old life and habits he would cling as long as the income tax and German bombing made it possible.

What had Rose and her friends really done to find servants, he demanded. He was surprised indeed to find that his unbusinesslike wife had her name down at all the registries, had advertised in at least ten Scottish papers, and answered countless advertisements of sisters, married couples, and working housekeepers in these journals. Rose had spent the afternoon at a Red Cross working-party, and could add to her statistics the experiences of her friends.

'Oh, some people have maids, of course, over forty, and the Labour Bureau tells us that we may each keep one servant if we can prove her essential. But none of these maids will stay if they're alone, or if they do stay they're old family treasures who need waiting on instead of doing the waiting. Emily Riddell has a hereditary cook and parlourmaid, and they keep her so busy doing housework and their odd jobs that she's only a wreck. All the young, efficient, married women are managing without any but a little daily help, and say that the difference in the bills and wastefulness is incredible. Of course they're lucky, for all their mothers had the sense to send them to colleges of domestic economy or give them some training. Why did our generation become so helpless, Stuart? Think of that lovely diary of your great-grandmother at Culmains!

> She can brew and she can bake
> And she can make a wedding-cake

all right, and teach her servants too.'

'Oh, of course, housecraft disappeared before the spread of machinery and the manufacture of mass-produced foods.' For a moment Rose hoped that Stuart might be led astray to his favourite theme of modern degeneracy, but he pulled himself up.

'Well, Rose, if all this is so, there's nothing to be done for it. We must shut this house and go into a hotel. There are some that might be tolerable.'

'But I'm afraid they're terribly crowded, Stuart. Someone had been to fifteen today, she told us, and only just got in to some poky place with one bathroom, and what she called a common table, when she was in despair!'

Stuart's answer was to scribble down a short list of possible hotels on a sheet of paper and go to the telephone to ring up the managers. It seemed marvellous to Rose that he could keep his temper and aloof courtesy as obvious refusals were returned to him by overcrowded hostelries, and she dared not intervene. For after all, Stuart must find out for himself, and she would never in any case have been cruel enough to shut him up among old ladies and aspidistras.

'Well, in God's name what's to be done?' he asked, irascible at last, as he left the telephone. 'Except for the station hotels – and we can't afford, and wouldn't like, such big places as a permanency – there seems to be no room anywhere.'

'Stuart dear, listen! Suppose we were Russians, Poles, Greeks, French, almost any continental people hearing this discussion, what should we say? "Why do these people make such an idiotic fuss? They have a lovely house, money enough, food enough. They are not so old and feeble but that they can hit balls with golf clubs round and round a golf course for hours any afternoon. Is it possible that they are spoilt enough to feel the end of the world has come just because the woman must try to do a bit of honest work for once?"'

'But – but –' Stuart plunged among a host of objections striding up and down the room. 'I can't have you opening the door to tradespeople!'

'If you ask me, that's the only part of my new job I'll do efficiently at first,' said Rose drily. 'Any fool can do that, Stuart, and why not? They won't bite me!'

'But – but – as if I'd have you carrying coals about and lighting the range at half-past six and cleaning out the basement.'

'Well, even if I did what is there to make such a song and dance about? I read some reviewer in the *New Statesman* who said that he wished that pleasant lady authoresses of the kind I love could get down to real life and sweat and blood and tears. Well, I see what he means about all of us, though I don't sweat as it happens, but I expect I shall cry a lot, and shed pints of blood, as I shall always be cutting myself. I'm sure of that because unluckily I'm one of the people things don't like. Knives cut me, kettles burn me, taps won't turn for me. I know all about the malice of inanimate things! But perhaps I'll conquer them and put them in their place – I do hope so. Anyhow it's a job of work which frees other women, and anyhow I'm quite sure there'll be no such thing as domestic service after this war, so why not be prepared? Dear Stuart, think of the mess the world's in, and the uselessness of people like me, and be sensible!'

'But you're not useless,' protested Stuart. 'Women like you uphold the standards of civilisation.'

'That's what Linda says, but do we? On the whole, women of my sort are moral (largely owing to a sad want of temptation in this Puritan city!), truthful because we've nothing much to tell lies about, and honest because we've everything we want. We've decent manners and have self-control, but any psychologist will tell you those are very dangerous old-fashioned qualities and must disappear. Most of the working women I know in Scotland are exactly the same, and when you call me a lady compared with them it's only because I've certain ways of speech and thought which mark one as belonging to a certain order, and have no value.'

'Nonsense, Rose. People like you, leisured people, keep culture and beauty alive in the world,' protested Stuart.

'Do we? We read, I suppose, that's to say we take an intellectual book out of the library and barely glance at it, and read novels continuously, either about the old city gentlemen found with knives in their backs in libraries, or about nice couples who live in Kensington with two children and three servants. That's how we support literature. We go to art exhibitions, but we don't buy pictures except when we have our portraits painted, and artists have no use for us. We go to concerts, but now the BBC's educating people in good music, people of any income who love music will go, and most of our young people want nothing but jazz and crooners. No, Stuart, I don't see that our happy, spoilt, leisured, cultivated upper classes are, or have been, any particular service to humanity or civilisation, or anyone but ourselves.'

'Is this all out of your friend Major Hosmer's book?'

'Only a little of it. It's largely the result of a long argument at the Red Cross this afternoon when I left half the dear souls convinced that I was no lady and a Bolshie. And don't look on Major Hosmer as my boyfriend, or a pick-up, Stuart! I had to make a story of it, but as a matter of fact Linda had met him on a committee, and as he called me little lady he will never tempt me from the paths of virtue! He's a darling, and you must meet him and you see if we follow his advice we needn't use the basement. If we had the water –'

'I know! I know what you said about that, but please understand once and for all that I won't have him messing about in my house over the electric installations!' said Stuart, rising and collecting his papers and pipe. 'I'll go in and see Martin myself, and have a chat about this heating idea of yours, but they'll probably cost the earth.'

'I shall pay for them out of my own money,' replied Rose with dignity. As Rose's jointure was alternately referred to as a pittance which obliged her to hand her dressmaker's bill to Stuart, or as an income large enough for her to finance the whole family abroad when she wanted to go and Stuart didn't, a grim smile from her husband was the only answer. 'You'll let me try, then?'

'You're so obstinate that I know you will. Besides,' he added, with the impotence of half the husbands in the same situation in Great Britain, 'if we can't get any servants or get into any of these damned pubs, I don't see what else we are to do!'

CHAPTER FOUR
DOMESTIC GENESIS

I will kindle my fire this morning
In the presence of the holy angels of Heaven
Ancient Gaelic Blessing.

On the first morning of her new vocation Rose decided that she had never in her life seen anything as repulsive as a house in the early morning.

It was an aspect of domestic labour which had never occurred to her before. The black-out of course enhanced the gloom everywhere, for now, at seven o'clock on the 1st of January 1942, she could not open windows and let in air. All over Europe women were creeping down house and factory, office and mess stairs, to wake the world and tidy it for breakfast, and probably most of them had not had time to make themselves a luxurious cup of tea in bed as she had! Nor, she was to realise later, did they begin getting up three-quarters of an hour earlier, so as to bathe, dress, and do their hair with their old meticulous care, as Rose had done this morning, simply because it had never occurred to her to do otherwise.

'Bravely, O pioneers,' shivered Rose, trying to recall Walt Whitman as she turned from the scent of stale tobacco emerging from the dark, close drawing-room. Her new role in life would be easier, she had decided, in her own erratic way, if she looked upon it as an adventure, however mild and fatuous an adventure it might seem to any efficient woman in the world. As she dressed she had repeated to herself – 'Sweep dining-room – give dust time to settle, Catrine says – how long is that? Sweep library and ditto – dust both and hall – lay breakfast and cook it.' It seemed a formidable programme but it had got to be done, for it had not yet occurred to her that you might eat and sit in a room which had had no benefit of brush or dusters.

In theory Rose had meant to pick up an immense amount of house lore from Catrine, and even Jessie, before they left, but how could she waste Mickie's leave in such dismal pre-occupations? Besides there had been no time, for the house in Christmas week had been its old self again, with telephone bells ringing, young people dropping in, trays of sherry and largesse of cigarettes and chocolates, Christmas gifts and flowers, poured upon the family by friends and well-loved tradespeople. It was only two days since Mickie had gone off south by the night train, avoiding farewells by filling the house with his friends to the last, and she had hardly dared to speak to her maids for those two days lest her eyes should fill with tears, as she thought of Mickie's last hug, and the maids should imagine that it was their imminent departure which she mourned. But sweeping was easy, she told herself as she rumbled the carpet-sweeper up and down the beige

self-coloured carpet of the dining-room. Jessie had despised the sweeper, saying 'To my mind there's nothing between a Hoover and a switch', and indeed the wretched thing seemed to drop out a loathsome gobbet of grey fluff more often than it picked up a crumb. Into Rose's mind came an odd memory of her old Aunt Ging in Ross-shire. Aunt Ging had a house-keeper who did the marvellous work of taking in local girls, three or four at a time, and training them in housecraft, and Rose recalled waking at six one morning, in the high, hard old four-poster, to hear Martha's voice outside her door saying bracingly, 'Remember, Maggie, there is a right way of sweeping a room, and there is also a wrong way of sweeping a room!' Certainly Martha would call hers the wrong way, and if that was Stuart turning on his bath water, already she must rush the horrid sweeper very rapidly over the library. 'At least,' she reflected, 'this makes time go quickly. The war may be over before I've finished doing the house once!'

It was at this point that a curious phenomenon obtruded itself on her notice. Like all her friends Rose plumed herself on having dignified and sparsely furnished rooms. They were not modern enough to have steel chairs or glass tables, but at least they had been in the van of reaction against such rooms as those which Rose had known at Seriton, rooms where the possessions of generations settled down comfortably as best they might, without any care or arrangement from their inheritors. But were her rooms so empty after all? Basically the dining-room mantelpiece only supported an Empire clock, and two great gaily coloured china birds, but on the shelf people had left photos, invitation cards, Christmas cards, pipes, ash-trays, and paper wrappings at their will; the Chippendale sideboard still presented lovely bits of inherited eighteenth-century silver with silver golf cups and prize cups of Mickie's – these she would put away, one by one so that Stuart shouldn't notice; a gate-legged table in the window was covered with pots of early bulbs, and in her first zeal Rose fondly imagined that one dusted under these every day. As for the library! Well, of course, it was the room nearest the hall-door, and everyone did put down everything as they came in, but no longer did she wonder that letters and papers disap-peared, for how could Jessie have been supposed to classify those which billowed over Stuart's desk and bookshelves and every table and chair alike? But there was Stuart's bath water running away, and she couldn't dust anything else if she were to cook breakfast.

'It won't be very easy to look upon this as either national service or a great adventure,' she thought ruefully as she entered the chief scene of her future activities. Catrine was openly sceptical about the possibility of cooking on the gay little electric stove, all white and grey enamel, with its hot-plate, grill, and tiny oven, or of keeping and washing up silver, glass, china, and pots and pans in one cupboard and one small sink respectively. But as it was quite obvious that no one woman could work in the basement and live upstairs, unless she were a professional mountaineer, Rose was deter-mined to manage somehow. And last night had seemed so promising, for Catrine, thawed, repentant, and unhappy at departure, had left a dinner which needed only the snap of a tap to come hot to the table: soup in a thermos, potatoes and

peas to accompany the cold chicken in a casserole, and an apple tart which Stuart mournfully predicted would be the last he would be able to get his teeth into for months. ('But I won't try pastry,' said Rose with dignity, 'because men are always funny about it – poor Dora Copperfield and Lady Jane Crawley both made pies, so I won't!') But this morning the little low room, where the small table abutted on the stove at one end, and only just left room to pass the shelves on the other, was depressing and smelly in the cold gloom. 'Bacon – toast – coffee, they must all be ready at just the last moment,' thought Rose, for hadn't Stuart often declared that he believed her cooks got the meal ready overnight? 'But not porridge I think! Stuart must do without it for once, there isn't time.'

A little complacence returned to her as she put slices of bread under the grill and got out the frying-pan. Catrine had left a large jorum of coffee ready in a white enamel jug, but with the zeal of early enthusiasm Rose decided that her coffee should be fresh for breakfast every day. The bacon pan was on the hot-plate, so she must trust to the coffee boiling on the grill in time, though she had been warned that this would be a slow process. How thankful she was that she had watched Catrine cook bacon once, otherwise she would have been alarmed indeed at the unhealthy bluish tinge which the fat was taking – like some obscure disease, thought Rose! And now the toast and bacon were ready to turn, and it was only twenty to nine, so what excuse had two maids for ever being late, she was asking herself, self-righteously, when she suddenly remembered that she had not laid the table for breakfast.

'And oh, Stuart,' she wailed later, 'I'd have managed all right, though you wouldn't believe how many things go on a table at breakfast! (It's like that game when you look at a tray for five minutes and then try to write down what was on it!) But the hyacinths were dead, so I just had to get a bowl of snowdrops from the library, and while I was arranging them on the table the coffee boiled over on all the bacon and all the toast, and it's browned the whole stove, and you must just have sardines for breakfast, if only you can open their beastly tin, for I can't!'

'But why bother about flowers or all these silver things?' asked Stuart, with admirable good humour, when Rose rejoined him, five minutes after her outburst, with Catrine's warmed-up coffee and some quite successful toast. 'If we're going to live like the working class let's do it properly, and put away all this stuff.'

'Well, it all holds hot water or salt or marmalade or something after all,' said Rose, 'and I thought you wanted to keep up our standards. Stuart, this bacon soaked in coffee isn't half bad: perhaps I've made a great culinary discovery –' But Stuart, who was unadventurous, thought it unlikely, and refused to try.

'Now don't clear at once as you did last night,' he protested. 'Come to the library and sit down and have coffee and a cigarette and a look at the papers first.'

This seemed to Rose, who felt already as if she had climbed Mont Blanc and played a hockey match on the top of it, quite admirable advice, if not wholly in line with the day of a normal working woman. But the question was settled for her by a deafening ring at the bell, which recalled Rose with a guilty start to the fact that of course it was her business to answer bells now.

'Milk!' said a taciturn and spotty-faced youth at the door. 'Couldn't get an answer below! Any empties?'

Rose ran to the pantry, as if the boy had all the County Council and ARP authorities up his sleeve, but she could only find one bottle to offer him.

'Should be four daily, and should be washed,' he said laconically. ('Four!' thought Rose in horror. 'And I told the maids they must make two do because of the milk shortage.') 'Could you give me the address of the young lady who's gone?'

'My daughter?' asked Rose, genuinely surprised.

'No, the young lady below stairs!'

Romance really did stalk in unexpected places, thought Rose. Catrine was thirty-nine if a day, and the spotty boy seventeen at most. Monsieur Blum would approve, she thought confusedly, as she ran obediently up to the drawing-room for her address book; or was his advice on marriage the sort of thing which had caused the collapse of France? Anyhow there was no time to consider the question, for when she returned the Milk had been joined by the Post, wanting 2d. extra on some tiresome letter, and a girl in uniform demanding waste paper, which necessitated a run to the basement to fetch a bulging sack. And barely had the three callers disappeared than the telephone bell rang with maddening persistency.

'Too bad of people to bother you,' said Stuart, looking up to speak to her from the *Scotsman*. It was the first time daily, for years, that he or she had uttered a word in that sacred rite of Stuart's after breakfast. Their old minister at Seriton had a gloomy way of saying of his acquaintances: 'Ah yes, he needed chastening, dear brethren, he needed chastening.' Was Stuart's chastening, in the form of sardines and warmed-up coffee, going to make him more human? Rose laughed at herself, as she felt at liberty to confide the telephone message to her husband, in spite of the *Scotsman*.

'Oh, it wasn't a bother, Stuart, it was a miracle! Mrs Loman at the registry office has actually remembered about me – wasn't it angelic of her?'

'Isn't it what she's paid for?'

'Oh yes, but when everyone's clamouring, and she's not nearly enough maids to go round! Anyway, she did remember. She says a woman came in asking for two or three hours' work every morning, and she remembered me, and though she knows nothing about this Mrs – Mrs Childe, she says she seems a very decent well-doing sort of body, and is sending her straight to me. Isn't it marvellous?'

'But, my dear, she may be a thief or drink, or Heaven knows what. I thought you never engaged anyone without a reference!' Stuart was so heartily relieved to think that his helpless wife would not be left to tackle her job alone that, with an unusual access of tact, he refrained from reminding her of her proud determination to manage her home by herself. But this sudden capitulation from her usual standards surprised him. He knew all about the references which she had hitherto taken and received from maids, as, like most husbands, he lived in dread of libel actions through his wife's outspokenness.

'She may be if she likes,' said the apostle of Labour, Ruskin, and Major Hosmer, 'as long as she does the drawing-room grate and carries up the coal! I don't begin to know how, and if I have to go down to the empty kitchen again I shall cry, Stuart. You know Catrine and I moved everything I wanted up to the pantry yesterday, and put everything else away, and there it is, gaunt and empty, with no glowing range and blaze of electric light (much as I've deplored waste), and no errand-boy having cups of cocoa, or charwomen with tea in a corner. There's nothing on the dresser but one lonely teapot, and I don't know how to bear it.'

'The post's come, did you know?' Stuart decided that a change of subject would be the best cover for this remarkable backsliding. 'There's a card from Mickie and a letter from Flora.'

Well, anyhow, this was the first morning, Rose recognised strangely, that she had not hastened to turn over the letters on the chance of a card from her darling. She rushed to the table now, to satisfy herself that it was only a request to send on various articles left behind, the penalty every mother pays for every child's visits, and handed Flora's letter to Stuart.

'You take it and read it at the office! I shan't have time to look at it,' she said as her husband opened the front door, and offered her a well-shaved cheek for their regulation morning kiss at parting. Stuart had never been a demonstrative husband and Rose often wondered why or how this curious custom had survived. 'Since there's no help, come let us kiss, seems to be the principle,' Tom had remarked once with an interested and analytical expression. But today Rose felt so grateful to Stuart for his good humour over the sardines, and so thankful that at least his protection was not to be withdrawn from her home, that she pressed her face quite warmly against his cigar-scented tweed coat.

'Come out to lunch with me or let's dine out,' said Stuart, urged to further heights of chivalry but Rose shook her head. Stuart would be miserable if he altered one iota of his daily routine, lunch at the Club at one, a drink there at six, and home to a bath and dinner. After all, restaurant and hotel dinners are for the most part the perquisite of the young and the Forces in Castleburgh, and she would not be such a coward as to run away from her duties at once.

A smart, brisk little woman, hurrying along the pavement with a large attaché case, slackened her pace, as she considered the couple on the doorstep. Mrs Childe, a Napoleon and Machiavelli in a life of intermittent work as daily help, had received the name and address of these prospective employers with some reservations.

'Laws House! Why that's a big place with a basement, Mrs Loman,' she protested. 'I wouldn't care for work there, not without there's a large staff resident and plenty help given. Still, if you make such a point of it, and the poor lady's in such a pickle, I'll go and have a look-see.' So, with this intention, her gimlet eyes took in every detail of Stuart's appearance: 'Good tweed suit, worn six years or so I'd say, and none the worse; shoes might be hand-made I wouldn't wonder; goes somewhere good for his hair-cuts, every bit the gentleman. Maids can only just have left for the steps were washed yesterday, I'd say. So that's Mrs Fairlaw, I suppose! Quite the lady and doesn't look too knowledgeable and wouldn't hustle me. Well, as I'm here I may as well give her a chance.' And so, on this fortuitous decision, Mrs Childe entered into Rose's life.

'Good morning, madam. I come from Mrs Loman.'

Rose started as the newcomer's prim little voice interrupted her speculations as to whether Stuart would think her heartless for handing over her daughter's letter unread. But then Flora's letters had so many requests and commissions in them, and carried so invariably several bitter stings for her mother and brothers, that Rose felt she had better not encounter such discouragement at the beginning of her day's work.

'Oh yes, do come in!' Rose hesitated, for how could she ask the new daily, perhaps the only daily in all Castleburgh, into the dusty library or the dining-room with its uncleared table? But Mrs Childe solved the problem for herself by darting into the pantry and saying, after one quick glance about her:

'Yes, I can see you do want help too, as Mrs Loman says! I'd better just get down to it at once –' already she was opening her case and pulling out shoes and overall. 'My charge is a shilling an hour, and I can manage daily from nine to twelve. We'd better clear and wash up straight away. I always say you should begin with the pantry.'

'How could I ask her for references?' Rose asked her husband later. 'I just felt it was very kind of her not to demand mine. And I can tell you that it's lucky for Jessie and Catrine they didn't depend on her references, for she made it clear as we went through the house that she thought very poorly of them. And anyhow I was too out of breath running after her to ask her any questions at all!'

'It's an odd little place this,' was Mrs Childe's verdict on the house when Rose led her upstairs, leaving the pantry in an order which Rose could never have believed possible an hour before. 'I like something up-to-date and cheerful myself, but I suppose you might call it old-world in a way. I'm partial to a bit of history myself now and again, but when it comes to cooking give me an Esse and no basement. Still, we must just do with things as they do with us, is what I always say to Mr Childe.'

That remark always seemed to Rose typical of her new ally and friend. She was, at the age of forty years or so, the offspring of a curious union between Scottish efficiency and canniness and the superficial refinement of the BBC and film producers. When she was at work, as Rose discovered later, she would lapse into broad Doric: today, as a visitor, she was giving a fine reproduction of what is known in Castleburgh as King Street English. Her face was lined with a life of cheerful hard work and worry but her nose was well-powdered: her hands were rough with housework but her nails were painted. Her hair was invariably tidy in its firmly-set perm; her shoes and dress were always neat, however dirty or energetic was the task at which she worked. Her manner varied between the respect with which she would have regarded Rose in her youth, as an authentic member of the Scottish county families, and the pitying contempt she felt now for another woman's ignorance and inefficiency. If the essence of a lady, in the true sense of the word, lies in the virtues of courage, honesty, and kindliness, Mrs Childe was a lady already: if the essence of vulgarity is the inability to face life and its vagaries heroically, Rose was at the moment, she considered, as common as she could be. In a revolution Mrs Childe would rise to any heights, while Rose herself would sink to any depth, for there was nothing Mrs Childe would not attempt, and very little which she could not achieve.

'We're both in a state of transition,' Rose told herself, 'but I'm going down the moving staircase and she's going up. It's well worth my while to catch her halfway and learn something from her!'

Mrs Childe was quite ready to instruct: there was no doubt about that. If she was going to help at all she was going to do it in her own way and at her own pace. Rose's idea of daily help had been founded on her former charwoman, now earning three pounds a week in munitions, who had 'obliged' the maid once a week for two hours in the basement, where she devoted presumably as much time to scrubbing as her passion for gossip, and the two square meals which she consumed, would allow. All her mistress had known of Mrs Gibbs was the number and needs of her family, which were curiously well adapted to the Fairlaws' discarded clothes, and the exact troubles and surgical re-arrangements of Mrs Gibbs's remarkable internal organs. Mrs Childe, she told herself, was of a very different kidney, perhaps because she still possessed two, and Mrs Gibbs, as Rose knew only too well, had but one left her!

'Right up to the top and work down's my way,' Mrs Childe announced, as Rose led the way up the winding turret stair.

'We needn't go up to the top though!' pleaded Rose. 'We're not using the top floor now as my family is away. There are only their bedrooms and bathroom and the linen closet and so on up there.'

'Still, you can't let them go dirty!' protested Mrs Childe, who fully intended to make a complete survey of the house while she was about it. 'And these old-fashioned places are just awful for collecting dust. Comes up through the boards I say. Now in my little bungalow –'

'But, Mrs Childe,' protested Rose, 'there's such a lot to do – there's the drawing-room grate, and coal to carry up, and all the rooms, and I must think about the food –'

'Oh well!' Mrs Childe, having satisfied her curiosity by peering rapidly into Mickie's room in the old tower and Flora's and Tom's rooms in the newer wing, was willing to make concessions. 'Suppose, when I was gone, you just take a duster and give them a once-over, we'll make a morning for a thorough next week. We shan't be able to get through a house like this without method, you know, madam. Were you not thinking of shutting up your drawing-room? That parlour downstairs is nice and cosy for two, and a coal fire's a nasty, old-fashioned, dirty thing when all's said and done.'

'I'm rather fond of this room,' Rose said apologetically. As Mrs Childe rapidly opened the shutters she glanced affectionately at the pieces of red lacquer from Seriton which looked out so graciously from the white panelled walls. She had spent such happy hours tracking down just the right shade of deep bright red for the arm-chairs and sofas, and though Flora said contemptuously that there was no unity in the room, and that Rose's collection of china birds spoilt it entirely, every corner of it was full of those associations which are so much more important than a period in a home.

'I was never one to care for blood-colour myself,' was Mrs. Childe's comment. 'I've got a suite myself with my own savings in my little bungalow – covered in Rexine, and very handsome it looks. Well, we mustn't stand here talking. I'll see to the grate while you go into the bedrooms. Look-see, I'll give you a hand with the bed first. Oh I see, another bath-room on this floor. And two beds in these two rooms!' Mrs Childe paused for one moment, looking forward evidently to comments to Mr Childe later on the probable marital relations of her new employers. 'And now, let me see, what were you thinking of for the master's dinner?'

Into Rose's mind flashed a caption of a French cookery book which had delighted the family once – 'Dinner to Recall the Affections of an Unloving Husband.' Her first effort was hardly likely to come under that category, she thought, however necessary Mrs Childe might think it, hiding a smile while she murmured: 'Well, I thought perhaps some Bovril, and there's some of the cold chicken still.'

'Hoots! Bovril indeed! I mean, madam,' the Scottish Mrs Childe vanished at once – 'you'd not be giving the master that surely! Why you'll be talking of giving him stuff out of a tin next!' Mrs Childe laughed so heartily at this joke that Rose prayed she had not noticed the long row of consommés and purées in the pantry cupboard. 'No, I saw the stock of that boiling fowl, and we'll make him a nice drop of broth – you'll know how to do that of course –'

'Well, I haven't done any cooking before, but –'

'Never done any cooking!' Mrs Childe regarded her new employer with contempt rather than pity or surprise. If she had asked straight out, 'Well, what *have* you been doing all these years?' she could not have made her meaning plainer. 'Well, well, we must get down to our work now – you get on with the bedrooms and after our elevenses,' said Mrs Childe with great meaning, for how could you be sure that Rose's fathomless ignorance might not even extend to the proper routine of a working day? – 'after our elevenses we'll just try to make time to give you a hand with preparing the veg and then you can warm up the white meat with a good white sauce, and if you devil the legs you'll have a nice *fricassée* for the master, and then just toss up a nice little savoury of cheese or such-like, and there you are!'

Rose was thankful for the interruption of the telephone bell before she could be pinned down to any more alarming culinary programmes by Mrs Childe. A high drawling female voice demanded Mickie's number just as the door-bell rang. By the time she had taken in the grocer's delivery, the telephone was appealing again, loudly, this time for a wrong number. 'It's a bell boy I want really,' she thought as the greengrocer called for empty boxes and a sack, and she ran back to assure a friend on the telephone that she was terribly sorry she could not take her place at a canteen at twelve that morning. She had done no more than sweep the bedrooms – 'and a good switch is what they want, not one of your la-di-da maids mop-ing about with a carpet-sweeper,' Mrs Childe insisted, when she was summoned downstairs to 'elevenses' (and another time she must mention that tea full of sugar and milk was abhorrent to her). As her entire staff had been invisible, in old days, for half an hour at least over this festivity, she was hoping for a little rest, but Mrs Childe, hot on the track of the servants' iniquities and Rose's ignorance, rapped smartly on the library door in five minutes, and escorted her mistress to the basement.

'You couldn't scrub veg in that there little contraption of a sink in the pantry,' she explained, 'and why you don't use this good kitchen premises, ma'am, instead of puddling away in that wee hole over that electric bag of tricks just beats me, it really does! Why that's as good a kitchener as I've got in my bungalow – it really is, and a gas stove too, and I'm partial to gas, and that's inlaid linoleum I can see, and a beautiful scullery sink. What ails you at it all, ma'am, that you're not using it?'

'But, Mrs Childe,' expostulated Rose, watching out of the corner of her eye to see whether you used hot or cold water for the ablution of potatoes and 'veg' and if you did or didn't use soap, 'I couldn't manage the stairs very well at my age, could I? And it would mean a lot more to keep clean!'

'Well, it's got to be kept clean anyhow,' said Mrs Childe decisively. 'You can't live on top of dirt, now, can you? We'll have to see about cleaning a piece every day. Now that'll do for veg and we'll take them upstairs, for I've still my hall and brasses to do, and I'll have to leave the stairs to you, and a good switch is what they need, 'm, and I'd better just put the broth on for you, you not being got into your ways yet!'

At least, thought Rose, after another period of intensive activity on the stairs – 'at least she doesn't waste time in gossip!' But there, it appeared, she was mistaken, for when twelve o'clock struck Mrs Childe dived into the pantry, to reappear at one minute past as neat and immaculate as if she were going to a lunch party, whereas her poor, dishevelled mistress felt she would never be clean or tidy again. And now Mrs Childe had leisure for all the topics which she had been hoarding all morning – the possibility of mending the Hoover (broken up by Jessie), what the cook had done with mysterious items called the colander and the swill-pail, the ages and whereabouts of Mrs Fairlaw's family, and a few general reflections on 'this nasty war, and what it's all about don't ask me!' . . . the probable future of society – 'and there'll be no more domestic service after this war, mark my words.' As this mono-logue was conducted standing in the chilly hall, even Rose was brave enough to open the front door, and thus speed Mrs Childe's departure, for the last topic led, by an inexplicable association of ideas, straight to 'me ovaries', and since this is a topic which leads to at least ten minutes' conversation in every class of society, something drastic must obviously be done at once.

'Well, I'll be in at nine sharp tomorrow,' were Mrs Childe's parting words, 'and we must get down to our work tomorrow, mustn't we? We mustn't just stand about looking round us and gossiping idly every day!'

'Idle gossip,' thought Rose despairingly, her feet and knees aching, her hair flying in all directions, her fingers freezing, and an appalling sense of hunger to crown her

depression. 'Idle gossip all morning! And we're to work harder tomorrow!'

She had looked forward to being left alone in her empty, echoing, gracious house; she had planned to allow herself half an hour perhaps at the long-neglected piano; she would no longer feel guilty if she settled down to a book till lunch-time after a morning of work. But how could she do so when her new tyrant's parting instructions were to dust over the top rooms, and drawing-room, do out the dining-room thoroughly as Mrs Childe hadn't had the time to touch it, and it *was* in a mess, sort out the silver, and wash out the dusters and dishcloths. She had incidentally sketched out a programme for Rose's lunch involving several contortions with a mincer and a bit of sausage, but even Mrs Childe couldn't find out if Rose threw away the sausage and lunched off roll and coffee!

'Oh House, House! how I hate you!' apostrophised Rose in pious imitation of Alice. 'Or do I love you?' she added penitently as a ray of winter sunlight fell through the turret window on the stairs, and she looked out from the tower to see the drying-ground golden green in the light and the shining line of the Firth above the glittering roofs of little homes below with smoking chimneys. It was like climbing to the top of the tree, and here was the nest, the three rooms which had sheltered her children. And now they had flown, 'and I'm quite sure birds don't go sweeping and dusting the twigs and feathers,' thought Rose rebelliously.

She looked into Mickie's room, and as she saw, by the crack of sunlight through the curtains, all the framed groups of boys in football or cricket elevens at school or Oxford, smiling or scowling from the lemon-coloured walls, she turned away and shut the door. If she once began to dust the bookcase, where *Just William*, T S Eliot's poems, Edgar Wallace and A E Housman jostled each other for pride of place, her upper lip would lose the very small stiffening left by her exhausting morning. It was not only the cherubic little boy Mickie, scuttling into bed in his blue pyjamas at her footsteps which would haunt her, or the schoolboy who reverted, so secretly and touchingly, to his old books and toys in the holidays. Most painful of all were the memories of days when Stuart had fumed over the sort of reports from school which implied that Mickie could work if he wanted to, only he didn't; the letters ending in light-hearted requests for cheques, and most of all, Mickie's meteoric changes of front about his future career – 'anything but a Castleburgh lawyer' was his usual conclusion, tiresome enough for a father with two sons to provide for and so admirable an opening in his own firm. Rose had tried to support Stuart in his solemn strictures, 'though you're infatuated with that boy,' as he would say angrily with raised eyebrows. All that seemed now so miserable, so pathetic a waste of happier days. If they had known how surely fate was to decide Mickie's future, she would never have heard the door bang in a fury, as Mickie rushed out of the library, or seen him go off to Oxford without a word for Stuart, however affectionately he hugged his stepmother goodbye.

Rose shut the door defiantly, and looked into Tom's room. She herself had tidied away all the collections of his youth into a cabinet, so it looked strangely tidy. For dear, jolly, placid

Tom had always been as untidy in his appearance and habits as he was orderly in his mental processes. He had always gone his own way imperturbably since his babyhood, and Flora had not failed to point out that this was a sure sign of their mother's neglect – 'for neither you nor I count with her, my poor Tom, compared with Mickie.' Tom must have been about ten years old, she supposed, when he rose once in the drawing-room, and suddenly, thoughtfully, and violently pulled Flora's hair, the only form of attack on ladies authorised by nursery lore. 'Kindly remember,' he said, in his most mature way, 'that Mother fusses over Mickie because he's delicate and needs her. I'd hate it, and she knows it, and some day I shall fuss over her!' And he was quite right, for as he grew up he developed not only a genius for mathematics at school, but that even happier gift of being the indispensable member of the family circle. If Rose had never wholly grown out of her instinct to protect her adored Mickie, she grew yearly more and more dependent on Tom's good sense and easy acceptance of home problems. If it had been Tom who was in the Air Force now she could not have looked into his room, but surely after Tom left the ranks he must be safe for some months in the OCTU, and she could bring herself to obey Mrs Childe and dust the room he would surely occupy again quite soon. Flora had done her best to spoil this family relationship, but here at least she had failed entirely.

All the old undercurrents of jealousy and suspicion seemed to crowd back upon her as she looked next into Flora's green and white bedroom. Never could she read of the Problem Child without seeing Flora's scowl! One of the few surreptitious actions of Rose's life had been to take her daughter to a psychoanalyst at the age of fourteen, in despair of their relationship to each other. She could still see the gleam of triumph in Flora's long, dark narrow eyes beneath her curly fringe when Rose herself was told to leave the room. 'At last I can tell someone what I really think of you' was expressed in every line of her fierce face and long, lithe body, in its short neat kilt and green coat. But whatever Flora had said – and Rose trembled to think of it – the doctor had been very kind when he interviewed the mother an hour later. It was true that for all the use of his words like father-fixation, compulsion neurosis, and traumas, he didn't tell Rose much that she did not know already in a vague sort of way. It was hard to believe that the loss of her father at the age of three months, and Rose's remarriage three years later, could have affected the child, but she did see how the latter fact, striking on the consciousness of an abnormally sensitive and jealous nature after a long period of subconscious revolt, had needed far more tact and understanding than her mother had ever given. As for Flora's relations with Mickie, well, old Nurse had summed them up when she announced, 'Just eaten up by the green-eyed monster you are, my bairn,' but the doctor made her realise how the jealousy of the care which Rose gave to the delicate Mickie had led Flora to develop such curious inhibitions about illness and pain that she would never give way to any complaint till she could walk no longer (she had been removed from one school by successfully disguising a measles rash till she had infected everyone else). That and other events in her early life ('And what?' wondered Rose) had given her a morbid interest in death which must be discouraged, or rather, sublimated.

That the girl was so hopelessly naughty and defiant at school – for it was after her expulsion from yet another establishment that Rose had determined to seek aid in such an unknown path as psychoanalysis – was all the exhibitionism due to the subconscious demand to make herself paramount in her mother's consideration, even though the conscious Flora seemed to feel nothing but dislike for and distrust of her mother. Rose had found that the diagnosis did help her to understand about the past and see her own mistakes more clearly, but she was depressed to find how little hope or advice could be given for the future. Flora could certainly have treatment, and the analyst could put her on to a first-class man in Castleburgh, but that would mean telling Stuart, and would Flora ever consent to go? Flora, who had conceived a passion for the analyst almost as great as that which she entertained for Gary Cooper, insisted that she would only receive treatment at his hands, so for six weeks Rose stayed with her at a private hotel in South Kensington, awaiting the miracle of Flora's transformation, while nominally she was looking out for another school for the girl in the South.

'I can do no more for her,' said the psychoanalyst at last, flushed and uncomfortable. 'The transference of libido in these cases is always an awkward factor. But I can, I think, manage to place her at Halwell Hall under the care of Miss Lowes, who makes a wonderful success of difficult pupils. I should advise you, too, to let her spend large parts of her holiday with her father's relations. It seems to be a fixation with her that she has not been allowed to see much of them.'

So for three years Flora cost vast sums at the school in Sussex, learning bee-keeping and Greek dancing, javelin-throwing and the care of pigs, and all those other activities vaguely classed as forms of self-expression, and spent most of her holidays with the one sister of her father, a lady whom Rose had found very uncongenial since she had married a rich stockbroker and parted entirely with her old environment and tradition. There was a contemporary cousin with whom Flora went to a finishing school in Munich, and with whom Flora shared a season in London afterwards.

'What does that lead to for a girl who's got to live in Castleburgh?' demanded Stuart with annoyance, and indeed it seemed to lead to little but tragedy.

Rose looked sighing at the portrait of Flora in her Court dress, too tall, dark, and heavy at that age to show her genuine beauty but already clearly a compelling personality. Her cousin May, a giggling little blonde, had been a success as a deb where Flora was a failure. Flora's aunt, selfish and uninterested, had let the girl drift into an odd bohemian set, and the experiment had ended by an urgent summons to Rose to remove her daughter from London before she got hopelessly entangled with a married man. The years which followed, while Flora was unable to forgive her mother for an interference for which Flora's victim was obviously grateful, had been almost the most painful in Rose's life. Flora's form of revenge was to attach herself devotedly to Stuart, and treat her mother, as Mickie said indignantly, as something the cat had brought home in the dark. When the war began Flora at once elected to go off to a Red Cross ambulance unit in the South, and until Mickie only too soon gained his wings, life was at last tolerable again. Poor, poor Flora! Rose pitied her child, and reproached herself vehemently, as she dusted the little china ornaments and old treasured scent bottles which made Flora seem a vulnerable, pitiful child again. Mrs Childe, she decided, had better look after these rooms in the future, as they had to be cleaned now and again, for no one could be a real world's worker when they were living through such emotional crises of the past.

But in the drawing-room, that more neutral ground, she really set herself down to work, thankful to be spared the grate, at least, through Mrs Childe's assistance. She had braced herself to it last night by that traditional Gaelic blessing:

I will kindle my fire this morning
In the presence of the holy angels of Heaven,
In the presence of Ariel of the loveliest form,
In the presence of Uriel of the myriad charms. . . .

But on the whole she preferred Mrs Childe even to that elusive and mystical army of helpers. As she switched rugs and dusted and polished, she tried to remember other such charming rhymes for household use, but it was probable, she decided sadly, that Highland housewives did little about their cabins but that sacred act of kindling. It was Lowland and English proverbs which came to her mind, and very dull they were too! 'Many a mickle makes a muckle. . . . Doe ye next thinge. . . . Blessed be drudgery. . . . If a thing is worth doing at all it is worth doing well. . . . There's no grease like elbow-grease. . . .'

'Darling, I won't keep you but I had to ask you!' Linda's voice on the telephone called Rose from the bathroom, where she was meeting her Waterloo with a tin of Vim – 'How have you got on? I waited till after lunch so as not to disturb your work!'

'After lunch? But the bell hasn't gone! Oh, of course it wouldn't, now I think of it,' said Rose waking to reality. 'Oh dear, I see it's long after two! I thought I was getting hungry!'

'Have you had nothing to eat yet? Rose, you must come round here and have something at once!'

'I couldn't, love. For one thing your maids would give notice, and for another I'm far too dirty and far too tired to try to clean myself. Oh, Linda, my hands!'

'But, dearest, you should wear gloves.'

'I did, but they all disappeared. There's a rubber pair I wore in the basement, I expect, as I was cleaning veg there (yes, dear, you speak of veg not vegetables in the underworld) and a chamois pair at the top of the house, and a housemaid's pair lost for all time in some bedroom I expect. Oh, Linda, dear, I'm having such an awful time with the bath. I shook Vim out on it in just exactly the way Jessie did, and all the stuff simply belched forth, and I can't scrape it up. Stuart will have to bath in sand like a sparrow, for water doesn't seem to move it a bit. But never mind! Anyway, the time has flown. Of course

I must confess I haven't been doing it all alone, oh, Linda, that angel Loman has sent me a daily woman!'

'Darling, how splendid –' (Linda was almost the only woman in Castleburgh, thought Rose, who wouldn't ask herself automatically – 'Why didn't she send her to me?') 'But why didn't she get to work and do the house herself? Is she any good?'

'She may be a treasure or a curse, I don't know. I only know that by ten o'clock I'd have asked Catrine and Jessie to come back on my knees, and now I'd welcome the Borgias if they'd give me some lunch. No, Linda, I don't mean that, and I won't come out; I'll go and get something to eat and then I'll rest, yes, I promise I will.'

'Well, dearest, tell me you've not been worrying anyhow, have you? You've not had time for that?'

'No, not really, except when I looked at Mickie's room. Linda, I made a rule for myself that I'd never think of him without praying for him, and I think that may help – no –' Rose's voice changed. 'Where I did waste time was standing in Flora's room ten solid minutes, worrying about that child.'

'She'll come through all right, dearest, I'm sure she will. My Wanda wasn't too easy till she married, you know.'

'But look at your Iona. Mickie and Tom both adore her. She's a pet, and the image of you, Linda.'

'She was terribly flattered and bucked all last week, but there's safety in numbers. She's just brought me letters she's written to both your boys, as she thinks her spelling is shaky – and is it or is it not, as she'd say! She's addressed them both as

"Deerest" you'll be glad to hear! I don't wonder her school reports for English were a little pained.'

'What does spelling matter? You just teach her how to cook, Linda, so that she knows how to mince up a little chicken with white sauce for the master's dinner. An Iona who could cook would be a pearl among women.'

'Do you know, Rose, I'd rather she picked up a little general knowledge. What can we do with these children who can't go abroad to get a little polish and a wider point of view? I'd rather she had your nice quirky brain, and took a little interest in any book that wasn't a thriller or about sea voyages.'

'Well, she can do that and cook. I mean to! I've put a bookrest in the pantry and while I'm scraping carrots, which looks to me, let me tell you, Linda, as if it would take hours and hours, I'm going to try to get through the sort of book one never reads, like the *The Faerie Queen* or *The Decline and Fall*. I did look out a Spenser in Tom's bookcase but of course it opened on the only canto anyone ever really reads – "Sleep after toil, port after stormy seas." Do the parsons who quote it realise that it's an impassioned plea for suicide, I always wonder? So I think it had better be Gibbon, don't you, or is *Decline and Fall* a little too topical?'

'Only too much so after the news of today,' said Linda sadly.

'Oh don't, dearest! The only thing to be said for my life is that I haven't looked at the papers yet. No, I just meant my decline into being a lady in reduced circumstances. And very reduced too, for how we ever got through the masses of milk and bread and all that the maids used to take I don't know!'

'Don't read Gibbon anyhow! What about Jane?'

'If only she'd lived longer and written more! If only she and Mrs Henry Wood had changed fate over that! There comes a point when you really do know her too well, whatever the Janeites say. I've re-read her three times since war began. No, I think I'll finish a detective book of Stuart's, the sort which tells you what he had to eat at every meal – you know: "Jimmy ordered an admirable meal of *sole meunière* and Maryland chicken followed by a rum omelet, and his guest was so far recovered by the time they were sipping benedictine with their coffee that she was able to discuss quite calmly the discovery of her husband's corpse in the bottom shelf of the linen closet." How I'm groaning to you, Linda! Tell me your news for a change.'

'Well, the maids seem fairly settled at the moment, but Ian goes off to fetch Grannie here tomorrow –'

'Oh dear! For a visit?'

'More likely the duration. Her servants all walked out on her, and she and Griffen had to take refuge at the Avie Arms. She and Griffen (you remember her trampled maid with a scone sort of face?) and the factor and the last gamekeeper were trying to shut up the house somehow when fortunately the Command took it over all of a sudden. It was lucky, because she'd probably have refused to leave if the servants hadn't gone, and then we'd have had her court-martialled.'

'Quite good for her,' said Rose casually. 'But why shouldn't she live on at the pub? It's quite good and the air's quite bracing, and we landowners should stick to our properties, don't chah see?' That last phrase of Grannie's had been thus rendered phonetically long ago by her irreverent son, and all the children of both families, who had always used the honorary titles of Aunt and Uncle to the former generation, spoke and wrote habitually of Grannie Don't Chah See.

'Unluckily she says now that families should cling together in such days as these! Ian thinks that the proprietor is very likely trying to turn her out, as she won't allow people to smoke in the lounge, and won't stay in her own sitting-room!'

'Oh my poor dear! All I can say is I'd rather wash up and switch floors – yes, I'd even rather prepare veg.'

'I'll probably have to do that too. The servants are sure to give notice, with Grannie ordering them about, and Griffen moaning over past glories all day. Don't you envy capable young women in uniforms with worth-while jobs?'

'Do I not! But I think you'll have a worse time than me, or I – which would Iona say?'

'And what about poor Stuart at dinner-time?' asked Linda as they exchanged laughing farewells, and Rose went to the pantry to fling bits of food anyhow on to a tray, and finish up almost the whole of Catrine's coffee, warmed up or not. And a few minutes later the door-bell and telephone bell, the urgent need for shopping and Mrs Childe's orders troubled her no longer, for the Apostle of the Dignity of Labour was sleeping on the library sofa as she had never slept in her life before.

CHAPTER FIVE
MARTHA

Dic nobis . . . quid vidisti in via?
Gloriam vidi resurgentis.
from The Paschal Mass

In the days which followed Rose discovered some answer to
the problem which had often puzzled her as to the conduct
and behaviour of the doomed in history: how could the
Roman aristocracy in the Province of Gaul or Britain, she
wondered, live on serenely in their villas, writing leisurely
letters, studying the classics, visiting and entertaining and
watching the harvest sown and reaped, while the tramp of
the barbarians was at their gates? How could gallants at the
Tudor Courts preen and swagger, when at any moment they
might be led off to the Tower and the block? How did the
aristocrats of the French Revolution laugh and trifle and play
cards as they awaited the guillotine? Well, at least she knew
the answer now. They just pursued the old tenor of their lives
because their habits, and the unconscious inability to envisage a change of habit, were too strong for them. They were

like snails dragging themselves along in their shells: they could not imagine life without them. It was the one point in common between people so different as herself and Stuart and Mrs Childe.

Rose could see no escape from her snail-shell, however wearisome or irksome it might be. This was her home and she must live in it, and while she did so habit, not to mention Mrs Childe, insisted that she must keep it clean and respectable. And yet during the bitter January of 1942, while bad news fell daily on her ears as certainly as the sound of good housewives scraping snow from their pavements in the black dawn, it seemed absurd to wash and sweep and polish rooms, as if they had any conceivable importance in the scheme of a nightmare existence. And, worse still, these things could loom so large that at times she even forgot the nightmare –

Do not let any woman read this verse;
It is for men, and after them their sons;
And their sons' sons.

Tom had said once that those lines were well calculated to ensure women readers for all time, but she felt now that if you substituted man for woman it would be just the prohibition she would attach to reading her thoughts. What would Stuart or Mickie or Tom feel if they could guess at her boredom and weariness, her self-pity and fuss over the effort to do a mere ordinary woman's work in the world? She could only keep her thoughts to herself, and despise herself in silence. When friends rang up and asked how she was getting on, she only gave laughing accounts of her idiotic mistakes. Very few of them really understood: most of them were still clinging to some lifebelt in the shape of an old maid or changing temporaries, and those in her own case were too busy for visits. And she had no desire really at the moment for the best gift which Heaven extends, for any accomplished female friend would inevitably wish to talk about Hong Kong and Singapore and the news which she could scarcely bear to read, or discuss the books about Poland and Nazi Germany which still came from the library and were returned unread. They would find her own petty struggles with her house merely contemptible. She could not even catch a glimpse of Linda, who was struggling with an epidemic of influenza in her household, and the worse infliction of Grannie Don't Chah See and her maid, and was far more to be pitied than Rose herself.

So therefore she crept on her round in her shell of habit, and Stuart did the same. He continued automatically in his old routine, and seldom, far too seldom, looked up to express his sympathy. To her horror Rose discovered that she was developing what was, she imagined, a working woman's mentality towards her husband. For one of them it must have been who, with an unbearable grudge in her heart, evolved the rhyme:

Man's work lasts till set of sun,
Woman's work is never done.

If the Fairlaws had turned out of Laws House into a flat or bungalow, or if some cataclysm had left them penniless,

Stuart might have woken up to feel it his duty to clean his own shoes, fill his hot-water bottle, or fetch his hot water and whisky at night. It was trifles like these, rather than the basic business of cooking and cleaning for him, which made Rose find herself regarding him resentfully as a great, idle, hulking fellow who was no use about the house. That was how the children's nurse regarded the big pleasant policeman whom she had married, only while Rose bit her lips Nannie spoke out, and by this time Bob Mackie was doubtless a perfectly trained husband. Stuart, even though he accepted the normal routine of life as natural, was perceptive enough to see that Rose's manner was carefully restrained and a little icy at times, but his well-meant suggestions for saving her work seemed, curiously, only to irritate her.

'I'm sure you'd feel better if you had a hot bath and dressed for dinner,' he said on the first evening, when he found his Rose, usually so slim and graceful in her long flowered silk tea-frock, standing with hair dishevelled in a stained overall over the pantry stove.

'Later on, Stuart,' she protested with glacial patience, 'I may come to be one of the wee wifies who run upstairs and put a blue ribbon in their hair and a smile on their front teeth before they welcome hubby home with a kiss to a dainty little meal. As it is, if I leave the thickening of this abominable soup for even a minute it will boil over or stick to the pan or something, and the potatoes and brussels sprouts will boil over too – they've done it ten times already!'

'Can't we simplify life a bit?' he asked a few days later, when looking over *The Times* at nine o'clock he saw Rose come into the library from washing up, and collapse into a corner of the sofa too tired to read or knit. 'Hurst was telling me they've shut their drawing-room and only have high tea. I'm sure you keep up our old ways too exactly. Can't you cut out some superfluous meals?'

'Just what?' asked Rose, trying without much success to sound good-tempered. 'You wouldn't do without your early tea now, even if I could. You must have breakfast before you go to the office. Mrs Childe has to have elevenses and I'm sure I'm very thankful for them. As for lunch I just put everything that's left over from breakfast or dinner into an enamel bowl and steam it very hot, eat it with a spoon, and have a huge cup of coffee. I've got rid of any standards over that, I can tell you – one bowl, one spoon, one cup to wash, that's all! If you want high tea you must be back at six, Stuart, because the only point of it is that then you give afternoon tea a miss, and I couldn't bear to wait later than six! And what's the point of high tea? You'd still want soup because you love it, and anyway it's the most filling thing you can get nowadays, and some sort of meat and fish and all the extras:

> There is jam, ginger-beer, buttered toast, marmalade,
> And a large pigeon-pie very skilfully made
> To consist almost wholly of beef.

Much more bother to serve and clear away than our dinner, and an endless race to the shops to get the pigeons and ginger-beer in queues –'

'But I never said anything about marmalade or pigeon-pie,' protested Stuart, who did not know his Hilaire Belloc as his family did.

'And then,' pursued Rose, 'after that, people as far as I can gather, have cocoa and biscuits and sandwiches at nine o'clock – another meal! At least after dinner I have only your hot water to get while I boil the kettle for the hot-water bottles.'

'Couldn't you get this Childe woman to come all day?' suggested Stuart. He was not a selfish man, but still it did not occur to him to suggest that he might take on this little job of boiling hot water at ten o'clock.

'No, she can't. She has to go at twelve, because Mr Childe is very particular about his bite of dinner, and she has her own house to look after in the afternoon, and as far as I can make out she goes to the pictures with Mr Childe every night because it takes his mind off his troubles for a little. Besides, I don't really want it! She's been in such superior service with all the dukes of Scotland that she's always had under-servants to train, and now that there aren't any more under-servants she's training me, and three hours is quite enough of it!'

'Well, couldn't we shut some room anyway?'

'Your library?' asked Rose coldly.

'Well, I thought perhaps the drawing-room –'

'So that I couldn't get classical concerts or have my gramophone records any more? Or you the news when we can bear to listen to it? And I don't mean it about shutting the library, Stuart,' said Rose, thawing rapidly with her rest, 'you must have all your papers, of course, and go on with your book. But the sad part of civilisation is that it makes people like solitude, and eat quite a little rather often. I could have been quite a respectable cave-woman with only one mud floor and wood fire, and one pot to boil for the gobbets of entrails you stuffed down once a day! No, we can't change much, and I must just hope that I'll get more efficient soon and learn how to keep my temper. It's difficult when one's a bit tired, and can't help thinking of all the horrible things that are happening.' All over the country, she supposed, as she reached her conclusion, such conversations were going on between the victims of a ridiculous civilisation. Society had never, it seemed, been able to free itself of its absurd trappings unless some final and conclusive smash shook it for ever out of its groove.

But if she realised clearly, and Stuart dimly, how absurd and fettering were the chains of habit in a world of war, Mrs Childe had no such illusions.

'I never wanted this tiresome war,' she would declare as she washed silver and china at incredible speed. 'I don't see that Mr Childe or myself will be any the better or any the worse whoever comes out top . . . it's a shame to think of my nephew Bob being taken out of his good job at Dowley's to go off to be a soldier, and my brother won't hear of my nieces, such superior girls as they are too, going into any of these services, as they call them, living cheek by jowl with any rough, common girl. And what I want to know is, what it's got to do with all of us anyway?'

Rose was far too wise to attempt any explanations, and when she murmured something about the defence of our Empire, Mrs Childe's immediate reaction was the earnest advice to buy rice and tapioca – 'which come from those parts, they say.' Any danger to any outlying fringe of Empire was a reason for hoarding to Mrs Childe, and for some inscrutable reason salt was included in this category – 'for the Store says there'll be a shortage soon and who can wonder if we haven't command of the sea? But there! Mr Childe says not to worry. He thinks those Russians and Germans will just kill each other off, and no loss either, for I never did like foreigners. And he wouldn't be surprised if the war was over sooner than we think. The stars seem much more hopeful, and a captain in the Merchant Service told the Fish, when Mr Childe was in the shop, that it would all be over by Christmas, and your boys safely home again!'

As for Rose's minute contribution to the war effort, Mrs Childe varied between declaring, when her old self was predominant, that it was a shame a real lady should demean herself so – and her sharp researches into photographs and letters and inscriptions on the Seriton silver assured her that Rose was a real lady – or vague prophetic utterances about there being no more service after *this* war, with the consequent determination to try to rescue Rose from the trough of inefficiency and helplessness in which she was drowning. From her point of view, that of a good upper-servant, it was not Rose herself who mattered, 'The Master' had to receive consideration in the nature of a good dinner and shining shoes, but the House itself was the supreme god, to which offerings of soap and Vim, floor polish, and most of all, elbow-grease had to be made every day. It was a point of view which Rose could just imagine if the house were your own, but that didn't matter to Mrs Childe. If you were in any way connected with it, your duty was to the House; and what Hitler did or those nasty Japs, whom Mrs Childe never had fancied, made no difference. And so, Rose supposed, she and Stuart and Mrs Childe would go on their ways as before till a bomb destroyed the house, or Germans battered in the front door. They were set helplessly in their ways. Saints and mystics, the young, the villainous and adventurous, would find some new way of life perhaps, but not elderly creatures of habit like herself and Stuart and Mrs Childe. While the shell remained they would crawl about as usual.

So it was that the dull blows of horror which fell upon Great Britain in the early months of 1942 stunned and incapacitated the mind, but left the body pursuing its usual ways. Rose remembered often how she had once, to her horror, seen a man dart out of the darkness of the pavements in Covent Garden, and snatch a pearl necklace from the neck of a woman as she stepped into her car. The string broke, the pearls rolled in every direction, just as in the East the great harbours and fairy islands of our Empire were being snatched from us, and scattered out of our possession for ever. The bystanders for the most part stood watching that theft helplessly, and when some more enterprising souls had whistled for the police, rushed in pursuit, and crawled over the ground in search of the pearls, the rest of them went home to supper or bed just as usual. What indeed was the use of doing otherwise? Save for economy and gifts to War Loan neither she nor Stuart could avert those unimaginable tragedies for an instant, and as for Mrs Childe she had no use even for those saving clauses. Empires might rock and kingdoms fall, but habits, it appeared, remained.

So every morning Rose crept downstairs in the stuffy darkness, for the smell of cooking from the pantry made the house far less inviting than in the days when everything was done in the basement, and from the time when she began to sweep the library till the moment at night when the clock struck ten and she crept, worn out, to bed, the house and its duties were never out of her mind. She had promised herself that when Mrs Childe's three hours of intensive training were over every morning she would settle down to a novel or to her piano, but that hope soon proved vain. 'Remember you should give the silver a good rub today,' Mrs Childe would say as she rushed off, smart and fresh as ever, 'and I'd not the time to O-Cedar the drawing-room and it needs it; and you'll have to run out for that washing soda, and those dishcloths would be the better of a wash,' and so great were the good lady's powers of suggestion and absent treatment that Rose went on with her tasks till nearly two o'clock before she threw her lunch together in the bowl, which did, she had to confess, bear a sad likeness to a dog's dinner. And after lunch there was often a rush to the shops near by, to return with a crowded bag: there were notes and letters to write, the laundry to attend to, mending to be done, and a lot of it, because it was unpatriotic now to buy new socks for Stuart, and all the telephone messages and minor business affairs which Stuart still left to her.

By half-past three she was so sick with fatigue that she took the receiver off the telephone, shut the outer front door, and slept, dead to the world, so dead that even a cup of tea hardly seemed to revive her. And directly after that she had to sweep and dust the dining-room, because she had found it was utterly impossible to do two rooms before breakfast, prepare dinner with anxious care and meticulous reading of instructions, weighing and measuring, and experimenting with the vagaries of the electric stove. By the time dinner was laid and cooked, served and washed up, any inclination for any mental activity but the reading of murder stories, or the simplest of her old favourite books, was out of the question. And even at ten her work wasn't over, for then she had to wash and scrub herself in her bath almost as hard as she scrubbed the saucepans, and brush her hair laboriously and dutifully, and go through all the toilet processes which seemed as essential to her as they would have seemed unnecessary to a working woman, in old days at least.

But none of this weariness was allowed to creep into letters to the boys. What did it matter if after a lifetime of ease and gaiety she was passing into an old age of weariness and boredom? They had had so little of a life they enjoyed so much, and what was her tiny sacrifice compared with the immense burden laid upon young men and young women? So to Mickie she wrote of Mrs Childe's endearing habit of letting her top dental plate fall on to the one below when Rose displayed some outstanding bit of ignorance or inefficiency, 'sometimes for the most innocent reasons like not knowing what or where a fish kettle is, or thinking she was talking rather impertinently about a damn cloth when it was really a damp cloth, or muddling up the brasso and polishing rags (a fearful crime!). Or sometimes more deservedly when she found I'd filled up the salt-cellars with washing soda, and when she had to prise open a Pyrex dish of stewing steak with a chisel, because I'd left it too long in the oven. She is a hard taskmaster, but then she goes at twelve and when I'm spryer and more professional I shall have some leisure, I expect, and at least I don't have to go out at all in this hateful weather, except to the local shops in Odd's Lane. Your father thinks I should have more fresh air and exercise, but if he saw me dusting the tops of wardrobes in the icy blasts which Mrs Childe decrees for the bedrooms he would retract it, I tell him. It isn't as if I had dear old Smuts to exercise any more – and I'm glad now that we didn't get another dog, though I miss one quite dreadfully at times. And I don't have to toil through snow and ice to war work any more for I literally haven't a moment. In short I'm house-bound, and there are moments when I really like it, for this is a friendly house, we've always agreed. The only real troubles of my lot are grease, which I do think, with snakes and wood-lice, really justifies a belief in original sin, getting up early, and, oh dear me, losing my temper with your father because there's no one else to lose it with! And don't think of me as worrying about you or the world in general, for my mind is so full of whether I remembered to polish taps and count the laundry, or what I'll try to cook for dinner and when I have to begin it, that I often spend hours without any coherent thoughts at all.'

And to Tom who shared her passion for solitude she wrote: 'The house is heavenly, darling – it is a castle or fortress now where I can lock myself up in complete silence. Often when the bell rings I just give a look out of my bedroom window, and if the beller looks boring, I just don't answer it. And I take the receiver off the telephone for hours on end, and I think I am well on the way to becoming one of those old women who are found dead in filthy houses which no one had entered for months, with a mattress stuffed with banknotes. (That part might well be true for we seem to eat nothing and spend nothing without maids!) You can understand how it's really rather fun to be house-bound, so I must confess to you that it was odious of me to be cross today when Daddy asked me to go to the memorial service of Sir John Loring tomorrow – "My first outing for a fortnight," I said, "what a gay one!" And of course he was horrified and of course I insisted on going to make up for being a pig. Daddy is really too busy, and it only seemed rather silly for me to go, because I only spoke to Sir John once and, as he was ninety and dotty, the only service I should have held for him would be the Te Deum and the Hallelujah Chorus! Now you see what a vixen you have for a mother – in fact, I expect I'm well on the way to a second version of *Lady into Fox*. Mrs Childe must have heard our conversation – I don't think anything goes on in this house that she doesn't hear or see – and has just asked me if I wouldn't like her "to iron my blacks". She looked awfully shocked when I said I didn't approve of mourning, and that my nails were black enough to make up for the rest of me – and so, alas, they are! Isn't it queer that I can't bear the feeling of being herded with a lot of people again, even just in pews in church? It is an odd life and it's all infinitely trivial, but it does pass the time and deaden one's imagination.'

All her life Rose would, she surmised, remember oddly how much against the grain had been her consent to go, in

Stuart's place, to the memorial service of which she wrote to her sons. It was stranger to think how nearly she had refused to go, and how easy it would have been to accept her husband's horrified apologies, when he realised what was the nature of the first entertainment which he was planning for his wife since she had become his maid-of-all-work. But Rose had shown enough temper to make her thoroughly ashamed of herself, and insisted on going to St Edwin's Church at three o'clock rather as an act of expiation than anything else. And it must have been that fate to which people refer so glibly, and in which nobody either believes or disbelieves, which led her to make the sacrifice and thus gain light from two new windows in her new, petty, unheroic life.

In a grey, well-cut tailor-made suit and little felt hat Rose chose as dark a corner of St Edwin's as she could find, and settled herself down with a shudder of distaste. This was Stuart's church to which she accompanied him on the ten or twelve Sundays of the year which he could spare from golf ('It's dreich weather, so don't fill up Mr Fairlaw's pew today,' was the customary advice of the head beadle to his underling). Rose's family had belonged by heredity to the great non-juring section of the Scottish Episcopal Church. The Seriton of that period had built a little chapel on the place, which had survived the destruction of the little old house in the eighteenth century. It had been served by a neighbouring town with visits from the episcopal vicar and, as Rose said, she had been obliged to attend the services and play the harmonium as assiduously as if she had been a parson's daughter. She was neither a *dévotée* nor a rebel when she made a long

visit, after the loss of her first husband, to his father and
mother in the close of a great cathedral. And at Mells under
the influence of her saintly father-in-law, and the beauty of
worship, so infinitely more impersonal and majestic than any
she had ever known, Rose found her stumbling way towards
the heart of Christianity. There in the old jewelled glass of the
east window was the great representation of the sacrifice
of God for man: there in the old panelled house was Tim's
father, nobly content with his son's sacrifice for his God
and his country. Rose had never repudiated her faith, for
the touch of poet and mystic in her made it easier for her to
believe than disbelieve, but after her visit to Mells it was as if
the sun had risen and poured light and meaning and colour
into the drab outlines of her pictured faith. But if her heart
had a new treasure she did not expect to share it. When she
agreed to marry Stuart it never occurred to her that he would
share the spiritual side of her life. Though the Scottish clergy
have wrangled for generations in the past over their various
creeds, the Scottish laity has met tolerance with tolerance for
years. On Christmas Day and at Easter Stuart politely accompanied his wife to her church; when the weather was too bad
for golf she accompanied him to St Edwin's. The rector of the
Episcopal church which she attended was too infinitely wise
and courteous and tolerant to criticise that which more fiery
partisans would call the sin of schism. Rose had sometimes
wondered if it would be difficult about the children, but as
they went away to English schools they inevitably came to
accept church services with their mother as more natural
ceremonies, and, as Mickie said easily, preferred serving God

in the open air with a mashie to any organised religion. They would accompany her, if she occasionally suggested it, to what they termed her God-box, but as she remembered her efforts to teach them in the nursery, and those touching moments when she had looked down on shining heads and bewitching necks in church, as their loud untuneful voices proclaimed the song of the herald angels, she reproached herself for having helped them so little on their pilgrimage through life. But the wise and human rector had always urged her to leave them alone, and pray for them rather than worry over them. 'For after all,' he said sadly very recently, 'we had hoped in the last war to become one of the brotherhood of European nations, and I fear our poor old creaking Church-of-a-compromise had done little to further that, just as she has spoken with no united voice on our social inequalities. Of course your boys are critical: of course they are irreverent: of course they are attracted by new shiny faiths of every shape and colour. But I know and believe that the spirit within the Church is alive and bursting its bonds, and that she too, freed from her bondage of outworn customs and riches, will be ready to play her part in a new world order. Not one of our clergy has been found wanting in the bombardment of our cities: if tribulation came they would, I know, show the courage and self-sacrifice of Lutheran, Catholic and Greek priests alike. Your boys must wander; all youth wanders, but they may come back to her, and anyhow are searching, I feel sure, for their own path to the City of God at the other end of the road.'

And since the war, Rose asked herself, counting the gilt stars on the blue ground above the pitch-pine, awe-inspiring pulpit, what had happened to her own faith? Some of her friends declared that they had lost theirs for ever, but Rose hardly thought of the question in such terms. The shock of the catastrophe seemed to have hurled her world into another dimension where past, present, and future alike seemed to have lost their meaning. She could not see the war in terms of right or wrong, of races or empires: she saw it only as a war of men against the machines which they had created for themselves.

'Men have made machines which are too strong for them,' her mind wearied with the old dilemma now. 'What's difficult is not to feel they are too strong for God as well. When you feel nothing but an ant in an ant-heap, waiting for an enormous, heedless foot to crush you, you can't even feel as important as the two sparrows sold for one farthing. "Thou turnest man to destruction" – though I expect some commentary would say it didn't mean that – and I expect we deserve it. Only when you're one of those on whom the ends of this world have come, because men have lost control of their own inventions, it's very difficult to look back to Bethlehem and forward to a Beata Urbs, because nothing seems to have eternal values.'

She had only discovered how far she had wandered into these dark mists of despair on Christmas Eve when she listened on the wireless, as she did every year, to the Service of Nine Lessons and Carols in King's College Chapel. Never before had the words of the bidding prayers, the simple stories in the different voices, and the exquisite melodies of the carols failed to bring joy to her heart. Even in 1940, hearing in fancy the echoes in the fretted roof and vaulted aisles, her heart had travelled back to the little town of Bethlehem and lifted itself to the beauty which must surely be left untouched in the world:

> 'O the rising of the sun
> And the running of the deer
> The playing of the merry organ . . .

That had been bound up always with the smell of bracken in the mist on December mornings, and the first golden glow of sunrise, through white birch-trees, on the stalls where cattle had knelt the night before (so the old story said) in worship of the newborn Child. But this year all those songs and carols and the very story itself seemed only part of the world's beautiful past which could have nothing to do with the real world or the future.

She had been frightened then to discover how far she was drifting from her old moorings, and how little her regular church-goings and ceaseless, urgent, despairing prayers for Mickie had meant to her intellect. 'But people should remember that they are responsible for their want of faith as well as God.' Canon Goring's saying came back oddly to her mind now. It was not, she told herself, because the problem was too vast, but because she was too small, that she was losing her way. She would retrace her steps, she must find her way back, for if she were to lose the hope that beyond the unreality of this nightmare world was the steadfast reality of another, and that man's spirit was as invincible as his body was vulnerable, she would be left with no reason for existence at all.

She must think, she had told herself that Christmas Eve, when for once the Cradle seemed so empty, the Mother so devoid of hope. She must think and read and pray, and find out for herself, for no other soul can help in times like these. 'Wishful thinking,' Flora would say, but phrases like that would not deter her. But the boys had been at home, and their leave passed in a whirl, and after that she was left alone to her new job. And in this job she had simply shelved her problems altogether. She could never go to church any more, for she had all the work of the house on her hands, as Mrs Childe never obliged on Sunday morning. Servants got out on Sunday night, of course, but they left the mistress to look after the master's dinner, and Rose could leave no one, even if her legs had been equal to the task of dragging her to evensong. She never had time for her old well-regulated prayers in the morning, and she was too dead tired to think at all by night. All her devotions, she discovered to her shame today, were kalei-doscoped into wild petitions sent winging helplessly through space to a God who might, or might not, be strong enough to protect her sons. She was no longer worried, indeed, by self-questioning over the reality and omnipotence of God, or her fainting hopes of immortality for those she loved: such thoughts merged almost at once into considerations as to whether you should or should not keep the lid on while you boiled potatoes, whether she had or had not ordered the marge, and what you did when you had to bake different things in a slow and quick oven simultaneously.

'So that it's all become utterly far away, like the tiny writ-ing of an airgraph, or a whisper down the telephone,' she concluded. 'It's not my fault really, for how can you think when you're a mere household drudge? I suppose my prayers for the boys go somewhere somehow – (Oh God, bless my darling Mickie, wherever he is and whatever he is doing, and bring him safely back to me again!) But how can I be expected to think out my faith or find a reason for any hope in anything beyond this? I am stuck down to my pots and pans and brooms for the rest of my life, and if you're shut in a dull stodgy basement – not a romantic prison – you have to be an exceptional sort of person to look out and see the stars, or look back and remember the sun and roses you used to know, or look up and see the gates of the City. I never could have been a mystic or saintly Mary, and now I can never be any-thing but a dense, inefficient sort of Martha.'

It was just at that point that Rose's spirit was suddenly stabbed awake. Absorbed in her thoughts she had not noticed that the doors were shut, the church full, and that the clergy-man had made his way from the vestry to the pulpit. It was thus, without warning, that the words struck on her ears, in the deep Scottish voice:

'And Jesus said unto Martha, I am the Resurrection and the Life. . . .'

To Martha! Rose suddenly found tears in her eyes and an odd lump in her throat. She had never noticed that, never realised that before. It was not the saintly Mary or the mystic disciple, but the busy, zealous housewife who had been thought worthy of those words which still arrest mourners of every creed, or no creed at all. Professed unbelievers or the careless materialist alike, if they avail themselves of those last rites which still have a hold on humanity, have to stand up and accept them without apology or explanation: 'I am the Resurrection' – just that and no half-measures, as it was said long ago to a woman who was cluttered up with material cares, and had little time or thought probably for spiritual realities. Was it because Martha was Martha that she needed and received such an awakening, or was it possibly because all service does rank the same with God that she was chosen? Rose did not stop to pursue that point, for still her mind reiterated the words: 'And Jesus said unto Martha,' (as if you would say anything to a Martha which you did not mean to be taken absolutely literally) 'I am the Resurrection . . .'

So she must start again, Rose determined, or rather she must go back to see herself, as Tom said, in a world of three dimensions, and believe that just beyond and outside it was a world of other spiritual dimensions, nearly tangible, nearly apprehensible for those clinging to Heaven by the hems. Why should she suppose that it was harder for her generation than any other to hear through the clang of engines and war the herald's song, or see, through the mist of all the blood that's shed on earth, the light of the Beatific Vision? These things were only a question of degree and number. The promise made to one woman alone on a hillside had rung out to millions through the centuries. Lines which she loved rang out in her mind above the paraphrase:

Because I know the spark
Of God has no eclipse,
Now Death and I embark,

And sail into the dark
With laughter on our lips. . . .

At this point Rose gave herself a shake and woke to her surroundings. She was ashamed that she could thus forget the poor old man for whom the memorial service was conducted, and devoted the remaining time to earnest prayers for his soul. ('How you must enjoy knowing that you'd be turned out as a Scarlet Woman if anyone guessed,' said Mickie once when she confessed to her practice, 'and who would, as a rule, be more annoyed than the deceased himself if he was a Presbyterian?') Then she got up and slipped away quickly, to evade the grim procession of chief mourners who would obviously be either in their own dotage, or endeavouring, if they were young, to conceal their relief that their charge was now safely handed over to Heaven.

Thus it was that, as she hurried as fast as her weary legs would let her, up a narrow, icy, wind-swept passage into a wide, wind-swept square she precipitated the other and obvious crisis in her life by almost running, head bent against the gale, into the arms of Major Hosmer.

'And say now, isn't that a bit of luck,' said that composed and self-assured warrior, offering Rose his arm in a way which she described to Mickie as purely medieval, 'I've called on you twice or thrice and had no luck.' (Rose had the grace to blush, for twice she had left the bell to ring as it might, after she had glimpsed a military cap through her bedroom window.) 'And now here you are, all tired out and run down and washed out, and I'm going to see you straight home, and come in if I may

to hear just how you're getting on in that gallant struggle of yours.'

'Oh well, I suppose Martha put up with callers in Bethany,' Rose found herself thinking petulantly as she smiled a polite assent. When you looked into the benignant, trustful smile behind those absurd, wide spectacles, you forgot about the Major's flat, sallow face and extraordinary clichés, and you really could not hurt him any more than you could hurt a child.

'Now that's good,' he said, placing her hand within his stalwart arm in a way which made her hope hysterically that none of her friends were in sight. 'I've a sort of hunch' – and here the Major spoke far more prophetically than he knew – 'that we shall have a great deal to say to each other.'

CHAPTER SIX
A WELCOME GUEST

I called the New World into existence
to redress the balance of the old.
Lord Canning

It was rather comforting, thought Rose, as she let herself into her dear, empty, echoing house, that though Major Hosmer might, by his own account, know all about housework, he would not have Mrs Childe's gimlet eyes for dust. In this matter of dusting, indeed, Rose had discovered that the mistress of a house had a definite advantage over her maids. She knew just where dust would show and could deal with it, whereas a fatuous housemaid would often scour a dark corner of the room, and omit such strategic points as the table in a sunny window, or the flap of the bureau opposite the corner of the sofa where her mistress habitually sat. Rose had never been addicted to the habit of speaking to the offender, so likely to produce the provocative answer of: 'Well, of course, 'm, if you're not satisfied with me it might be best to give you my notice at once,' but she had discovered that, as she had never noticed such details as the legs of the gate-legged table in the dark corner, or the top shelves of Stuart's bookcases in old days, she need not be too conscientious about them now. Certainly Major Hosmer seemed in no mood to be critical for he looked round appreciatively saying: 'Now this is kind of you. I do very much appreciate seeing the interior of a high-class Scottish home!'

'I expect what you really want to see are my electric gadgets,' smiled Rose. If only she didn't feel so tired and if only she didn't want so much to be left alone to think about Martha, she would have suggested getting tea for her visitor! But that, it appeared, need not worry her.

'Now see here,' said her guest, 'you're done in and all out. What I'm going to suggest is that you let me loose in that little kitchenette I saw at the end of the lobby, and see what sort of tea I bring you. Remember I've knocked all round the world in my time before I took to medicine. I was steward on a liner for six months, as well as managing my shack all alone, later on, so leave it to me.'

'But you don't know where things are,' protested Rose, trying to struggle to her feet.

'No, but I can guess. There'll be a tin marked "Cake" and another marked "Bread", and butter in a red crock, and tea in the tea-caddy. And now, see, have you such a thing as a gas-ring in the house?'

'There's one in the dining-room, but we never use it now,' said Rose. 'You see there's the hot-plate on the stove for the kettle –'

'Very slow and extravagant,' commented her guest. 'Just

you use your ring for tea-making and quick boiling generally. Now, if you'll give me a match, for I'm no smoker and don't have any, I'll put it to this gas-fire and the ring in one. Now you lie back, and open your mouth and shut your eyes and see what the king will bring you!'

As a matter of fact Rose only lay back on the sofa, trying hysterically to imagine Stuart forcing his way into a strange woman's house, and getting to work in her pantry. Even this experienced Major Hosmer would, of course, probably crash half the tea-things, and take hours to produce a meal, but Stuart! . . . She was still smiling at the idea when the stout, deft Major reappeared, as if by magic, with a tray laid with an elegance which Rose would never have bothered about, and almost before she had murmured her appreciative thanks he was gone, and returned with the tea made already, and a plate of hot buttered toast.

'But no maid I ever had would have been so quick,' gasped Rose in admiration.

'Just horse sense,' said the Major. 'These poor boobs in caps and streamers fill a big kettle to the brim from the cold-water tap, whereas if you're in a hurry hot water from the hot tap, and not too much of it, is the secret. There's no risk with a copper boiler, you know.'

'But how do you know my boiler is copper? I always understood the water in boilers was rusty with iron!'

'They couldn't have put the thermostats in your boiler if it wasn't copper,' explained the Major briefly. 'And those electric grills are good value, though, mind you, I don't care so much for the ovens. The heat comes too slowly and lasts too long. If I were you I'd put that rice pudding I see prepared in a pot to steam on the gas-ring right now, instead of baking it. If you're having that fish fried you don't really need a hot oven tonight at all. Now tell me, how are you getting on with your chores?'

'Not too well, I'm afraid,' smiled Rose, feeling for the first time the incredible pleasure of talking over her new career with someone who really seemed to feel interested. 'You see, I made the mistake of engaging someone with High Standards, and she keeps me so busy cleaning the house with her all morning that by the evening I'm too tired to want to cook. And then, though she's an excellent cook herself, she doesn't believe in cookery books, so she leaves me with a lot of directions I only half-remember, and then when I look things up in my five, no six, cookery books they all give different directions again!'

'Well, I think I can ease that difficulty for you right here and now, Mrs Fairlaw,' said Major Hosmer very seriously. 'You see, I've studied the point theoretically, and what I find is this. One school of cookery tries to make as much labour for you and as much show as they can (and to that I'd be tempted to assign all these scientific teachers of cookery), and the other sets out to show you how to do the best you can with as little labour as possible. You can't combine the two sets of instructions.'

'I suppose that's what I do,' said Rose ruefully. 'Now take soup, though I don't think anyone would want to take mine! Mrs Childe, who's always telling me that she knows a trick or two worth all the cooking schools, tells me to put all the veg – I talk about veg to her quite naturally now – to simmer for hours and hours. Well, about tea-time I look in the *Diploma Book* and it tells me I am to brown them in boiling fat. So I boil fat and take them out of the pot and put them in fat, and for a few minutes they remain horrid damp little bits of carrot and turnip, and then suddenly they turn into little heaps of black charcoal! Then the book says: "add water", so I put in the water they boiled in, and at once I have a minor display of fireworks on the stove. And then I remember all Mrs Childe told me about thickening, and put in some horrid brown stuff like chocolate, and some flour which covers me and the floor and everything else on its way to the pot, and in the end there's just a nasty burnt, sticky mess which the good books would describe, I think, as "the consistency of paste". They love those sort of phrases and I don't really know what paste is like – it's such ages since I used it for sticking photos of the children into albums! Cooks have such odd minds, and what my boy Tom would call visual images – they're always saying "the size of walnuts" or "the size of thimbles" – things I never think about! And they all have such bad indexes – every one of them – I suppose cooks are so used to mixing their materials that they can't help mixing up their pages – and even the war books expect you to have things like tomatoes, and milk, and eggs, which you can't get! But I really mustn't bore you with the sorrows of a would-be Martha any longer!'

But Major Hosmer was not bored, that was quite evident.

'Little lady,' he said so impressively that Rose managed not to wince, 'you've got my sympathy every time, and if you let me drop in round about this hour some evenings I can put you wise on some points, better than your Mrs Childe. For a lady of your intelligence and perceptions wants reasons for her actions, not just instructions. There are books which explain to you why you should do what you do, and I'll make it my business to try to find one for you. For, believe me, I do think you're making a gallant struggle, and it's courage that always gets me right down where I live.'

'I don't know,' said Rose. 'What is it Esmond says: "To be brave, that is nothing: everyone is brave: but to be successful, in that there is something divine"; that's what I feel about my soups. And now,' she rose decidedly, 'I'm afraid I must stop being a hostess and get to my job. I must black-out the house and light the drawing-room fire. My husband likes to work alone here in the evening.'

'Now isn't that just too bad when we were enjoying such a nice old wives' talk,' said Major Hosmer with a hearty laugh. 'But, say, let me help you, for there's nothing I don't know about lighting fires. And perhaps after that you'd let me give a hand to that soup!'

How, wondered Rose with a strong inclination to giggle, was she to get rid of this strange guide, philosopher, and friend before Stuart returned home? How could she ever dislodge him if he was once free of the pantry? – and she had a sad feeling from the sounds below that he was nobly washing up the tea-things, while he waited for the drawing-room fire to burn up properly. For he had managed to light it with one match, as he had foretold, and thrown in a hasty exposition of how Mrs Childe should build it up (as if Rose would ever dream of handing it on!) and sketched out an arrangement for extending yards of piping from the gas stove in her bedroom to the fireplace, with a gas poker at the end of it, so that she would need paper and wood no longer. If only, thought Rose, he could be cashiered and disgraced, and cured of calling her 'little lady', how lovely it would be to have him as a handyman about the house, and above all to hear him putting Mrs Childe in her place! But what Stuart's feelings would be, if he came home and found an utter stranger in uniform putting artichokes through a sieve in his kitchen, she could hardly bring herself to imagine.

But she need not have troubled herself, for when she had finished struggling with blinds, stiff shutters, and refractory curtains, in the dark empty rooms on the top floor which made her heart ache so intolerably, she looked into the drawing-room to find Major Hosmer standing, immovable, his face set in new stern lines before a photograph.

'Pardon me,' he said formally. 'May I ask if this young lady is a relation of yours?'

'Flora!' Rose's eyes followed her guest's to the latest photograph of her daughter. Flora loved to be photographed and sent home the results, Rose sometimes imagined pitifully, because she had not many friends who wanted them. This one in uniform, with her chin raised, and face fined down by hard work and war conditions, gave a forceful beauty to the girl's rather heavy features. 'Do you know her? A relation? Why, of course she is! She's my daughter!'

'Your daughter!' The Major turned and looked Rose up and down in a new, critical, and appraising way. What the matter was she could not imagine for the moment, but at least he did not look like calling her 'little lady' any more.

'Yes, by my first marriage. Of course you would not know from my surname now –'

'No, I know her as Flora Graylle naturally. And I didn't know that her relatives resided in this city. I'd an idea from her conversation that her mother lived in some old place in the country –'

'We used to, in my old home. But that was a long time – I mean, some time ago, when Flora was – well, quite young.' Rose had always recognised that Flora's perverse insistence on her connection with Seriton was rather because Mickie had no lot or part in Rose's home or family than from ordinary snobbery, but she hardly knew how to put this to Flora's strange friend.

'It was my own mistake probably – because she spoke with affection of some old family seat. Yes, I do know her, Mrs Fairlaw. I saw a great deal of her when my ambulance was attached to her hospital down in Eastminster. I saw her a great deal when we were working in the blitz there, and let me tell you that she played a very brave and heroic part. Many a worker who won a medal deserved it less than your daughter.'

'Oh, I know, I know!' cried Rose. 'Of course she didn't tell me a word but I heard from her friends!'

'And so you see you have reason to be proud of her after all,' said the Major in so severe a voice that Rose gasped involuntarily. 'Yes, yes, I must confess that it's a great surprise to me to find that this is Flora's home and that you are Flora's mother.'

'You saw a good deal of her, I gather?' Any ordinary acquaintance of Rose's would have understood from the change to conventional politeness in her tone, and her move to the door, that he must make his farewells, but the Major stood his ground.

'I think I'd like to tell you straight out, Mrs Fairlaw, that I've studied psychiatry in Cleveland, Ohio, as well as taking my ordinary degree. So that though I didn't get a very clear impression of the externals of Miss Graylle's life she did give me the privilege of hearing the story of her inner life, and sad hearing it was too.'

At once Rose understood the change in the Major's manner. It was only too easy to see what a recital of injustices and inhibitions, neglect, and neuroses, Flora would have poured out to so sympathetic, and in some ways surely so simple, a listener as Major Hosmer. No wonder he had been surprised to find that Rose was the cruel, misunderstanding mother of Flora's tale, for probably Flora had given some impression of a virago six feet high and twelve feet broad, as well as the picture of the old country home which she had left at the age of three, and couldn't really remember at all.

Rose's curiosity so far outran her dignity that she found herself asking, as the flames began to light up the cream walls, and give a faint semblance of warmth to the long chilly room, 'What did you think her mother would be like?'

'Mrs Fairlaw, I couldn't answer that question without violating a confidence. Nor would I wish to, until I've had more opportunity of correlating my impressions with those confidences. There is, of course, no doubt' – the Major seemed to be addressing himself at this point – 'that in the case of a highly sensitive introvert, with that slight disintegration of personality which comes from a severe trauma in early years, one has to discount certain exaggerations and unintentional distortions in their diagnosis of their surroundings. . . .'

'In other words, Flora bunged him up with a lot of lies about you,' would have been the boys' comment on this wonderful sentence, thought Rose. But, as it was, her course was plain to her.

'Well, I think we should just say goodbye and leave it at that, Major Hosmer. I'm glad to think Flora has a friend, as wise and understanding as you. I know there have been many mistakes in her upbringing, and I blame myself very heartily, and I do hope you'll be able to help her to make a whole of the wonderful character which her heroism shows her to possess.'

'Now that's generous, Mrs Fairlaw, very generous,' admitted Major Hosmer. 'But, mind you, though I don't think Flora responsible for any misconceptions about her home life, it would help me if I knew how far those misconceptions were justified. Now if you agree, I believe the best thing for Flora would be if I put my hand right down on the table, and told you what your daughter suffered, or imagined she suffered, in your care.'

'Oh, no!' Rose shrank back into the shadows by the mantelpiece. 'This is Flora's affair! I've no wish to excuse myself at her expense. It would be fatal for her to know you'd met us and talked her over with us!'

'That's a very understanding remark, Mrs Fairlaw!' Evidently every word she said made Major Hosmer more sceptical of Flora's outpourings, and Rose tapped her foot with annoyance.

'I really think you'd better go!' she said, for indeed short of such direct speech there seemed no way of getting rid of her guest.

'She seemed fond of her stepfather,' mused the Major. 'Perhaps if I could talk it out with him –'

'Oh well!' Rose tried not to let her dismay at this suggestion appear obvious. 'I don't know. Like most Scotsmen, you know, he isn't very explicit about personal relationships. We old-fashioned people let these things slide – wrongly as you'd say, I expect. He knows that Flora has been an anxiety to me, and that I rub her up the wrong way, but I don't think he'd ever admit to anyone outside the family, or inside it, or even to himself for that matter, that anything was wrong but a little incompatibility of temperament.'

'Criminal!' said Major Hosmer simply and finally. 'Simply criminal. Why at that rate he must need my help as much as Flora! He must be a mass of inhibitions, and so are you, I venture to imagine, Mrs Fairlaw!'

'We like them,' said Rose a little hysterically, moving to the electric lamps. From down below came the sound of Stuart's latchkey, and what he would say if he found her with a stranger in the firelight discussing her husband's inhibitions, she could not venture to imagine.

'See here, Mrs Fairlaw, let me speak straight,' said the Major, moving towards the door at last to her infinite relief. 'In an ordinary way I'd agree with you that the girl's my patient and I must leave her to put me wise about her own case, trusting that she'll see the truth more justly when I've got right down to the root of her complexes and eradicated them. But it's not as simple as all that. From what I saw of Flora as lately as a fortnight ago, when I slipped down to Eastminster on leave, the girl's in some kind of emotional crisis, and may need – who can tell? – your help, or at least the help of your husband, if she won't ask yours. I couldn't aid her this time: there was a barrier which was, I must own, a very great surprise to me after the intimacy of our former relationships. I said to myself at the time: "Percy Hosmer, that girl needs someone with a closer knowledge of her background than you can have, and it's up to you to find it," so I think the best thing I could do would just be to have a good straight talk with your good husband, if he'll give me the opportunity.'

Never did any husband or father look less likely than Stuart Fairlaw to embark on any polite greeting, far less on any intimate conversation, than Stuart, as he looked into the drawing-room on his way to his dressing-room, surprised at the unusual sound of voices.

For Stuart, though he had neither the wish nor the capacity to make his feelings obvious, was suffering in his own way from the upheaval of his household. Rose, recognising that to such a creature of habit she must endeavour to maintain old customs, did manage to provide him with a well-set and, at times, a well-cooked dinner. The house was still warm and comfortable when he returned to it, and the papers on his desk had never been treated so reverently. His shoes were well cleaned and his clothes cared for, but Rose's real affection for him was just devoid of that touch of mutual understanding which would make her realise this was not enough. He hated to see his pretty wife grow thinner and more lined every day:

although she gallantly aimed at looking neat and well-cared-for, she was no longer a decorative asset at the dinner-table. Her conversation too, like that of all pioneers, turned almost exclusively on the dishes she laid on the table, and on Mrs Childe's gossip; though she simulated interest in Stuart's daily news, her mind was obviously straying to the stove. Like many husbands and wives they had left off exchanging their views on the war, for Rose's bitter, blank pessimism refused any comfort from the optimism which he had either entertained or simulated for so long. It was useless, he felt, for him to utter his sympathy when she flung aside the daily papers at breakfast, with a tight-lipped gesture of misery, as she read of yet another loss in the Pacific or inscrutable hints of disappointments in Libya, or disaster in the Atlantic. It was useless too, he considered, to repeat again and again how he hated the drudgery of her life, for he was too sensible, and too little intimate with his wife, to realise that Rose could have listened to such protests again and again with gloomy pleasure, and gained new courage from them. Their fears and anxieties over their children were a sealed book between them: they had been ever since Mickie first nonchalantly announced his intention of flying, and Tom appeared in a private's battle-dress. All he could do for his wife, Stuart supposed, was to keep his own business worries and financial cares from her, without realising that she could have had no better tonic than to be asked for sympathy. Altogether, in short, his home-comings nowadays were not so cheerful that he could be expected to welcome a stranger, planted in his drawing-room, announcing in tones which were audible even from the staircase that he intended to have a very, very long talk with Flora's stepfather.

'Pleased to meet you, sir,' was of course Major Hosmer's immediate reaction to Rose's anxious introduction.

'I met Major Hosmer, Stuart,' she said, 'with Linda – she's a friend of his, and now I find to my surprise he's a friend of Flora's,' she added in answer to Stuart's bristling eyebrows. Anything more obvious than that Stuart did not reciprocate the pleasure of meeting the Major was impossible to imagine.

'Have a drink?' suggested Stuart, for though a guest might be unwanted, and whisky scarce, a Scotsman remains hospitable against his will.

Major Hosmer, it appeared, however, was averse to whisky, not because he advocated total abstinence, but because he had seen the evils of rye-drinking in America. 'No, it's just a talk with you both I want,' he repeated. 'I've been telling Mrs Fairlaw that I am not only Flora's friend but her psychiatrist at the moment, and I feel you two could help me very much in untying some of her knots. Now, see here, we're all three busy people and I may be called away from Castleburgh any minute, so I've got a proposition to put to you –'

'Well, as a matter of fact,' said Stuart, driven to desperation, 'I usually have a bath and dress for dinner now, and so –'

'Don't let me interrupt you!' Major Hosmer interrupted, holding up his rather podgy hand. 'I know the value of routine to a busy man. But my proposition is that this lady, who looks to me tired out, should tuck up her toes on the sofa and you go off and dress, and leave me to cook and serve up

your dinner. Madam here will tell you I'm as interested in domestic economy as in my job, and there's nothing I'd like better than to get my hands on a stove and do a little practical work for a change. I'll cook and serve it and share it, if I may, and after that we can settle down to a real pow-wow.'

'Stuart!' whispered Rose at the dressing-room door a minute later, 'do you suppose those books on social etiquette tell you how to get rid of a guest who insists on acting as cook and parlourmaid at dinner-time? There should be, for I hadn't an idea how to get rid of him, neither had you!'

'The fellow's mad,' replied Stuart briefly as he emptied the contents of his pockets at his dressing-table. 'Do you suppose he's making off with the silver?'

'Oh no, I'm sure he's a heart of gold!' replied Rose vaguely. 'And anyhow I do feel it's important he should tell us all he can about Flora.'

'Is the fellow in love with her, do you suppose?'

'He's interested in her at any rate. And he seems to think she isn't too happy just now.'

Rose had diagnosed Stuart's attitude to his stepdaughter accurately enough. Stuart was sorry for the girl, because she didn't get on with her mother, and though he couldn't understand her attitude to Rose, he had a legal habit of assuming that there were always faults on both sides. But he would never forgive Flora if he discovered that she had been disloyal to her home and relations; and washed her dirty linen in front of this American fellow.

'But oh, how much easier it will be to be tactful and lady-like,' reflected Rose as she enjoyed the old luxuries of a bath and dressing for dinner, 'now that I feel a little like a lady again.'

After all her task was not difficult. Even Stuart thawed after the unwontedly excellent dinner. The Major had transformed Rose's vegetable soup into mulligatawny; the fish emerged crisp and golden and whole from the frying-pan, instead of in the flaky scraps Rose produced, and was served with a sauce worthy of Ambrose. Leaving the rice pudding to its fate, the cook produced a wonderful Bombay duck, for 'gentlemen,' he said beaming over his spectacles at Rose, 'prefer savouries, and we're two to one.' Soothed and mollified, Stuart followed his usual routine of closing his eyes for a few minutes after a cup of super-excellent coffee, and a glass of Kümmel which he had insisted on producing for so invaluable a guest. And no more happy arrangement could have been made, thought Rose, as it enabled her to get through the Major's questionnaire about Flora's traumas without arousing Stuart's hostility at what he would have dismissed curtly as this psycho-rubbish.

'And as you sit there, looking like the Heart of the Home,' said the Major, in obvious admiration of Rose's shining hair and pretty flowing silk gown, 'I can just figure out to myself what's at the root of Flora's neuroses.'

It was far easier to talk to Major Hosmer than to the psychiatrist long ago. For one thing she was aided by the album of family snapshots with its frequent representations of Flora, sullen and glowering in the midst of happy laughing groups, and still more because, as they talked, she began to have a clearer picture of Flora as she thought herself to be. After all it was plain, in the light of the girl's recent exhibition of courage and initiative, that Rose had failed always to get the best out of her daughter –

'It's like my wretched stove,' she said sadly. 'I put everything on very carefully with its button at the orthodox pressure, and then I come back an hour later to find that I forgot to put it on at the main. I've never managed, I see, to turn on the main switch with Flora. But I must leave you to talk about the present trouble with Stuart while I go and do the washing-up.'

'But it's done,' said the Major, shocked. 'As if I wouldn't have finished my job!'

'Not everything!' gasped Rose. 'Oh, I don't mean to doubt you, but you see when I began I thought it was just a question of washing glasses and silver and plates, and Mrs Childe has taught me there's so much more! She makes me wash out the bowl I washed in, and then the cloth I wiped it with, and then the dishcloths I used, and then the sink and the cloth I wiped that with, and then she gives the floor what she calls a once-over, and then washes the cloth she used for that. I always feel it's like someone beginning to make out a train time-table, and trying to get back to the first train that has to run.'

'Oh yes, I'm wise to all that!' laughed the Major. 'And if I may say so, Mrs Fairlaw, that's all rather symbolic of the work in the human mind which interests me and my colleagues. You've got to get right through all the processes and clean up all the influences at work, however remote and unnecessary they seem. You'll say of course that your daughter, at the age of three, couldn't resent your second marriage, or your absorption in your delicate boy. Believe me, her subconscious mind would record deeply the transfer of interest from herself to others. Then again, you couldn't begin to understand the effect on an introvert of living in such a family of extroverts as I gather you to be. You meant it for the best when you all laughed at her or ignored her sulks and jealousy – oh yes, I can read her story, for it's common enough unluckily – in photos like this one in your album –' The Major pointed to a group where Flora, sullen and scowling sat with her back to her laughing brothers, defiance in every line of her kilt and long bare legs. 'All these passionate friendships and admirations at school you tell me of prove, as you say, that she was capable of very, very deep affection and was striving unconsciously to sublimate her jealousy, but you see you were all so different from her that you didn't begin to know how to help her. You mothers all need education in psychology, I guess, and thank God it's beginning to be recognized now. In any case you did your best by taking her to consult an expert. It was just bad fortune that the fellow was a disgrace to his profession, and used his influence to make the poor child fancy herself in love with him.'

'Nonsense,' said Stuart, opening his eyes suddenly and speaking very loud. 'She simply threw herself at the fellow's head, and he had to ask my wife to take her away. I must say that, in justice to him, and I won't be responsible for any libel against him. He was a fool, I think, mind you, but he was certainly an honest man. And now, Major Hosmer, forgive me if I've indulged in forty winks after your excellent, your marvellous, dinner, and tell me what's wrong with poor old Flora now.'

'Well, remember I'm speaking from observation in one meeting only, and I know nothing of the facts, but it seemed to me pretty clear that the poor girl is in trouble – Oh no, my dear friend' – the Major added hastily, as Stuart leapt up in his chair with an explosive grunt of horror – 'I forgot you had a narrow technical sense of that phrase over here. I've no grounds for suggesting that, but it does seem to me that she's in the throes of some psychological disturbance, and that it's due probably to her immediate surroundings. "You need a good change of environment," I told her straight out. I didn't suggest her returning home because I'd gathered from her, if you'll pardon me, that she can never be sure of her welcome – that's her fixation, you see.'

'Well, it's a damned lie,' said Stuart in less technical language, feeling for his pipe. 'My wife's given untold thought and anxiety to her daughter with little return for it, and though I'm fond of the girl myself, and can manage her well enough at times, it's no use to pretend that she doesn't make an infernal nuisance of herself.'

'And it's because she senses that, that she feels she has no welcome at home,' replied the Major steadily. 'You, my dear sir, if I may say so, are not at all sensitive yourself –'

'Thank God, no,' interjected Stuart.

'And Mrs Fairlaw is, as far as I can judge, one of those rare characters who are sensitive only in their external relations. She has no understanding of the morbid passion for affection, the jealousy, the alertness for slights and neglect, however imaginary, which characterise your daughter.'

'"God help the man who's tied to our Davie!"' quoted Stuart profanely.

'I beg pardon? Oh well, forgive me if I don't catch the allusion. The point I want to make is this, that I think Flora is pretty badly in need of help and advice, yes, and of external authority, judiciously applied –'

'Do you mean she's making a fool of herself over some man?' demanded Stuart, whose phraseology was sadly limited for an interview with a psycho-analyst.

'I don't know, sir. I tell you I know none of the external facts. All I know is that if she were my daughter I'd do my best to get in touch with her right now.'

'If you wouldn't mind going to your club for a day or two, Stuart,' suggested Rose timidly, after a pause which all three felt to be impressive, 'I could run down to Eastminster –'

'I doubt if you'd be the best person to deal with her just now,' said the Major apologetically.

'You mean I should go?' Stuart's eyebrows went up to the ceiling at the idea that he should leave his under-staffed office, and race off south to track down an emotional disturbance in his stepdaughter. 'Oh well, as a matter of fact I've got to go up to Town in a fortnight to a board meeting, so I suppose I could fetch up at Eastminster for the week-end, and kidnap the girl and bring her home, for I gather that's what the Major suggests. At least she can help you about the house, Rose!'

Rose passed over that remark. Stuart had made it before his sons, when it had been received with shouts of amusement, for everyone knew how lazy, selfish, and untidy Flora was in the house. But Stuart had a real admiration for his tall handsome stepdaughter, and his conventional belief that any daughter must be a help to her mother took an unconscionable time in dying. It was only the revelation of Flora's disloyalty to her home and mother which made him so outspoken in his condemnation this evening, and he was always ready to hope for a better state of affairs.

'No, on the contrary, I think you will have to exercise the greatest tact and patience to get her away at all,' said the Major gravely. 'It's just possible she might come if she felt her mother right down needed her, or if she's entirely at cross-purposes with her superiors. That's what may be the trouble, you see – I don't begin to know. But I do know that if someone doesn't win her confidence, and get her away, I foresee grave psychological dangers.'

'Infernal cheek of the fellow to give us advice about our own daughter,' yawned Stuart, when at length the Major made his farewells. 'I will say though, that if he's as successful with his brain tests as he is with his fried sole he can't be altogether a fool.'

'I think he's very wise in many ways. I know you feel psychology is just common sense in fancy-dress language, but he really has given me a lot of new light on Flora's character. I never saw that what she needed was someone dependent on her, someone she could devote her life to. I believe if I'd been an invalid –'

'Well, it's no use your developing spine trouble or arthritis now she's off on her job, my dear!'

'No, no! But perhaps if I see my mistakes more clearly we'll get on better in the future. Stuart, don't you think you should run down and see her at once?'

'If I'm to go south every time Flora makes a fool of herself I'd better get a season ticket,' returned her husband caustically. 'All that girl needed was to have been spanked good and plenty long ago!'

'That's what Cousin Mary would say, but it's not in the least sound, Stuart. What Flora needed, what you all needed I expect, was truer understanding. As the dear little Major talked I realised that I've been house-bound in every sense all my life. For it is being mentally house-bound to expect a family all to share your point of view. I just expected Flora to understand us, and felt it was her own fault if she wasn't happy.'

'Well, good Heavens, the girl was all tied up in knots herself too – if ever anyone was what you choose to call house-bound it was Flora!'

'Yes, but it was my job to help her to get out. Don't you feel when you talk to someone like Major Hosmer, from a new world, who's had no ties of possessions or heredity like us, that you're in a big sweep of open country, breathing fresh, clean air, instead of huddled in a little room over a fire?'

'Give me the fire every time,' said Stuart obstinately. 'You've been too sympathetic to Flora all her life, if you ask me, and the girl's thoroughly spoilt. Cousin Mary had plenty of common sense about that as well as everything else. By the way, Linda wants you to lunch with her – Tuesday I think it was – to help her with Mary and the old lady. They never saw eye to eye you know, and I gather they find Grannie a bit difficult about the house. Now don't say you can't manage it. You must get out more – no, I don't mean to memorial services! House-bound indeed! This house is too much for you, that's all!'

But the phrase lingered on in Rose's mind as she relapsed on to the sofa with a novel. It belonged not only to herself, not only to Martha in Bethany, but also, surely, to all the unhappy individuals and races all over the world. Peoples, countries, empires, shut themselves up in their own domains, refusing to consider the views on which others gazed from their windows. And these things seemed to them a virtue, for when you said that an Englishman's house was his castle, or that a woman was house-proud, you said it with self-satisfaction. But there could be no hope surely of any world of peace till everyone flung open all their doors and windows wide, and came to know each other's ways and views. And that, concluded Rose, had only happened once in the world's history, when, out of her fuss over her mourning, and food for her guests at a funeral feast, Martha had gone out to receive the challenge to death and mortality. Oh, if only Flora and all the world could hear it and believe it, and rush out of their prison houses into the sunshine of hope! If that could only happen, and peace dawn again, how contentedly would she and all the Marthas of the world go back to their drudgery – 'though she certainly hadn't three bed, three sitt, and two bathrooms in Bethany,' was Rose's conclusion as she opened her novel, and settled down contentedly to the discovery of the corpse in the library.

CHAPTER SEVEN
PRESENT AND FUTURE

Where are you going? Who
Is summoning you away
From those you love, fair maiden?
Your father's roof so early are you leaving
Alone, as for a journey?
      Leopardi (trans. RC Trevelyan)

'Servants! I don't know what they're coming to!'

Rose gave a little sigh of disappointment as she advanced into Linda's big cheerful drawing-room, and heard old Mrs Carr-Berwick's high-pitched drawl. Had she braved Mrs Childe's disapproval, when she announced she was going out and would leave the drawing-room undusted and the dinner unprepared, so that she might catch Linda alone before lunch, only to find the old lady in occupation? Bed was the place for old ladies of eighty-five, recovering from influenza, or, indeed, for poor Linda, who looked worn and pale as she rose with her arms outstretched to greet her friend.

'Dear Rose can tell us all about servants' feelings,' she said.

'You know I told you she was doing all her own housework now, Grannie?'

'Yes, and a pack of nonsense I call it,' said the old lady, extending a withered yet wonderfully smooth cheek to her daughter-in-law's friend. 'Why don't you get hold of two or three good girls and be done with it? It's all the fault of you young women that there's any trouble at all. You've spoilt them, don't chah see? I never had any trouble, because I would never stand any nonsense and kept them in their proper place.'

It is the privilege of age to be inconsistent, and neither of the two so-called young women commented on the fact that it was Grannie's entire failure to keep her staff which led to her being installed, like a rapacious cuckoo, in her son's home, 'though thank Heaven,' Mickie commented irreverently, 'she's not likely to lay many eggs at her age!'

'Oh, but I don't think either bullying or spoiling maids has anything to do with it!' It was silly perhaps to bother to disagree with Grannie, but Rose's recent life had led her to so many reflections on the servant problem that she had to air them now that she was sitting, a lady again, as Mrs Childe would remark, well-dressed and well-cleaned, even to her nails, in Linda's sunshiny room. Or was it the glass of sherry, that forgotten luxury, which was too much for her discretion? 'I've been thinking so much about it, Mrs Carr-Berwick, and I'm quite sure the answer is that it's not work for people of intelligence nowadays.'

'That's it !' interposed Grannie triumphantly. 'I've always said all this education would be the ruin of the country!'

'It's not exactly education I mean, though I suppose that's developed people's reasoning powers. 'Give me a reason!' Tom used to say when he was small, and I can see lots of reasons why good, intelligent, capable girls were content with service in the past. As long as there was no machinery or ready-made food a maid went to a big household as girls go to a factory nowadays. When you read diaries like Stuart's great-grandmother's, Mrs Carr-Berwick, you see that girls learning to bake and brew, and make candles and spin and sew, did really learn a trade. And they were the centre of an estate which gave work on the land to their fathers and brothers, and later to their husbands, so there was a reason for it all. Even in your days I should have seen, if I'd left home for service, that I'd get better food and more leisure than in my own home where my mother had probably a round dozen of children, and my father earned ten shillings a week. And as you saw the mistress of the house busy at the same job, you would feel that she was a worker, in her own way, and deserved to be waited upon –'

'Dear Rose, take care! She's getting purple!' murmured Linda. Grannie, stout, erect, and autocratic, was so well-preserved from the tip of her vast white toupée to the toe of her expensive hand-made shoes that one was liable to forget she had passed the age of argument, till you noted that her shrivelled hands were shaking, and the plump cheeks which sagged into her ample chin were beginning to take a mauve tinge.

'So I just mean that people of our generation are at fault really!' Rose hastened to atone for her diatribe. 'We don't have big, useful, factory sort of households or big families any more. And we've used our unearned leisure to elaborate life, and have more and more indulgences, haven't we?'

'I should think so!' Grannie, appeased, started off on a favourite diatribe. 'Early tea for everyone if you please! I don't say that ladies of my age, or ladies expecting a happy event, haven't always expected their own woman to bring up their breakfast to their rooms, but I never had a cup of early tea in my life till I was seventy, and now I understand young people, even young men, expect it. Nor sherry before lunch indeed! Why, afternoon tea was still a new meal when I was young! And then all this smoking and jazz and films and late hours and London Seasons, and no family prayers,' said Grannie, becoming a little vague in her contribution to the problem. 'I don't wonder that a judgement has come upon us all. Why, it was all written in the Pyramids, don't chah see?'

'Oh, Grannie, you are so right,' interposed Linda who had found the adventures of the Lost Tribes and their probable future one of the most trying features of Grannie's convalescence. 'You all set your servants such good examples and we don't!'

'Especially by doing no work,' urged Rose. 'Of course an intelligent girl asks herself why she should give all her time and energy to work for a woman who could do most of it herself if she were active, and hadn't our absurd big houses. The tiresome part of any house is that it insists on having all its work done just to be undone, and done again next morning. The tiresome part of cooking is that you spend hours in producing something that disappears in three minutes! Think how maddening that must be when it's done for someone who's idle and useless! I think there may always be kind-hearted people who'll wait upon the old and helpless, and there'll always be enough to wait upon men who go out to work, because they're helpless too, but I don't see why any modern educated girl should tolerate carrying breakfast up to people like Wanda and Flora, just because they've been dancing all night while the girls themselves had to be in at eleven.'

'Eleven! Very lax!' commented Grannie. 'Me dear husband always held evening prayers on the stroke of ten so that we could be sure the whole household was in safely for the night, don't chah see? He wouldn't even trust the butler or the housekeeper!'

'Of course I quite see they want more freedom,' said Linda, pursuing her own thoughts. 'But after all, we do give them a great deal more now!'

'I don't think it is freedom they need so much as a purpose in life. I don't say that the general run of domestic servants would think it out quite like that. People like my Catrine and Jessie just felt vaguely I think that our sort of people had had their turn, and they are going to have their turn soon.'

'Then they were extremely foolish young women,' said Grannie. 'There'll always be rich and poor in the world as long as it lasts.'

'Yes, but revolutions are made by people who just think it's their turn to have all the money and leisure, even though there's no real hope of their getting it in the end. But I don't think the young girls who've been in the Services will feel quite like that. I think they'll merely feel that obviously everyone will have to look after themselves for the future, as they're prepared to do on their account.'

'But then, darling, they'll be just as bored with their own housework!'

'Oh no! Even I can see already that it's not as boring to dust and polish things if they are your own!'

'But don't you think they like looking after all our pretty things?' persisted Linda.

'Not much! For one thing I don't think they do think our old furniture and pictures and silver particularly pretty. They form their ideals on hotel lounges and the rooms of millionaires in American films. Mrs Childe thinks my things from Seriton in the drawing-room are dusty old stuff, and wonders I never thought of buying a suite.'

'But still, when you've nice maids of the sort we used to have,' pleaded Linda, 'you do all live together as one happy family, don't you think?'

'Not really, darling. Our sort of people are rather like the British who've taken on governing half the world. We've gone about thinking how kind and just and pleasant and useful we are, and how we must be loved and valued, and yet it's pretty clear, in India and in the registry offices here, that the subject peoples don't look upon us from quite that point of view.'

'India! Me dear husband always said we should have trouble with India when we took to giving them all this absurd education, and giving them a hand in the Government. What these native peoples require is a firm hand, don't chah see? Ring the bell for Griffen if you please, Linda, my dear! I must go and get ready for luncheon.'

'Thank Heaven!' cried Linda, as the old lady made her majestic departure on the arm of her maid. 'There's nothing Griffen couldn't tell you about subject peoples, I'm sure! Now, Rose, dearest Rose, tell me all about everything. I know Mickie and Tom are all right because Iona got letters from them both this morning. She showed me Tom's but she said she'd keep Mickie's for me till later when Grannie wasn't about. I do hope your Mickie isn't going to break her heart or anything, Rose darling! Certainly she didn't look heartbroken when she went off to her canteen at twelve. She sent you her love, and said you weren't to let Cousin Mary sit on you, and to wait to see her till she came back. Oh dear! That's Mary's bell I expect. Mind you outstay her and talk to me afterwards, Rose! It's the only chance because, thank Heavens, Grannie does lie down in the afternoon, don't chah see?'

'I will and I'll let Grannie talk to me about British-Israel all through lunch. It was stupid of me to air my silly ideas like that, but when you live as I do you do see the domestic point of view.'

It was a tradition in the Fairlaw family that when Stuart, who like most Scotsmen admired and avoided his notable female relations, told Mickie reprovingly that Cousin Mary was the salt of the earth, Mickie rejoined with his impish smile: 'Well, personally I like sugar better.' Some such feeling was already clearly uppermost in Linda's mind as she sat, looking a little flushed and faded on her drawing-room sofa, gazing at the two cabbages, the copy of *Time and Tide*, and a mass of rather exhausted snowdrops which her new visitor handed over to her as she entered the room, emptying out her bag like a conjuror. They were all nice things in their way, of course, but not somehow what you wanted in convalescence. Not half as welcome as the little pot of primulas and the copy of the *Daisy Chain* which Rose had chosen for Linda's entertainment.

But Mary Macfie was a notable woman, there was no doubt about it. In her early fifties, of a type produced by her class and generation alike, she was erect, alert, and forceful as she had been for the last thirty years. Heir to the tradition of pioeer women, she had taken her degree long ago at a Scottish university, and proceeded from her father's comfortable and cultured home to enter fervently into the philanthropic, literary, and political interests of her native city. 'The Curse of the Committee and the Gorgon of the Guardians' was Tom's description of her, after her best efforts to interest him in local government, and with the outbreak of the war her activities naturally doubled. Her father was dead, her house in the care of three sour, faithful old servants, and never, said Rose in a it of unjust annoyance, was there anyone who enjoyed the war more than Cousin Mary! The entrance to her house was blocked by bags of wet sphagnum moss and bales of wool and her ARP equipment; some committee or other seemed in perpetual possession of her dining-room; her tables bristled with agendas and minute-books and reports. In such intervals as occurred in her busy days she would go off with a spade to dig in her allotment: her car was dedicated to the use of the WVS. And Poles, Canadians, French and Belgian soldiers were sure of a welcome at any meal and at weekends. With true altruism, she had disposed of almost all her wardrobe to these unhappy peoples, or to bombed areas, so that it seemed to Rose and Linda as if since August 1939 she had never worn anything but the same pepper-and-salt tweed and black felt mushroom hat, with the addition, in winter, of a sealskin coat, the legacy of her grandmother, worn into a black and brown patchwork but still a gallant whole. Her grey eyes behind their rimless spectacles looked out on the world from her long, rather equine face with something of the gimlet quality of Mrs Childe's, only it was, Rose recognised uncomfortably, the laziness and dust of the soul rather than her surroundings which Mary espied.

'Well, my child!' was her greeting to Rose. 'I'm so glad to see you. How goes the great experiment?'

'Oh, sometimes well, sometimes badly,' responded Rose casually. Here was no such receptacle for her confidence as she had enjoyed in Major Hosmer.

'Poor Rose, she must be most terribly tired,' said Linda, looking at her anxiously. 'I think you look terribly fagged and thin, darling.'

'It's bound to tell upon her at first, at her age,' was Cousin Mary's comment, as she rubbed her long chin vigorously in a characteristic gesture. 'But you'll soon get the hang of it, I expect, and be all the better for the exercise. Good news of the boys, I hope?' In accordance with Linda's and Rose's general theory, Cousin Mary omitted to wait for any answer. 'I think, Rose, I must put your name down on our list for offering weekend hospitality to the foreign forces up here, as you're bound to be about your house a good deal, I imagine.'

'Oh, no, please, not yet, Mary!' The horror of the idea roused Rose to unusual vehemence. 'If they came to tea on Saturday or Sunday Stuart would hate it, and foreigners always stay on to supper, and there'd be nothing for them to eat.'

'Mary wants us to have them to stay,' murmured Linda in a voice which showed how little enthusiasm she had for the project.

'What's that? Someone to stay?' Grannie advanced into the room leaning on her ebony stick, followed by the wraithlike Griffen, carrying the old lady's handbag, knitting-bag, gas-mask, and library book. 'You should keep those maids of yours up to the mark, Linda, lunch is two minutes late already.'

'Lunch *is* served madam,' put in the parlourmaid pertly from the door.

'And so it should be, so it should be,' said Grannie undaunted. 'Shall I lead the way, Linda? Very nice to have some visitors! Linda's an absurd way of saying it's impossible in wartime. I've lived through wars enough without giving up hospitality! Who wants to come here, Mary?'

'Officers of the foreign forces, Grannie,' shouted Mary on the assumption that all old people were both deaf and stupid. 'Do persuade Linda and Rose to do their duty.'

'Certainly not! Spies, the whole lot of them,' returned Grannie sweepingly. 'We couldn't hear of such a thing. Why, I've got all my jewellery and silver in this house, don't chah see?'

'And I can't,' pleaded Rose, 'for you haven't an idea, Mary, how much work there is in a house for just two people!'

'Probably because you make Stuart far too comfortable,' said Cousin Mary with disapproval. 'He's inclined to be selfish and lazy over the war effort, you know, and contact with educated, polished members of the foreign forces would rouse him up.'

'It would, but it might be the wrong way,' said Rose drily. 'How are all your committees and canteens, Mary dear?'

At that, fortunately, Mary was drawn into a rapid summary of her own activities, coupled with searching criticisms of all those with which she was not connected. It gave Rose leisure to enjoy to the full the pleasure of a well-cooked, well-served meal, with the preparation of which she had had nothing to do, and she had to rouse herself with a start when Mary demanded of her suddenly, with her rather irritating term of phraseology:

'And how goes the canteen, Rose?'

'I don't know! I don't go now,' admitted Rose.

'I should think not,' put in Linda loyally. 'The poor dear's life is one long canteen!'

'There's too much drinking nowadays!' put in Grannie suddenly. 'I don't know why you want to encourage it, Mary. Your dear mother was a keen temperance reformer.'

'Only temperance drinks, Mrs Carr-Berwick,' shouted Mary. 'My dear Rose, you can't call the care of your house and Stuart war work.'

There is no more fatal faculty than that of seeing ourselves with the eyes of others. Poor Rose realised at once that tonight she would lie awake, to see a Daniel come to judgement in the shape of Cousin Mary's long, severe face and stern, glittering eyes. After all, it was perfectly true! She might be busy, she might be exhausted, but could she really pretend that her work had anything to do with what Cousin Mary would describe in a minute as Woman's War Effort? Still, she was aggrieved enough, for the moment, at the want of recognition of her labours, to protest:

'My dear Mary, all my three maids left at the beginning of the war to marry men in the Forces, and they're all having babies as hard as they can! The next three were all called up to the Forces, and the two I got instead volunteered for Munitions, though they were older women. So I feel that I've given eight girls who have left me to the service of the country!'

'You didn't give them, my dear!' remarked Mary with unpleasant accuracy. 'They went either because they had to, or wanted to! No, no, my dear! Service not self should be our motto and who are you serving but Stuart and yourself?'

'But, my dear Mary,' remonstrated Rose, feeling quite brave after such unusually good food, 'remember it isn't as if we lived in a blitzed or forbidden area. This city is crowded to the brim with people like you who work or want work. I told them at the canteen I'd try to come if they wanted help, but I gathered that there was a positive queue of people waiting to take my place –'

'*Not* at our Open All Night depot,' said Mary rolling her eyes severely. 'I can assure you of that –'

'Well Stuart puts his foot down at that anyway.'

'And so does Ian,' chimed in Linda with the same defiance. 'He says that chucking out drunks is no job for women who won't see fifty again!'

'I should think not indeed! What you need, Mary,' said Grannie maliciously, 'is a husband to shelter behind.' ('And a pretty big one he'd have to be,' Rose's eyes signalled to Linda.)

'I can't imagine myself tied to a man who interfered with my duty,' replied Mary briefly and truly. 'But I suppose, Rose, that you still go to your working-party?'

'No, I don't! I can knit for Mickie and Tom at home!'

'Quite right, quite right,' put in Grannie. 'Me dear husband always said that a woman's place was the home, and there were none of these European wars before women began screaming for the vote. It upset everyone and made them quarrelsome, don't chah see?'

'My dear Rose, War Comforts don't cater for extravagant young officers,' said Mary, refusing severely to be drawn into an argument with Grannie on this original theory for the causes of the war. 'They cater for men whose mothers are working women and too busy to knit.'

'Well, I'm a working woman and Tom's a private,' replied Rose, as Linda got up to lead the way to the drawing-room.

'No, I won't come upstairs, dear,' said Mary. 'I mustn't frivol any longer. I must fly to the Red Cross, and then I've my job at the WVS, and I shall be at the canteen till midnight.'

'Oh, Mary, you are wonderful,' sighed Rose, her conscience wide awake. 'And you're right too! I must find time for some war work!'

'Gadding,' said Grannie severely, 'simply gadding!'

'We must just hope there'll be no siren to-night or I shan't even get my rest then,' pursued Mary, rightly ignoring her implacable foe. 'Never mind, I'd rather wear out than rust out!'

'What that young woman needs,' repeated Grannie as she went off to her room in charge of Griffen, 'is a husband. I told her mother: "Get that girl married or she'll be a public nuisance, don't chah see?" but she didn't listen to me. Well, I'm going to have my rest anyhow. I have the sense to keep myself well for the sake of the country.'

'Both wonderful people,' sighed Rose when she and Linda were left alone together, 'and yet both of them would be among the first to adorn the lamp-posts in a revolution, I fancy.'

'Oh well,' said Linda comfortably, 'Grannie's only a relic of feudalism, after all –'

'And Mary really belongs to the transition stage of women when they had to be rather uppish and self-consequent to be noticed at all. One can see that the next generation men. And even if Mary is trying at times she's always right – perhaps that's why she's a trial? She's quite right when she says my job is selfish and narrow, and that I'm not helping the war effort at all, and yet – oh, Linda!'

'Is it so very awful, darling? Worse than you imagined?'

'Yes and no! There are compensations, you see. After my daily "do-s", I have the house to myself. No one can run up from the kitchen to say the fish hasn't come, and can I fetch it? or that the plumber's below wanting to see me about the

leak in the gas pipe. And the shops are so kind and good that I nearly always get what I want sent to the house, and if I can't I just go without instead of going out to join a queue. But, oh, Linda! the things you don't realise that a House wants! You know one dusts tables, but did you realise one ought to dust cornices and doors and tops of furniture and stair balustrades? I've put away most of the silver, but what there is goes black on me every other day. And the brasses! That doesn't just mean ornaments but all the door handles and the front door –'

'And stair-rods,' said Linda. 'And maids do love brass, don't they? They think the front door the most important thing in the world, and the worst housemaid likes to settle down and rub up the rods, and yet one never sits on the stairs or outside the front door, so what does it matter?'

'It's the neighbours. I know that from Mrs Childe. "What'll next door say if she sees our brass like that?" she says. And oh, Linda darling, the bells! I believe the baker really judges just the moment when I'm sitting down with a novel and cigarette after lunch, and the people who want to know the way to trams, or want rags or old clothes or money. And the people on the telephone who ring up wrong numbers. And one's friends ring up from their comfy beds to ask how I'm getting on, and I have to answer them, shivering in the dining-room. And the way everything in a house reminds you of something else you've got to do! You start up from the hall, and remember you must carry the laundry up, and when you're halfway you see you didn't dust the chest on the half-landing. And two steps higher up you remember you left the apples stewing and must run down to take them off. And that reminds you that you must telephone to the greengrocer, and while you're doing that you remember you ought to fill up the salt-cellars, and when you take them to the dining-room you see the flowers are dead, or you didn't finish polishing the floor that morning. And when you get back to the laundry basket you find you must get the book to count it out, and then you notice you haven't taken the shoes to clean. And of course, as Cousin Mary would say, none of these things are of any sort of use to the world at all, and yet I suppose they've got to be done!'

'The real truth is that it's all so difficult because you're only beginning and have never done it before,' said Linda soothingly. 'And by the time we've all lost our maids and are at the foot of the ladder you'll be terribly efficient. I shouldn't wonder if you won't have to teach Cousin Mary what's what, for her old pussies can't last for ever, and no modern maid would stand the hordes about her house all day long. But, darling, you do look as if it were all too much for you.'

'I know I look a fright, but am I suffering from heart disease or anaemia or anything becoming? Not a bit of it! I've had a frightful cold which gave me faceache – just like one's housemaids, and oh, Linda, I was never sympathetic enough! – and spots on my face like an evacuee child; and it left me without any sense of smell, so that I stood stupidly just like our cooks when something's burning or the gas is escaping, saying: "I can't smell anything, ma'am!"'

'If Mary had heard that saga she couldn't have thought you lazy,' smiled Linda.

'Not lazy but useless. She's always thought us rather cumberers of the earth you know, Linda, and so I expect we were – don't chah see!'

'It's so odd, you know,' said Linda thoughtfully, 'that when one married one thought it was a full-time useful job to look after a husband and house and servants and children, and try to keep them all well and happy, with just a few good works thrown in, because it's so dowdy not to have some after all! And now one looks back and wonders – wonders whatever earthly use it was – "For this had I borne him", added Linda in a whisper of tearless bitterness, as both of them sat staring into the fire thinking of Geordie, dear, absurd, loud-voiced, hearty Geordie who had loved fishing and shooting, trees and flowers and birds, and had never returned from Calais. 'It was sweet of you to send those roses for his birthday last week, Rose darling – it was because of that poem about names of roses in *Punch* wasn't it –'

'Yes,' said Rose clearing her throat. 'I wish I'd cut it out – something about –

I would call mine Calais
For one who loves roses
And died in Calais –

Oh, Linda darling, I shouldn't talk to you about him!'

'Yes, you should. Nothing is harder to bear than the way reserved Scottish people can't talk about the dead. Ian and Wanda and even Iona don't – it seems to me a real death when our darling Geordie mayn't even be whispered about

any more. Oh, Rose, do you remember that old Gamp I had, twenty-two years ago now! I think you had her for Flora – and how she sat in my bedroom chair crooning:

Oh if I were the King of France,
Or better the Pope of Rome,
There'd be no fighting men abroad
And only peace at home!

No, don't mind my crying – it does me so much good to talk of him to someone like you who remembers him as a baby and little boy, and yet as a soldier too. It's wrong to try to stop the wound by forgetting it – it means one would come to forget him – Oh, Rose, I was looking up that speech of Constance's when I was ill, and I came across something earlier that was truer than all the grief part – she thinks how they'll grow up without each other and says:

When I shall meet him in the courts of heaven
I shall not know him.

It's far better to cut oneself to pieces at first and keep them alive and talked about every day!'

'Linda dearest! –'

'Rose, forgive me, now I'm crying I may as well make a thorough job of it – tell me, for I must talk to someone; what do you really think about Heaven and all that? At first I didn't really doubt. Geordie seemed to me so alive that I wouldn't have been surprised if he'd walked into the room, but now

– after all these months of silence – that's gone. And I don't really see what one's got to pin one's hopes of the future on. Do you notice that parsons very rarely talk about immortality nowadays? Is it because they've given up Hell that they're a little nervous of Heaven?'

'I think it's more,' suggested Rose hesitating, 'that the old imagery gets in the way a little. I mean the modern ones don't look upon golden streets and white robes as anything but allegories, and yet old-fashioned people would be shocked if they said so! And I suppose all the discoveries about space and time and dimensions, which I don't understand in the least, make it all harder for them to find the right sort of images. I was thinking about it a good deal yesterday, Linda, as a matter of fact!' And haltingly Rose produced her meditations on Martha. 'I don't suppose it will help you in the same way – words and thoughts have to be one's own, don't they? Only it seemed to me not only rather a nice message to someone like me who's just an inefficient Martha, but rather a splendid challenge to the whole world that's always busy about the things of the moment. There's no explanation or apology, you see, just the challenge. I think that's what Christianity ought to be. Not, as most of us would say, "Well, I don't know what you think about it and of course one hardly knows what to believe, but one does hope there may be something beyond after all." . . . Just the certainty – "I am the Resurrection and the Life".'

'Yes, Rose, I do like that. And I think it helps to talk. Though as you say one does get the oddest comfort in the oddest ways. Poor old Ian advised me to read his favourite

Bozzy to distract my thoughts and I didn't want to one bit, because I think Johnson must have been quite dreadfully tiresome, and I'm for Mrs Boswell all the time in that dreadful visit to Edinburgh, and anyone could be witty if they were as rude as he was! And yet it was so strange! – I'd been worrying as we all do, I'm sure, about what happens when our children cared so little, or seemed to care so little, for religion as we were taught to see it, and I opened straight on a question in a note in the *Life* which has made all the difference to me:

> Between the stirrup and the ground
> I mercy ask'd, I mercy found.

But I expect that sounds – well, meaningless to you.'

'No, I love it. I talked to my father-in-law about that when Tim died, for Tim didn't seem to care a bit, you see. And he said it wasn't finding but seeking that meant anything, and everyone had their own approach to the truth.'

'Yes, I see that about great philosophers, or men of science, or artists of any kind. You wouldn't expect them to accept things meekly as we did. But then they do pursue the Truth in one way or another, and our boys – well, they were just happy people who didn't care!'

'I don't agree, Linda! They all had lots of ideas of their own, and talked a lot about their theories. Oh yes, I know they'd have seemed terribly blasphemous to Grannie, but what does that matter? I know the dear old Canon used to say that anything was better than the old stilted goody-goody style of our youth. He said too that if the mass of people have no use for the Church it is partly her own fault for getting so tied up with the educated, leisured classes. We cling, you see, to Gothic cathedrals, Italian pictures, and the old beautiful Elizabethan language, which mean nothing to the man in the street, or the woman in a council flat. And if anyone ever tries to popularise Christianity by making films of Bible stories, or putting it into modern English or holding vulgar, rousing missions, we all shiver and say how dreadful. And yet it wasn't a bit the creed of cultured leisured classes in Galilee!'

'Oh, Rose dear!' Rose had strayed off into abstract speculation to distract her friend, and she had succeeded, for Linda was sitting up now and wiping her eyes. 'Have you discovered another sinful side in our wretched characters? You are getting Bolshie since you took to housework!'

'Aren't I?' said Rose proudly. 'Anyway I do see how silly it is of parsons to worry working women to go to church, when Sunday is the busiest day of the week with one's husband and family all at home. But, Linda, talking of class religion, I really do remember Tom and Geordie laughing together once about the amount of Old Testament they had to learn at school. And Tom said, "My dear fellah, don't you realise it's only fellahs who've been at public schools who know who Jehu the son of Nimshi was", and I remember Geordie saying "A gent am I, for I know who begat Zerubbabel." It's ludicrous, I know, but I suppose we shall only discover it all again as the faith of slaves and outcasts when things are even worse. And yet, since I got that sort of message, as I felt it, about Martha, I do dream a good deal more of a new Heaven and a new earth.'

'Pie-in-the-Sky, they'd call it,' murmured Linda sadly.

'Oh, darling, what do words or even creeds matter? They are all taking their share of the Greater Love, and as the Canon would say, if you accept the Gospel at all can you believe in a God who loves His sons less than their mothers do?'

It was odd, thought Rose, when she tore herself away at last, after a long exchange of sad yet laughing memories about the boys in old days, that people didn't talk more about the things that mattered. Perhaps it was one of the stupid results of over-civilisation that you shut yourself up so firmly within yourself. Certainly no such inhibitions troubled the Mrs Childes of this world or her maids in old days. They would cheerfully expose all the skeletons in their cupboards at their first encounter with her, and as far as diseases went Mrs Childe liked nothing better than to tell all her bones. Was reticence a good thing or a bad thing, she wondered, as she put on her overboots in the hall, and then forgot her unprofitable musings as Iona burst in at the front door, rosy and smiling, followed by her retriever.

'Oh, Aunt Rose, I nearly missed you!' she cried. 'And I told Mummie you must wait for me! May I walk home with you please? It's absolutely frightfully important. Mimi, drop that boot! Look out! don't slip on the steps! Do hang on to me!'

'Darling Iona! You are so nice and solid! I feel as if I had Mickie looking after me!'

'It was Mickie I wanted to talk to you about,' said Iona, with few traces of maidenly coyness. 'I couldn't get hold of Mummie before lunch, and I'd a feeling anyway that Mickie

would like you to know first of all, but he couldn't very well write to you about it till he'd got my answer. You see, the truth is Mickie and I think of being engaged!'

'Mickie, darling!' Rose nearly slipped into the drifted snow in her surprise. 'But we always thought it was Tom!'

'Oh, I love Tom awfully of course!' Iona accepted the remark as calmly as ever. 'But not that way, and this last leave he seemed quite taken up with Zoë Macfie, you know, with that nice platinum hair. But Mickie! Oh well, Mickie is different from everyone in the world, isn't he?'

'Well of course I think so,' agreed Rose warmly. 'But, Iona dear, won't your father and mother think you far, far too young?'

'Well, I'm practically eighteen, and after all, there isn't much time ahead for certain, is there?' asked Iona, with an acceptance of the world around her which pierced Rose's heart. 'As a matter of fact, I asked Daddy at breakfast what he'd say if I got married, but he only ragged of course, and said he wouldn't allow it till I could manage my pronouns properly. So then I'd die an old maid like Cousin Mary,' ended Iona sadly.

'Then Mickie hasn't written to your father or mother?'

'He couldn't write to them or you very well, till he knew what I'd say, could he? I'm just going to post my answer now! It's ten sheets –' Iona, who was known for her hatred of the written word, said this very proudly. 'I expect the spelling's a bit queer, but he won't mind, will he?'

'No, no, indeed, and I expect you can spell "Yes" all right, darling!' Rose hardly knew what else to say as she stumbled

along in her snowboots beneath the leaden skies. Iona was slipping along beside her, hanging on to her adored Mimi's lead, the plump rosy cheek nearest Rose slightly distended by a peppermint, her eyes alight with happiness, with no trace in her candid beautiful immaturity of that maidenly reserve, rapture, or doubt which Rose still vaguely expected of girls in love. Wanda, Iona's elder sister, certainly hadn't shown them, but then Wanda was as tough as nails, and never had betrayed any emotion. Iona had given no such impression of toughness, because she had always accepted life with such radiant, equable enjoyment. It wasn't because she was too stupid to realise the risks of war – that remark about not having much time for certain proved that, and it wasn't because she had no personal experience of sorrow, for she had adored Geordie and turned, temporarily, into a ghost of her former self when he was killed. No, it must be just that the child and so many other children, hoped Rose, had grasped the secret of wringing out of the world all the happiness they could still find in its odd moments, and making for themselves a life out of death, as touching and pathetic to older, hopeless people like herself as bunches of spring flowers on a child's grave. And what was Iona but a child and had she the least idea of what love or marriage meant?

'It was a bit awkward when Cousin Mary met me on my way back from that old canteen and asked what I was going to do when I was called up,' volunteered Iona, almost as if in answer to Rose's thoughts. 'Because I hope I won't do anything for a bit as I'd much rather have a baby. Wanda thinks I'm bats about that – she said she never could after some biology class she went to at school, but I think it would be simply thrilling. But of course what Mickie and I want most of all just now is to see each other again as quick as we can, and get what he calls hitched up as soon as possible!'

'Well, you can't do that till Linda knows, Iona darling. I'm sure you must go straight home and tell her the moment she's had her rest and tea. I believe it will do her all the good in the world really to see you so happy and so – so sure of yourself. And nothing could be better for her than to go off with you and stay at Bindleton and see Mickie – there's a very good pub there, he says. You see while she's been ill she's been thinking about the past. Get her right away to think about the future. I know Dr Harvey will be wise and understanding enough to let her go.'

'If only she doesn't go on the "too young" tack –' said Iona doubtfully. 'Do you think there's much in that, Aunt Rose?'

'I married when I was twenty-two and I was a widow at twenty-three,' said Rose with the candour which Iona's clear gaze seemed to demand. 'But I wouldn't have missed that year for the world, even though –' and even as Rose spoke the thought pierced her that if she hadn't rushed into marriage and motherhood she would not have brought poor Flora with her unhappy temperament into the world. She must ask the Major if he thought her youth and fears and agonies had been responsible for Flora, for already she looked upon the Major as a possible confidant for every problem.

'You'll have to come down to Bindleton for the wedding too, anyway,' said Iona, recording Rose's verdict with no apparent diminution of her steady equanimity. 'He says it would be better than wasting a day's leave coming up here, and he wants to go straight to London for our honeymoon and have a real binge. Won't it be fun, Aunt Rose?'

'Wouldn't you like the country better?' asked Rose curiously, for both Iona and Mickie had always seemed such country-loving children to their families.

'Oh no, I don't think so. We might get rather hipped, wishing we could be going to settle down in a home of our own to breed dogs and stock trout, and all the things we always planned to do, with Ken and – and Geordie you know. We shouldn't feel like that in London because we'd never want to live there, you see, and we'd keep awfully busy with shows and dances.'

They had reached the gate now, and Iona turned to run back, fired suddenly by the thought that she could not keep her secret from her mother one moment longer. It seemed only a moment since she and Tom had run in together at the gate of Laws from their first little school, and as Rose went in and lit the gas-fire in the library Iona's confidences seemed incredible. But then as the pleasant silence of the old house and the warmth of the fire surrounded her, her heart grew lighter. The old hall and stairs at which she was gazing seemed to be looking back to all the passing generations they had known, and assuring her that the length of time in which they had lived and loved did not matter at all compared with the intensity of that life and love. Mickie's mother looked down from her portrait, perennially radiant and young, her hand brushing those shadows backwards, as if to signal to Rose across the darkness that her few months of rapture in those very rooms must really count for more than the long procession of little joys and sorrows and discontents which other long-lived wives had known. All she would have asked for the son who inherited her beauty and gaiety was love like hers before, if fate willed it, he too bade farewell to life. 'You'd love Iona,' Rose confided to the portrait, 'and you wouldn't grudge Mickie to her for a moment. I can't understand how people ever can grudge their sons to their wives. You'd want him to have the best of everything in life just as I do!'

Was it, or wasn't it, a good thing, she wondered, that at this point the clock struck and recalled her to her duties? It was probably for the best, though it was of course depressing to go upstairs and take off her pretty clothes and get into an overall again.

Her work had certainly helped to keep her from all the worry she would have devoted to Flora's problems, and she must make it keep her from any but the most immediate aspects of Iona's news. A wedding was just what every working woman loved, and she would make plans about it and forget everything beyond. So she finished her housework and went to the kitchen for this solemn ceremony of 'the master's dinner'. The Major's advice had really helped her, and she had some soup made under his instructions, thank goodness. And there was mince from the butcher which did not look nearly as repellent as his usual wares. She was to stir oatmeal in it when it boiled to make it go further, said Mrs Childe, and at once Rose scented a symbolism which seemed to dog her domestic life. There was nothing like good stodgy work of the oatmeal variety to smooth down the emotions of one's heart. 'And put a few raisins in that scrap of rice and a bit of marge the size of my thumb and you'll have French rice pudding,' Mrs Childe had said. Well, she must look upon this marriage as a raisin in the dull texture of life and keep her thoughts to the immediate future. 'But oh bother all the beastly things,' thought the unregenerate Rose, even as she recognised, with justice, these duties did make time go and steadied your nerves, so that when Linda's tearful emotional voice came to her down the telephone she could be quite bracing and sensible, after a short exchange of sheer sentimental joy and rapture, and unacknowledged foreboding.

'Yes, dearest, of course you must go and see Mickie and talk it all over with him at any rate. Of course you can be spared and you can just pack off your mother-in-law to the Romany – as if we old people mattered one scrap just now!'

'You wouldn't get her to agree to that!'

'Well, no, and she's a bit old to learn, but you must go and settle matters. What does Ian say?'

'Well, he's just come in, and he's been stamping all over the room, and saying that it's impossible, and Iona is far too young, but Mickie's a splendid fellow, and why don't they get married in London instead of dragging us off to Bindleton! What does Stuart say?'

'He's not in yet. I hope it will distract him because we're both worried about Flora. I wish I'd had time to tell you about that, but after all, talking doesn't do much good. It's all through that dear odd Major Hosmer that we heard of it.'

'Oh, Rose, is he in love with her? How splendid! Because they'd go and live in America after the war, wouldn't they?' Linda certainly had no illusions about Flora, and none of that love to spare which the Major advocated so warmly.

'I couldn't tell if he cares for her – you know how he just seems to see everyone as a case, but I suppose you could be in love with a case! Anyhow it's early days to think of America, but I gather from him that she means to come home for a bit.'

'My dear!' Linda sounded aghast. 'I say, don't you think we could get her to take Grannie off to a nursing-home, and let him psycho both of them.'

'Lovely,' sighed Rose. 'Hasn't Grannie worked off most of her energies on Mary though?'

'Not a bit. She's just been scolding Ian because America won't go to war with Japan, and went deaf when he explained that they were. And when Iona tried to tell her about Mickie – for she's so bursting with pride, dear baby, that she wants to tell everyone – Grannie said she would give her her pearls, and she gave them to Wanda you know, and Wanda has popped them. There'll be a shambles, as Iona says, when she looks for them, and thinks I've stolen them. And the house-maid's given notice because she doesn't like Griffen, and who can blame her for we all hate Griffen. And she keeps saying she's coming to dance at the wedding, however, Ian says he'll put a stopper on that. She's sitting now writing to the Scottish Command to say what cuttings they may take from her herbaceous border, and how when she goes back there after the war she means to manage with a staff of six.'

'Now that's what I call a stiff upper lip at eighty-five,' said Rose admiringly.

'Yes, but it's only because she doesn't realise that her world has vanished! Sometimes I think it would have been better for her to have been bombed with her house on the top of her.'

'Oh, I think that's carrying a love of home too far! Good-bye, dearest. Isn't it too lovely that we're co-mothers-in-law?'

Rose hastened her farewells at that rather abruptly, explaining that she heard Stuart's key in the door. It was odd to realise that her heart should have leapt at such a solution of her troubles with Flora, whereas Stuart, she knew, would probably be grieved if his stepdaughter put the Atlantic between them. And then on the other hand, though he was fonder of Mickie, and prouder of him than he had ever been in the difficult years of his boyhood, his first comment on Rose's news was the query: 'What do they propose to live on?' Still, that was, Rose admitted, a very natural preoccupation for the father of a family in these difficult days, and though he muttered some protests on the lines that Iona was too young, and it was a pity to tie her down, and that it was better for the boys to get on with the job and leave marriage till after the war, he retracted his theories after one glance at Rose's pitiful gesture of despairing protest. Certainly step-relationships had taken a very odd turn in their family, but no longer could she brood anxiously over the problem. Stuart's meal must come first, and it was perhaps the salvation of unaided women all the world over that there was always some job waiting for them to do. She could not even worry over Mary's strictures till the mince and the oatmeal were safely amalgamated, and had found their way to Stuart's interior.

CHAPTER EIGHT
THE TANGLE OF LIFE'S WOOD

What need, White-Winged, to follow them
With well-strung bow and fluttering hem
Adown the tangle of life's wood?

William Morris

It hardly seemed credible that within a fortnight of that day
Rose should be sitting at her bureau, late in the afternoon,
issuing invitations and making arrangements for Mickie's
marriage to Iona in the following week. Mickie's impetuous
charm and Iona's placid determination had somehow con-
quered all their elders' demurs about youth and risk. While
the parents hesitated the young couple had given way gracefully on all the minor points. Mickie would relinquish the
idea of being married at Bindleton, all the more easily as he
found he might, in his own vague phrase, have to make a
speech to the lads from a propeller. And, at that, the church
in London and date were somehow fixed as an inevitable
sequence. It was to be very quiet, of course, Mickie entreated,
but again he gave way gracefully, as all the outlying relatives of

the Fairlaws and his mother's family woke to life in the south and demanded invitations. Stuart was such a respecter of family feelings that there was a lot to arrange, and not for the first time Rose found how incompatible were the jobs of a maid-of-all-work and her social existence. Stuart was not of much help, for his knack of remembering remote cousins and long-forgotten acquaintances merely added to her work. Regardless of the risks of war and revolution in general, and Mickie's job in particular, he and Ian Carr-Berwick drew up settlements and trusts which would provide very nicely, Mickie commented, for the future of the tenth child of their ninth grandson, but didn't seem to promise them much of the ready for the moment. Stuart's profound conviction that Mickie would forget some essential legal preliminary for the service, to be held in St Dubricius', near Sloane Square, occupied a large part of his conversation, and the one redeeming feature of the affair seemed to be that the date was timed to suit his board meeting, and his subsequent visit to Flora. Such were his ways of camouflaging very much the same sentiments as those which tore at Rose's heart, but with her mind so full of Mickie and Iona, and the tragedy of youth, Rose was not in a mood to do him justice. She was anxious about Tom, though his comments on the engagement certainly did not suggest a broken heart. 'A very good thing to bring a nice, sensible, strapping wench like that into the family,' he wrote, but not yet had Rose cured herself of her pre-war habit of imagining heartaches where none probably existed. She was worried too at the prospect of a visit from Flora. In old days her return home usually resulted in threats

of notice from the cook, 'because I was never spoken to in my life as I was by Miss Flora in the hall', by the parlourmaid because Flora was always unpunctual, and by the housemaid because she never could get into the young lady's room till eleven, and hadn't time for all that washing and mending and dancing attendance on her. Flora would still certainly give a lot of trouble, and Rose herself could not give notice! To feel like this about a daughter's visit was not only heartless: it showed how clearly she belonged to the normal order of working-class women who expected their daughters to go off at the age of fifteen, and not come cluttering up the house any longer! It might be shameful, but it was natural, and she could only console herself by thinking that it was useless to worry till Mickie and Iona were safely married. Flora had vouchsafed no reply to the news of the engagement, or to subsequent letters giving the date and details of their plans for the ceremony. It didn't seem likely that she would come, strained as her relations with Mickie had always been, and if she did she would certainly come in the mood of the bad fairy to the feast. All these preoccupations were in Rose's mind as she ticked off the list of wedding presents to the bridegroom, which overflowed in the library, so that when the front door-bell pealed at six o'clock she went and opened it, automatically expecting yet another wire from Bindleton about the time of the marriage ceremony, or what Mickie would call the God-men who were to perform it. But instead of the familiar boy in uniform she saw, in the gathering darkness, Major Hosmer, smile and spectacles all complete, standing before her with the air of one who is quite certain of his welcome.

'Now aren't you just too busy! I can see that!' said the Major as she led him rather reluctantly into the library, explaining that she was up to her eyes in correspondence, but of course she could spare him a few minutes. 'Now, Mrs Fairlaw, in an ordinary way I'd just make my farewells and hope for a better opportunity, for indeed I heard about your son's wedding to Miss Carr-Berwick, and quite understand what a fluttering of the dovecotes there must be over this happy event. I'd like to offer you my best congratulations on it, for I hear that each one of the pair is as charming and worthy as the other –' The Major rose, solemnly offered Rose his hand, and reseated himself. 'But I came to see you today, and I'm venturing to interrupt you now, because I have just received a piece of information which I should, I feel, hand on. It's from your daughter Flora.'

'Oh dear!' Rose had been sitting purposefully at her desk, but now she rose and came to the big leather arm-chair by the fire, feeling a little cold at heart. 'Nothing wrong I hope?'

'Now see here, Mrs Fairlaw, I don't think so, but I do feel I should interview your husband as well as you over her predicament. That's why I came late so as to find him in. But now I discover you hurrying off your letters for the mail I'm going to ask your leave again to let me act as your servant, and get your dinner set all ready – oh no, I won't suggest sharing it when you're so busy! And then when Mr Fairlaw does come in we can thrash this matter out all together without wasting your time. Now do say you're agreeable –'

'Oh, Major Hosmer, you're too kind! Indeed I ought to get

those letters off, but it seems so rude – and to let you do my work again! It's taking advantage of your kindness.'

But the Major did not think so, and marched off to the pantry with an air of eager anticipation. Rose turned back to rush off the thank-you letters she was writing for Mickie – with the rather rash promise that he would write himself when he saw the beautiful chafing-dish, electric lamp, or thermos flask in question – feeling too much relieved to worry over her absurd aide-de-camp. 'It's just "little goat bleat, little table appear", she quoted to herself from the old fairy story. 'I don't care what Stuart says or thinks.'

It seemed fortunate that Stuart was very late that evening. The Major had come in at the sound of her steps in the hall, carried off the letters to the post, and was standing beside her in the pantry showing how to make 'roux' for thickening soups, when the sound of a latchkey was heard. But immediately after it Rose peered cautiously round the door in dismay, for Stuart was talking to someone who was accompanying him in to the hall.

'Mary!' Rose emerged in surprise, thankful that the Major did not follow, asking to meet her friend at once. 'Have you – have you come to look us up?'

'I've come to test the great experiment, my dear!' Mary's crisp voice rang out heartily in the shadows of the old stone hall. 'I met Stuart and told him my poor old Eliza was laid up and I was dining in a hotel, because I know no one likes to have their staffs upset by an unexpected guest. So the dear old boy suggested that I should come here, as after all you've no one to give notice. It's all right, I hope?'

'Oh yes, Mary, if you and Stuart don't mind going rather short. I've got a visitor already and only a little fish!'

'Who's here?' asked Stuart, gazing across at the military hat and gas-mask in the hall, and speaking with unfortunate distinctiveness. 'Not that – not the Major again?'

'Yes,' replied Rose repressively. After all, if Stuart felt at liberty to ask people home without warning, just because they'd rather give trouble to her than other people's maids, she wasn't going to let the Major go unrewarded by his own efforts. 'Just run up and take your things off in my room, Mary – I'm too busy to come! – Dinner will be ready in a minute – you won't have time for a bath, Stuart, I'm afraid.'

'Couldn't you put it off half an hour?' Stuart asked as Mary disappeared. The Major was still absorbed apparently in the pantry.

'And let me sit and entertain them for half an hour and then have the dinner spoiled? No, Stuart!' Rose's whisper was almost fierce. 'And Major Hosmer,' she called in a louder voice, 'here's Stuart! And you must please let me serve the dinner, and pretend it's mine, so as to impress a cousin of mine who's just turned up!'

The Major's disappointment at relinquishing his favourite task, and Stuart's lack of welcome to him, were not promising omens for the dinner-party, and when they all assembled in the dining-room, over the bowls of soup which the Major insisted on serving, their evil presage was amply justified, for Mary and the Major, as Rose began her introduction, stiffened themselves, and exchanged such hostile nods that it was quite evident they had met before, and failed to enjoy the experience. 'What a row they must have had somewhere,' thought Rose. 'I never imagined that the dear little man could look so fierce!'

By every social tradition, of course, Mary might be trusted to ignore her battlefield with the Major (for surely there had been a battlefield) on such neutral ground as this, and Rose's odd party might be trusted to consume dinner without bloodshed. It was the day on which the Admiralty admitted the deterioration of the position in the Atlantic, and Stuart's gloomy prognostications as he let his soup grow cold would surely keep the conversation off personal topics! But she was reckoning without the more direct methods of a younger civilisation, for, when the Major sprang up to help her to change the plates, and hand round the fish pudding and vegetables, which had in his hands become things of style and beauty, instead of the apologetic mess Rose was liable to produce, he seized the distraction to bring his forces into action.

'I'm very, very pleased, let me assure you, Miss Macfie, to have this opportunity of meeting you again, and make it clear that I have no feelings of personal injury at the very outspoken attack you made upon me at our committee.'

It was useless to expect that breeding or conventions would let Mary accept such a remark either with non-committal courtesy, or with a non-controversial and frigid acceptance of the olive branch. By the time Rose had returned with the salt and pepper which she had forgotten, the protagonists had clashed swords, and Mary was appealing to her Cousin Stuart in the voice which had fired a thousand committees:

'Let me just lay the facts before you, Stuart, and then Major Hosmer can have the benefit of an unprejudiced and reliable legal opinion. Even you, I imagine, Major Hosmer, have some respect for our famous Scottish justice! Major Hosmer and I are both members of that small committee which inaugurated the hostel, in Maybury Terrace, for the wives and relatives of foreign or colonial officers serving in Castleburgh. It was founded on a basis of generous donations, and is run now most capably by a matron of my own acquaintance: it has justified its existence not only by meeting a felt want, for there is rarely a bed to spare, but also by managing at last to pay its way apart from the rent, heat, and lighting which are most generously provided by Mr Tonks, the owner of the house. For some time the work of the committee has been almost nominal, but unfortunately last month a very serious crisis arose. Miss Hills, the matron, had to report to me that she had allocated a double room to a Canadian captain and his wife: they seemed quite a decent, pleasant couple, but on their departure she happened to notice that the name on the woman's ration card was not that of her husband, and her identity card revealed the same truth.'

'Spies, of course,' said Stuart shortly. It was one of the trials of Rose's lot that she had to restrain her desire to discuss every detail of the meal she had achieved with those who consumed it, and tonight they might all have been eating shoe-leather for any attention they gave to the food. Still, Stuart as he uttered this triumphant diagnosis, did take a large second helping.

'Not at all,' replied Mary hotly. 'Pray, Stuart, don't let this spyphobia of yours get possession of you.'

'Perhaps it's the reasoned opinion of our famous Scottish legal system –' the Major interposed with spirit.

'My dear sir! Pray let me continue my story, and you can present your own case afterwards. On inquiry the couple admitted the truth without shame. "X", as we may call him, has a wife in Toronto; "Y", as we may call her, met him on some job in London, having known him all her life, and the two agreed to use our hostel, our own hostel, for –'

'Well, their honeymoon,' suggested Rose hastily, fearing the more explicit phrase which seemed to be hovering on Mary's lips.

'I suppose there's some ruling against that sort of thing in the constitution,' suggested Stuart, as he followed the Major's lead by getting up and helping to change the plates. How Mary greeted this rather tepid response to the exposure of sin Rose did not hear, as she hurried to the pantry, but on her return with the miraculous pile of cheese pancakes tossed up by the Major, and still fresh and sizzling from their retreat under the low grill, the Major himself was holding the field.

'There's the story told quite fairly from your point of view, Miss Macfie, but you must let me add the details which throw a rather different light on the story. "X", as you call him, has been tied for years to a neurotic, invalid wife who spends her life in a sanatorium, and has never pretended to care for him. Over here and lonely – and you can't any of you imagine what that loneliness is, still less,' he bowed to Rose, 'what such kindness, yours, means to the lonely – he met this friend of his childhood, a woman as solitary here as himself. They agreed that he must be loyal to his wife in name, and only met as friends. Then he was ordered up to the North, and shortly afterwards got his embarkation leave. I won't say where he was going, but he expected imminent danger anyhow. She knew that she could give him a week's happiness and that she had her one chance, perhaps, of fulfilling her womanhood.' (Rose stole a glance at Mary and quickly dropped and retrieved a spoon a little noisily.) 'Now if you'd been in their place' – his gleaming spectacles swept the table – 'wouldn't you have done just what they did? You're a lawyer, sir,' the spectacles focused on Stuart, 'but you're a man as well.'

'Quite,' agreed Stuart in his driest voice. 'But at the same time I gather that one is under some contract to this – ah – institution – only to use it as a hostel for – ah – genuine relations and marriage partners. There can be no legal excuse for breaking such a contract. They should have gone to a hotel.'

'They couldn't have afforded it! Under Miss Macfie's capable management the hostel caters for these officers at a remarkably reasonable price.'

'So I imagine', said Mary in a voice which made Rose start nervously, 'do bad houses!'

'I have really no information on that subject,' said the Major, meditatively, betraying no such symptoms of embarrassment as his hosts. 'But, come, Miss Macfie, you must know that that wouldn't have been a practicable proposition for two such decent, respectable people as you yourself admitted the matron thought "X" and "Y" to be.'

'I doubt if your argument holds good though, Major.' Stuart was little in sympathy with his cousin at the moment, but his sense of kinship and patriotism, as well as more abstract reasoning and a growing prejudice against his other guest, led him to incline to her side. 'At that rate you'd condone the theft of a loaf of bread because a man was hungry!'

'I should, and for much the same reason, that there's something fundamentally wrong with society if its laws condemn a man to starve.'

'Or the theft of a hundred or a thousand pound banknotes?' persisted Stuart.

'Not at all. You've passed now out of the range of a human being's natural demands and cravings into the selfish wants created by an artificial state of society. Oh yes, I know you lawyers must protect property while it exists, but how much will there be left to protect after this war, when, as far as I can see, the peoples of the world must turn upon their rulers? All such laws will have to be changed, or at any rate modified completely, and in the same way men will have to find out some better basis for the relationships of the sexes –'

'Oh well, of course, if you deny the sanctity of marriage –' Mary brushed away the dish which the Major offered her for a second helping, as if she were brushing him too into a limbo of outer darkness.

'I don't. There is, there must be sanctity in sex-relations if we're not to lapse into barbarism.' The Major was happily unconscious of Stuart's embarassed annoyance. 'Put it this way, Miss Macfie. Imagine yourself growing up on a desert island with normal *libido* and no inhibitions – (let me get that spoon for you this time, Mrs Fairlaw) – your sole companion a youth of sterling qualities and reasonable good looks. Would you refuse to mate because there was no lawyer to tie up a settlement, no priest to register vows before God? Of course not, I should hope not. Now we psychiatrists know that half the married couples in the world suffer from frustration and misery because the laws of Church and State alike aren't based on a proper conception of human nature. They're based,' continued the Major, having reduced his audience temporarily to a stunned silence by the picture of Mary's probable activities on a desert island, 'they're based on a mistaken insistence on the rights of property (though no decent man looks on his wife as a chattel any more) and the integrity of the family, though what integrity there is about a family when husband and wife are at loggerheads I've yet to discover. And the only remedy man has devised for this mess of his own making is this preposterous business of divorce, which lets the rogues and the heartless get free without a qualm, and keeps the well-meaning and conscientious still tied up in hopeless knots. Oh, believe me, after this war we'll see drastic changes as they did in Russia.'

'That happy land of free love, adultery, and abortions!' Mary was certainly freeing herself of some of her usual inhibitions in conversation tonight, thought Rose, as she jumped up to fetch the coffee and break up this appalling dinner-party.

'Let me assist you, Mrs Fairlaw!' The Major sprang to his feet too. 'Now forgive me, pray, if I've held forth too long! You see I've got my own angle on all these problems, and I've studied reports from Russia very carefully, though I haven't been there to see for myself. But as I make it out after a time – after a time, mind you, when you had a pretty primitive state of savagery – the proletariat there has settled down much like other countries. When husband and wife love each other and raise a family they stick together, and when they don't they part with considerably less washing of dirty linen than we have to put up with. I don't say they're even on the road to solving the question yet, but they're a bit nearer than the old countries.'

It seemed to be an accepted routine in the Major's eyes that the rest of the party should adjourn while he washed up, but Rose tonight insisted on staying in the pantry to help him, though Stuart's expression showed that he had grave doubts as to the safety of leaving a woman alone with so loose a thinker. He even came in and picked up a dishcloth distastefully himself, till Rose, with a significant glance, urged him to join Mary in the drawing-room lest she should offer her help as well. There really was not space for a debating society in the little low-roofed room, and how could you keep protagonists from throwing dishes at each other's heads when there were so many lying about?

'Major Hosmer,' she ventured when they were alone, 'I'd like to know what kind of solution you hope to find for all these difficult questions.'

'I haven't,' admitted the Major. 'The only working policy I can see is a society governed by the Christian rule of loving your neighbour as yourself. If husbands and wives stuck to that they'd make a better job of it, for I once read a very remarkable article on the meaning of the text which insisted that the verb implied "try to love" just as "believe" implies "try to believe". If married people kept on trying to remember why they once thought each other so lovable they'd make a better job of things. And then in a really incompatible marriage they'd ask themselves if taking their own freedom hurt others – children or the other partner – in a way they wouldn't like to be hurt themselves.'

'It would be difficult to make a legal code out of that.'

'Sure thing, but then I don't think the law's an idea of how to deal with marriage. For one thing, except for murder it's the only crime for which you get a life sentence – as a witty lady of my acquaintance once remarked – "and even for murder you can shorten your sentence by good conduct." Mark you, Mrs Fairlaw, we're in such an age of transition that it's of no use to worry much over the present position. I'm quite sure that after this war we'll see very strange alterations in the laws and government of this country. But at least we needn't join the party who commenced pelting stones at that woman in the Gospels.'

'What happened to "X" and "Y"?' asked Rose, with the usual feminine tendency to relapse from the general to the particular.

'Why nothing. They were leaving anyway and they'd had their week. Miss Macfie – who strikes me as an autocratic woman, though one who's successfully sublimated her repressed sexual instincts into philanthropy – wished to get at them somehow by charging Miss "Y" with false impersonation, or "X" with bigamy (which incidentally he hadn't committed). But that wise old minister on our committee persuaded her we'd only make ourselves look very foolish and give ourselves a bad name. But it was me she really got her knife into, as I was perhaps rather outspoken on the subject. Though I never intended,' added the Major polishing a saucepan vigorously, 'to bring a blush to any lady's cheek!'

Miss Macfie was, however, apparently chary of her blushes, for as they entered the drawing-room, the Major carrying the coffee-tray, she began to make her farewells. It was obvious from Stuart's appearance that this seemed to him an excellent moment for parting with their other guest, but the Major was quite impervious to any hints.

'No, I'll not make my getaway yet, if you'll forgive me,' he said cheerfully. 'I've still got to come to the real purpose of my visit, a letter to me from your daughter. It arrived this morning and I said to myself after thinking things over from every angle: "Now, Percy Hosmer, you've got to go see Flora's parents about this right away."'

'It's very kind of you,' said Rose dully, while Stuart still fidgeted by the door. 'Stuart dear, do come and sit down!'

'Well, can we see this letter?' was all Stuart's comment.

'No, sir!' Up went the Major's hand. 'It's a very natural request but I decided before I set out that I'd no right to do that; in a sense it's violating the confidence of a patient. No, I fear you must just take it from me that the pace of the crisis we feared has quickened up a bit, for your daughter writes me that she can't stand the place, and that she's given them notice rather than let her enemies combine to ask her to send in her resignation. I should say,' said the Major reflectively, 'that there were a good many feathers flying down there, but anyhow that's beside the point. What concerns us is a remark of hers to the effect that she has no money and nowhere to go, and so she expects she'll just have to come home to you.'

'Most gratifying for us, I'm sure,' observed Stuart coldly.

'Now, Mr Fairlaw! Let me implore you' – and needless to say the Major did it with an uplifted hand – 'if there's one thing we must all do, in dealing with this unhappy girl, it's to avoid any sort of bitterness. If there's one thing that can help her now it's love, freely outpoured, asking no return. Now does she know that you were intending to visit her next week?'

'She shows no sign of having either read our letters or attempted to answer them for the last fortnight,' rejoined Stuart. 'I shan't write again, but simply wire her the time I mean to arrive for an interview –'

'Oh, but I think that's a mistake,' said the Major eagerly. 'My idea is that you should go far more than halfway to meet her. Since I've had the privilege of getting acquainted with you and Mrs Fairlaw I've had to revise my opinion of Flora's case very radically. I realise the self-deception which she indulged in about your attitude to her, but just because she wilfully refused to accept, and stubbornly rejected, the love which I sure know you offered her, it's all the more important that you should give her every chance of recognising it. I'd say to you, sir, take the example of the father in the parable, and while she is yet a great way off go forth to meet her, and fall on her neck and embrace her.'

A vision of Stuart, in the oriental robes and turban of the *Child's Illustrated Bible*, and Flora's reactions if her father employed such tactics, made Rose choke down a laugh, anxious as she was feeling over Flora's communications; and even

Stuart, she noticed with relief, was smiling a little, though his eyebrows were bristling, as he said:

'Now suppose, Major, we cut out all this vague talk about love and forgiveness and you tell me just what Flora has been up to!'

But that the Major refused to do, either because he would not, or, as Rose thought probable, he could not. So often in old days she had received letters from the girl at school, full of hints of catastrophic disaster and threats of running away, and so often they had resolved themselves into a quarrel with her best friend or a rebuke from some mistress on whom at the moment she had what the boys called a crush. All that seemed clear was that this particular row was bad enough to make Flora willing to return home, temporarily at least. And Rose could hardly decide whether the prospect of having another inmate as difficult as Flora to cook for, work for, and wait upon was more appalling than the fact that she, Flora's mother, viewed this prospect with such unmitigated dismay.

'D'you suppose there's some love affair behind all this?' Stuart put crudely the question which was disturbing his wife's mind also. There had been cases enough of that in the past, for not only was Flora one of those unhappy people who give without inspiring affection, but she was possessed, it almost seemed, by a genius for falling in love with people who were most unlikely to return her passion; old, comfortably married lawyers, the family doctor, an actor visiting the city, a staff officer engaged to her greatest friend. When, on the other hand, some suitable young man seemed likely to succumb to her dark commanding charm, Flora became so reserved and repellent that there was a hasty retreat.

'That I couldn't answer quite definitely, but I'd say it was likely,' admitted Major Hosmer. 'There must be no questioning of course, and it's very, very important that she should not feel she is observed.'

'But that's the difficulty!' Rose spoke despairingly. 'If we do question her she's always hated us for our curiosity, and if we don't she complains of my want of interest in her! It's always been like that, and oh dear, how I've mismanaged things!'

'Now, Rose, I think you're exaggerating.' Stuart got up, knocked out his pipe and looked purposefully at the door. 'Flora's had a hard time and done well, and I'm proud of her, and she feels it will do her good to rest at home for a bit. I expect that's all that's at the bottom of this fanfaronade – she always did exaggerate – and it'll be a help for you to have her to work about the house for a bit. After all, she'll have to register soon, now that this thing's burst up – I doubt if that'd have been a reserved job in any case – so she'll have to get down to something else and forget all this storm-in-a-teacup.'

'And I hope very much,' added the Major, 'that while I'm here you'll let me be of all the service I can, Mrs Fairlaw. It's wonderful what a willing interpreter can sometimes do in these cases, and I'll put all my free time at your service.' And the Major's help about the house, it was obvious to Rose, from Stuart's expression, would be about as welcome to him as Flora's erratic, self-satisfied bullying or neglect would be to her mother.

'Look here, you'll have to get rid of that man's visitations somehow,' said Stuart when he had managed to shepherd their guest to the front door at last. 'I mean it's past a joke letting him make himself free of the whole house. And I can tell you that Mary has the lowest possible opinion of him.'

'They don't seem to have clicked certainly,' was Rose's evasive reply.

'I should think not! What woman of her age wants to have a fellow holding forth to her on her sex frustrations, and a colonial too!' added Stuart as if this were the last straw. 'D'you think the fellow's in love with Flora or not?'

'I thought at first he was in love with her. You see he's seen her in a heroic light. Oh, Stuart, I wish we could get a glimpse of that Flora! It shows I've never appreciated her.'

'Well, if you want this house stiff with incendiary bombs, so that you can see the best side of your daughter, I don't,' rejoined Stuart, going off to the library, while Rose was left to fill the hot-water bottles, with the gloomiest anticipations of the future. More and more it seemed to her that every human being was in some sense what she herself was literally, nowadays, house-bound, tethered inexorably to a collection of all the extinct memories, and what the Major would call inhibitions, with which they had grown up, bits of mental furniture which they dusted and inspected daily. 'And we all have our kitchens too,' she thought with the erratic fanciful-ness of fatigue, 'where we hash up our motives, and warm up our own opinion of ourselves, and hoard all the goods we've inherited or got hold of instead of wishing to share them. And there are barriers between us all, or most of us. Stuart couldn't

get into the Major's house. I'm not really at home in Stuart's! And as for poor Flora. All her doors and windows are locked and shuttered, and I've never been inside since she was a baby. Oh dear, oh dear, how are we all to get out?'

CHAPTER NINE
BITTER LIPS

But gnawing Jealousy, out of their sight
Sitting alone, his bitter lips did bite;
And trembling Fear still to and fro did fly.

Spenser

A week later Flora Graylle sat in the comer of a third-class carriage in the crowded train which was speeding north from Kings Cross. She had got a corner seat by moving the bags which had been placed there to retain it, and refusing so fiercely to stir in favour of their owner that the timid little gentleman had retired to the corridor, muttering useless threats. She had not provided herself with any food, and when the kindly old lady opposite had offered her a sandwich, refused it with such contempt that its owner could take no pleasure in her own meal. And that, as Tom would have said, was Flora all over.

As a matter of fact Flora's scowl was not in reality fixed upon the eatables in paper bags. It was due partly to the short sight which she was too vain to remedy by wearing her

spectacles, partly to a long-sustained effort in her youth to look as remote or disdainful as a music mistress whom she adored, and partly because she was indulging in her favourite occupation of going back over her past life, to prove to herself how the neglect and cruelty of her relations had contributed to the dark clouds which now encircled her life, and utterly obscured her future.

Nothing would have shocked or horrified Rose more than to hear that story unexpurgated. She had realised, of course, even before Major Hosmer made it so clear to her, that Flora convicted her of mismanagement and want of love, and that Flora's jealousy of Mickie was at the root of her troubles. But of the other unhappy incidents which Flora claimed to be the cause of her complexes she knew nothing. And it was difficult to know what faith you could have in Flora's theories when she let hints drop now and again about the dark cloud cast on her life by her early acquaintance with death, and yet, as Rose privately assured herself, she could not possibly remember the death of her grandfather. That was true enough, but as a matter of fact Flora at the age of three had undergone an unhappy experience of which her mother knew nothing. Rose, worn out with weeks of nursing the old gentleman, was sent to bed by the old family doctor till the funeral, and Flora's old nurse, who had taken charge of three generations at Seriton, determined privately that she would take the child to see her grandfather, before, in her own phrase, he was coffined.

'Is Mickie to come too?' asked Flora, for though this episode happened before Rose's second marriage, the little girl was already jealous of the beautiful, adored baby.

'Oh no, Miss Flora! He's nothing to do with the house of Seriton!'

So it was with gratified pride that Flora stumped into the big dimly lit room. She had often been taken in before, for her grandfather had a tragic interest in the last descendant of the line, and she had always disliked intensely the smells of disinfectant, the vision of the old man propped up in bed in a Jaeger dressing-jacket, with his sunken, yellow, unshaved face and heavy breathing. And now the room was transformed into a bower of flowers, and in the midst of it lay her grandfather, beautiful in the masked serenity of death. 'Just a glimpse to remember him by' was all nurse decreed, so all that Flora carried away was a sense of the calm and beauty, and, above all, the importance of being dead. From that moment death had no terrors for the insensitive, self-consequent child.

She had never mentioned that episode to her mother, but she had spoken frequently of her sorrow at leaving Seriton. That seemed incredible to Rose, as the child was so small, and indeed, though Flora had the far-reaching, vivid memory of the introvert, she could remember nothing of her goodbyes to the house or grounds. What she did remember was her old Nannie, weeping in the hall, as she said: 'So my little missie will be the little lady of Seriton no longer!' Small as she was a sense of degradation and cruel deprivation of her rights had weighed upon Flora for months. Her tempers and fits of weeping were put down to grief for parting with old Nannie, who chose to be pensioned off rather than accompany the family to 'that poky little place in Castleburgh'. Rose could not understand it, for the two had always been at loggerheads in the nursery: it was her first introduction to Flora's habit of hating people in their presence and idealising them in their absence. And she had no idea that Flora remembered those days as 'the time my mother turned out my old nurse when she sold my home to strangers and married again!'

Rose, worried by Flora's grief and anxious to please Nannie, tried to atone by sending the two off together on a long-promised visit to her father-in-law, old Canon Graylle in his old house in the cathedral close of Mells. How could she foresee that on the very first evening Flora, lying awake in the odd canopied bed, watching the shadows of old Nannie, and the older housekeeper of the Canon, thrown by the fire on the wall, would hear something to influence her whole life?

'Yes, all alone he's lived, Mrs Day, since his wife left him twenty years ago.'

'Was she ill for long, poor lady?' asked Nannie, as she raised a teacup to her lips, and settled down to a recital of symptoms.

'Ill! No! Did you never hear? Fancy that! Why no, the poor lady put an end to herself!'

'Killed herself?' Nannie's horrified hissing whisper thrilled Flora most agreeably.

'Yes and she did. The river it was, and when they got her out –' The voices sank lower and presently Nannie creaked over the bed.

'Fast asleep,' she reported, having seen Flora's long lashes at rest below her eyelids, under her dark fringe. 'Well! Did you ever! And what reason had she?'

'Well, they said it was her baby's death; she'd only the one after your little one's father and that was stillborn. But I don't know. She came of a very good family, one of the Erskons of Erskon she was and it runs in the family – her grandfather I believe and some gentlemen further back as well. You never can tell with these old families.'

Flora knew all about people killing themselves, for had not Nannie herself read to her how King Saul fell upon his sword 'because he did not wish to live after the Ark of God was taken.' She knew all about old families from Nannie too, and how desirable it was to belong to a real old family, so the story impressed her immensely with the sense of a high and hereditary doom which she could weave most delightfully into the stories about herself in which she indulged every night. Most children at one time or another picture relations weeping round their deathbed, deploring their former want of appreciation, but in Flora's story the death was always suicide, and the penitence of the mourners proportionately greater.

It was just after Flora's return from that visit that Mickie fell ill, and though Rose might blame herself now for her utter absorption in the struggle for life and death, and acknowledge that Flora, left very much to her new, cheerful, casual Nannie, had some cause for jealousy, she never imagined, as no nature untouched by jealousy can imagine, the fierce resentment in Flora's heart. It had been bad enough when Mickie was the fat, adorable, smiling, golden-curled baby whom everyone noticed first, but at least her mother cared for her then, and was part of her life, instead of someone who was always vanishing into Mickie's sickroom. With her instinct for

drama Flora decided that Tom was neglected too, and constituted herself his guardian Big Sister. And Tom was quite willing to accept her attentions and obey her whims meekly, in the role of Little Brother, until Mickie grew well and boisterous again, and went off to the little school which Flora also attended. As soon as Tom was promoted to going to the kindergarten the fame and exploits of the great demigod Mickie, aged seven, bewitched his little brother, and Big Sister found her protection, her games, and her reading aloud impatiently brushed aside. It was after this that Flora grew so miserable and so intolerable that Rose, by the advice of all her relations and the old family doctor, sent her off to a little boarding school in the Borders. 'My brother robbed me of my baby brother's love, and my mother turned me out of the house,' was Flora's record of that period of her life.

Of course her foolish dreams and jealousy and fits of black sullen gloom were not the sole, or even the main, pattern of her life. She grew tall and strong and athletic at this first school, and in the next school, recommended by the London psychoanalyst, to which she accompanied her cousin at the age of fourteen, she was on the whole happy and popular. So many other girls had more or less violent 'crushes' for mistresses or older girls that Flora's overbearing and exacting affairs were not unduly conspicuous. Rose, in her renewed youth and gaiety after Mickie's recovery, had accepted easily the prevalent belief that she could laugh and tease Flora out of her silly jealousy, and had failed lamentably. But contemporaries can laugh where parents cannot, and though Flora was still swayed by fits of passion and sullenness, her memory of her schooldays was usually docketed in her mind as 'the first time I was ever really understood'.

'It was the same old story when I grew up!' Flora would tell any confidant of the moment who was willing to be bored with the story of her past. 'She packed me off to London to my Aunt Olive, as she wouldn't take the trouble to come herself, and she ought to have known I was too young and gawky at seventeen, and that Aunt Olive and her silly smirking little daughter would never care a damn about me if I wasn't a success!' It was simplest to forget how earnestly Rose had opposed the whole scheme of that London season and how fiercely Flora had fought for her own way against her mother and stepfather alike.

She passed lightly in recollection over her first foolish love affair. She could never forgive her mother for interfering, and 'spoiling my life' was her general label for the episode. What she could not forgive Rose, in reality, was the relief with which her mother was greeted by the married admirer with whom Flora had taken refuge, and the cheerful, casual way in which he had handed Flora back as a silly little schoolgirl who hadn't an idea what she was up to! Flora had thirsted for revenge, and had taken it, pretty thoroughly as a matter of fact, by the unpleasantness she inflicted on the family circle for the next few years. She made a consistent fool of herself, and of them, in their small circle of society, by her silly crazes for married men, and her contemptuous rejection of any suitable advances. She preferred to turn in memory at once to the years of war in which she had found herself. For, as Major Hosmer could see more clearly than her exasperated family, part of Flora's difficulty was that of a nature with primitive powers and emotions flung into an artificial state of society which gave it no scope. Even when she was completely at loggerheads with her mother she would dream of rescuing her from flood, fire, and disaster: even when she hated Mickie most she would have gladly murdered any fallen German airman who might once have shot at him in the air. When the blitz fell upon Eastminster again and again she knew all the joys of battle, and she drove her ambulance furiously, broke into burning houses, dug by the side of men for the wounded, and carried them tenderly into safety. Not for her was the patience or humility to kaleidoscope such qualities into the humdrum round of life, or even to see such procedure was desirable. She only considered that she had proved herself of finer mettle than the little world of her friends and relatives, and demanded yet a wider field for her courage and daring.

It was a pity, a sad pity, as Major Hosmer was to say, shaking his head later on, that she found this opportunity only in befriending Count Guy Poliaski.

'How on earth can you make a fool of yourself over a horrible bullet-headed dago like that?' her great friend and colleague, Miranda, had asked disdainfully, when the girls got back together from a night club to the room they were sharing in a hotel in Knightsbridge on their leave.

'Because his people have given their all for us,' replied Flora with glowing eyes, 'because he's lost land, castle, wife, and children, all that he has, and has escaped here to fight his country's enemies to the death. Most of all, perhaps, because people like you, Anda, throw such hideous cowardly aspersions on him.'

'Well, I only said he looked Teutonic,' replied Miranda reasonably, 'and so he does! But of course if you've fallen for him –'

'His country has fallen for us!' Flora stood at the shrouded window looking to Miranda's irreverent gaze rather like a Joan of Arc who was mistaking a siren for a heavenly Voice. 'That's why I may feel it my duty to give him my all!'

Even to herself Flora could not pretend that this sacrifice, which absorbed the last three days of her leave, was anything but distasteful to one of her fastidious and austere nature. She had played with the idea of love for so long that its reality, in the society of a hard, cold, and, as she was to imagine later, desperate man, was only endurable in view of the sufferings of Poland. The awakening was naturally all the more crushing when it came, delivered without undue sympathy by Miranda.

'I suppose you've heard,' she announced on Flora's return from a day in London, 'that your Guy has disappeared. When did you hear from him last?'

'Not since I got back a month ago,' returned Flora. 'He told me not to write because he had a secret mission.'

'Well, that was true anyway! Tommy Hartnell says he's in the Tower! He's been arrested and his rooms have been searched anyhow. Flora, you weren't really ass enough to go off and stay with him when I left you at the Clarice?'

Flora had no wish, as the train sped northward through the bleak villages of Yorkshire, to recall the royal row which had followed. She might flatter herself on some of the home-truths which she had shot broadcast at her friend, but the fact remained that Miranda had won her point. Flora must get out of their unit lest she should get them all into disgrace, and get back to Scotland where, under the aegis of a respectable legal family, she would be best placed if she became involved in any way with the researches of the military intelligence into Guy's past. And on the whole, Miranda vouchsafed, Tommy Hartnell had thought it unlikely, for Guy had been mixed up with so many women that they couldn't be expected to track them all down.

'Let my son get out and get you a cup of tea!' said the old lady, still pitiful and still unsnubbed, as the train stopped in the dripping murky gloom of Newcastle station.

Flora did not even acknowledge the remark, for now her thoughts were turning to her only other refuge, to her friend and adviser, Percy Hosmer. But would he be a refuge any longer now that he had, by his own account, made acquaintance, if not a friendship, with her stepfather and mother? Even the most self-centred people cannot deceive themselves all the time, and Flora was aware, in her more truthful moments, that her picture of the home, and that home itself, might not tally in the eyes of her friends.

It was that, incredible as it would seem to the old lady opposite, which troubled her far more than her recent exploit. She had hardly noticed the little Major in the days of their early acquaintance, till his outspoken appreciation of her courage, and obvious devotion, satisfied her cravings for admiration. And then she had been tempted to pour out her heart and all her history to him, and discovered, as Rose had done, the wonderful sensation of sympathy and understanding which he gave. He had never spoken of love to her: that would have been out of the question, from his point of view, while she was his patient. The fact that he had not done so had turned Flora's liking into real affection until he had gone away without a word. And then she had met Guy, and in the turmoil of her heart offered him, out of pity and self-sacrifice, what the Major had despised. That was how she saw her story, and it was one which the Major with his advanced ideas would, she knew, understand and condone if he loved her. And if only, if only, her mother had not poisoned him against her! So she mused as the train rushed past the red soil of Haddingtonshire and the red cliffs against the misty curtain of pallid sea. So far her one preoccupation had been to reach home at all costs, but now she began to wonder, as sudden storms of rain began to dapple the waves, what hope or help lay before her when her goal was reached, either from her family or from the Major.

The rain was falling briskly on the glass roof of the station as Flora emerged from the overheated carriage. Her bag was heavy, but she scowled at the porters and in consequence failed to get a taxi. That loss fitted perfectly into her morass of self-pity: it was only natural she told herself that no one should meet her, and she must drag her heavy bag by tram. For as she had telegraphed, surely Stuart, who had always taken her part, might have managed to meet her. Probably Rose had dissuaded him, she told herself, her dreams of that reunion with her mother already fading into thin air.

Like all selfish people Flora had never taken the trouble to envisage the new state of affairs at Laws House. Certainly no memory of it came to her as she tugged the bell violently, three times in succession. Someone must be there, for hadn't Stuart written that they were returning on the night of Mickie's wedding day, and how dared they keep her waiting at the door when she was so wet and ill and wretched? She was cold with fury when at last the door opened and a tiny crack of light illuminated the gloom.

'And who's there?' asked a voice almost as defiant and aggrieved as her own, when she replied autocratically:

'It's Miss Graylle! Open the door at once and take my bag upstairs. And tell my mother I have arrived though she doesn't seem to be expecting me.'

'She's not! We're not expecting company!' Mrs Childe was utterly perturbed by this unexpected intrusion. For the fact of the matter was that she had no business in the house at all, and now that she was discovered what would happen if this young madam took upon herself to send for the police? Not indeed that she had anything to reproach herself with, no indeed! Mrs Fairlaw had told her before she left for London that Mrs Childe had well earned a holiday, and paid her full fees very prettily, and nothing to do for it but just look in and forward letters, so that the kind woman had made up her mind to give the poor lady a nice surprise. Mrs Childe had been watching her pupil all these three months with an odd mixture of admiration for her grit – for stick to her work she did – pity for her obvious fatigue, and tolerant contempt for her inefficiency. 'I can keep the hoose up to the mark,' she told her husband, 'by just putting her to a different room every day, and giving the rooms she did yesterday a thorough today. But, oh boy, the kitchen! You see, I've no place there, as you may say, with her doing her bit of cooking for breakfast and supper, and me only there for my elevenses. She does her best, and she remembers all my hints, I will say that, about how to use soda or Vim or soap, but she's no strength in her wrists and no knack of it at all! You wouldn't believe it. You should see what the pots and strainers and dishes are like after she's been scrubbing at them for an hour! No difference at all, and it's all I can do not to snatch them out of her hands. And the cupboards and shelves all needing a good wash over instead of the little pokes with a duster she gives them now and again!' In view of this pathetic inefficiency Mrs Childe had therefore determined to give the pantry-kitchen and its furnishings a real good spring-cleaning, and wash over the neglected basement which was going from bad to worse through neglect. It wasn't only that she wanted to please Mrs Fairlaw either, for you never knew that she wouldn't have her head in the air dreaming, and hardly know one end of a sweeper from the other: it was the house itself which appealed mutely to Mrs Childe for order and shining cleanness. She had an artist's passion, as it were, for shining utensils and spotless woods and speckless floors. So therefore she had put in a most enjoyable two days' work – Mr Childe was told he must just go and get his dinner at the new British Restaurant round the corner – and she had just been making herself a nice hot cup of tea, resting and enjoying the results of her labour, when Flora appeared wet, dishevelled, and bad-mannered at the door.

'Who on earth are you?' For a moment Flora almost wondered if she had come to the wrong house. Instinctively she had expected to come in from the darkness without into the turret hall gay with flowers and lights, the scent of wood fire and the sound of the wireless from the drawing-room, and a voice of welcome from the library, while an impeccable maid carried her bag upstairs to unpack it. And instead of that here was this odd, self-possessed, impertinent little woman in an overall, holding open the door to show only a glimpse of darkness and deadness within.

'I'm caretaker to Mrs Fairlaw, and I don't know that it's my business to let anyone into the house without orders. There are a lot of queer characters about!'

'Go and get my mother at once,' retorted Flora, pushing past the woman into the house. Why didn't a door somewhere open at the sound of her voice?

'How can I when she's still in London? She wired to me she was taking another twenty-four hours there' (and just gave me time for that laundry, reflected Mrs Childe) 'and no orders given about any visitors expected here, daughter or no daughter.'

'As if you could keep me out of my own home!' said Flora contemptuously. 'I shall certainly report you to her for your insolence on her return.'

'Well, there won't be any return I can tell you! Not while you're about the place and that's a fact,' retorted Mrs Childe, whisking into the pantry and flinging on hat, coat, and gloves with incredible rapidity before she picked up her attaché case. 'I'm glad to assist your mother, but I've no use for such a madam as you about the place!'

'You'd better show me what you're making off with in that bag!' Ill as she felt Flora was yet able to know just how to annoy an enemy, and she was successful beyond her expectations. For Mrs Childe flung open the case to reveal an overall and a pair of shoes as she snapped out:

'That finishes it. You can tell your Ma she needn't expect me about this house again!' and darted out into the rain, slamming the door behind her.

How long she sat on the chest in the empty hall, too miserable to move, Flora had no idea. If she had not been so wretched, and assailed by such fits of shivering, she would have picked up her bag and gone to a hotel, and left Castleburgh next day for ever. (That she would first have to get some money out of her stepfather was the sort of trifle Flora never allowed for in her calculations.) The fact that she had always despised the Laws House and never pretended to look upon it as home was forgotten now. After all, it was the only one she had ever known, and now it was empty, bleak, and desolate, with no welcome for its child in her hour of need. The creaking of the wooden floor in the library, the loud tick of the clock on the stairs, only seemed to accentuate the death-like silence and desertion.

And then another sound struck upon her ears and she started up, her heart hot with anger. Someone was turning the latchkey in the outer lock: her mother had come home and she should know what Flora thought of her welcome! But it was not Rose, and Flora gasped with surprise, as Tom's shaggy head and rain-damped spectacles came peering in round the door.

'Hullo! Hullo! Are you the family ghost or Flora? Well, this is a surprise! You're the last person I expected to find here. What are you doing and why weren't you at the nuptials?' Tom banged down his bag, shook his raincoat, and turned on more lights with a heartiness which made Flora shudder.

'If you're back why isn't Mother back?' was all she deigned to ask.

'Because, my love, she and Aunt Linda suddenly decided to be girls together in London for another day and come on up by the night train. I came today because I'm just posted to my depot, and have to leave to report there at ten tomorrow morning.'

'And do you mean she wouldn't even take the trouble to come back and see you off? Just as she didn't bother to come back to welcome me!'

'I'd say the reason for that was that it's probably your telegram to her on the hall chest, and that it only arrived after she left home. I didn't tell her about my move, if you want to know, or of course she'd have come back and missed her bit of fun. Tact that was, my dear, the famous Thomas tact. As I'll be able to hop down fairly often now, I expect, I didn't see why I should spoil her chance of a binge with Linda. I say, you're looking like something the cat brought home in the rain! Hadn't you better get dry and go to bed?'

'What it comes to,' pursued Flora unheeding, 'is that she put Mickie before you and me as usual.'

'Come, come, my good woman, it was his wedding! Even Mickie doesn't get married every day of the week! If you're on leave why on earth didn't you join the wedding party? It was a grand show, and everyone bore up bravely including the bridal pair, though Heaven knows what they must have been through among the primal hordes of relations! I know I've never been kissed by so many women over sixty in my life! Why on earth didn't you make it?'

'I'm not on leave! Oh, Tom, do you remember the days when I was Big Sister and you were Little Brother?'

'I do. But' – said Tom with firm kindliness – 'if you ask me, I think sob-stuff is out of place after a long journey. Did you come straight up from London today then? We must have been on the same train. But I went round and got a snack at the Medici as I gathered we were clean out of slaves. Have you had nothing to eat?'

'No, I couldn't eat anything. Stop making polite conversation! I only wanted to tell you that I've chucked my unit and have nothing to look forward to in the world!'

'Toughers,' said Tom, suppressing a yawn. 'But you know I always thought they wouldn't exempt you on that job. Which of the Services are you thinking of? No, I don't mean to be heartless, old girl, and I'll go to the pantry and make you what the NAAFIs would call a nice hot cup of tea, but –' Tom returned after negotiations with the kettle. 'I don't think you're in a fit state to pour out the sad story of your life, and it wouldn't be any good with me, for my experience is that it's always finance at the bottom of it all, and I can't help you much out of my heroic pay. Better have it out with Mummie or Father really, you know.'

'Never!' said Flora briefly, her vision of finding a comrade and helper in Tom vanishing as abruptly as it had come.

'I know as a matter of fact that there's only one way for people like me, cursed from birth, and that's just to make an end of it all.'

'Oh no, I think you're wrong there, Flora! I mean, I suppose you might say that all our lot are cursed from birth, if you want to be melodramatic. We don't seem to have any choice for the future beyond being bumped off or surviving in a perfectly foul world, where we have to work eight hours a day and spend the rest of the time larking with the proletariat. That's what makes this such a ruddy war, selfishly speaking, that people like us are really fighting to put an end to the world we knew, and a damn good world it was for us too! Still, it only makes it worse – there! It's boiling! I suppose I must go steady with the tea! – if you keep a whole pack of secret sorrows and grievances too, and you've always been a one for that, you know, Flora. And it's pretty cowardly just to let the whole lot combined lead you to the gas oven, specially with all this fuel shortage. Buck up and again I say unto you buck up, and drink up your cup like a good little girl. Why, we were all as proud as peacocks when you did the heroine stunt in the blitzes, so you can't go loose about the upper lip now, even if the boyfriend has proved a dud or the bank balance is low, and I imagine that's the sort of thing that's eating you. Now go to bed with some aspirins, woman, and I'll come and tuck you up.'

Somewhere as if from very far away the consciousness came to Flora that Tom was trying to cheer her by taking her further into his confidence than any human being before. Just for a moment she clung to him as he sat down beside her with his teacup on the chest in the desolate hall.

'Oh, Tom,' she muttered, 'why should this all have happened to us?'

'Lord knows!' Tom had done his best but he wasn't going to let Flora pull any of the doomed generation stuff over him. 'Anyway, it's no use to make a song and a dance about it. Look at me! Didn't I only today see the only girl I ever loved, except two or three others, led to the altar by my rival and brother? And did I flinch? I did not flinch. I obliged with a solo rendering of "Shall I Wasting in Despair" in the vestry! Heavens! That's the telephone! You go and get into bed and I'll answer it. . . . Yes . . . yes – No, it's not Mrs Fairlaw, it's her son. . . . Oh yes, Mrs Carr-Berwick.'

Over the telephone Tom began to make appalling faces at his sister as a loud, quacking noise from the other end echoed in the hall. 'Well, don't chah see, something must be done!' urged the voice. 'I understand from Linda that the maids would be back tonight, so as Griffen, my woman, you know, seemed to be sickening for influenza, I sent her off to her brother's, and gave up my room at the hotel – I couldn't be left alone at the hotel, don't chah see, because I'd have had no one to wait on me. And now I find my son's house empty; and an impertinent note from the cook that their engagements won't allow the maids to return till to-morrow. I can't possibly stay alone in the house. It's out of the question, with no one to wait on me, and all my jewellery in my bag and all these burglars about. So I thought the best thing I could do would be to ring Rose up and ask for a bed. I've kept my taxi at the door and I'll come round at once.'

'Oh well, Mrs Carr-Berwick!' (Tom put his hand over the

receiver, and indulged in a short outburst of blasphemy – 'and what am I to say, Flora?') 'Oh well, as a matter of fact there's no one to wait on you here. I've just got up from London and though my sister's here I think she's got 'flu of a very infectious kind, and there are no maids or beds made up! . . . Confound and blast, Flora, the old beldam's rung off! I suppose she's hopping straight into the taxi and will be here in a moment. Look here, let's run away or hide!'

'The world's mad,' said Flora shortly. 'Think of that awful antique buzzing round the town in a taxi trying to find someone to take off her false hair and put away her false teeth!'

'What you might call a diehard,' agreed Tom still aghast. 'By the way, I gather there's someone called Mrs Childe who'll come in tomorrow morning and get breakfast. She can wait on the incubus.'

'No, she can't!' said Flora curtly. 'She was here when I arrived and behaved abominably, and when I told her off she gave notice at once.'

'Oh, Flora, you have torn it! Good Heavens! I gathered from Mums that she was her guide, philosopher, and friend! Well, all I can say is that whether you've 'flu or not you must pick the old Carr-Berwick to pieces tonight and put her together again tomorrow, for I won't – Lord, there's the bell already! Hail, blithe cuckoo!'

Flora turned to run up the winding stair, but she was so stiff and so tired that she was not quick enough. The dowager's quick eye lit upon her vanishing form at once, as she advanced into the hall leaning on her stick, leaving Tom to pay off the taxi at the door.

'Here, you! Who is it? Flora Graylle? Why are you up? Your brother said you had 'flu. Why isn't your mother here to look after you? As far as I can see Linda, my daughter-in-law, and she are gallivanting about in London like a couple of school-girls. Most unsuitable, and I'm sure at their age if I had an invalid to look after I was glued to my house, literally glued to my house!'

'Pity she isn't now,' muttered Tom, dumping down a heavy old-fashioned dressing-case. 'I suppose Mrs Carr-Berwick had better have Mickie's room, Flora?'

'Oh, I can't go up any more stairs,' said the old lady decid-edly, opening the nearest door on the first-floor passage. 'This will do very well for me! Your mother's room? Well, she won't want it till tomorrow, and I shall be getting home early I trust. And you, my dear,' she turned upon Flora, 'had better sleep in there, in your father's dressing-room, because then you'll be there if I want anything in the night, don't chah see?'

'Flora's ill!' shouted Tom at the old lady indignantly, 'it's she who'll want waiting on!'

'Of course if she needs anything I'll get it for her,' said the old lady with dignity. 'Now just undo my case, my dear boy, and Flora shall just put out the few things I want. I told Griffen to leave them near the top. What! Are you making yourself my valet? Very kind of you, I'm sure! No, not that Bible but a Testament with a vellum cover – the gift of my dear husband – dear me! I hope it isn't in one of those bags which you left downstairs. I couldn't sleep unless I had it by my bed. Flora, I think you had better lay out those shawls and my nightdress – we can't expect a young gentleman! – yes, the

sponge-bag, and my soap, yes, I shall want all those brushes –
and now my medicine chest and my photographs, and I shall
feel quite at home!'

Well there you are! thought Tom, when at last he had
satisfied the old lady, and looked through the door into the
dressing-room to see if Flora was safely in bed. There was a
picture of the old world, utterly and crassly selfish, expecting
to be waited on hand and foot, cluttered up with a mountain of
fatuous hereditary possessions and faded photos, hanging
itself, an intolerable burden, round the neck of youth. No
wonder a generation like that had fostered revolutions and,
by Jove, he'd like to be about in a revolution with a lamp-post
handy to string the old pest on! Eighty-five, and alive and
kicking in a world of war and rapine and destruction, raising
Cain because she couldn't find me dear husband's Bible!
Well, the times might be bad, but he'd rather belong to them
than to a period which bred an old tumour like that. And
what on earth was the old fool saying now, as she stalked into
the dressing-room, telling Flora to undo the catch of her
lorgnette?

'You're Flora, ain't you? The gal that didn't get on with
Rose? Well, I expect there were two sides to that question!
Both she and my daughter-in-law always seemed to me to be
weak, incompetent, selfish young women. Men's women, as
we used to say, who always put the men of their family first.
Not only the family, even, for your Cousin Mary was telling
me Rose had got some man hanging about this house now,
quite absurd at her age.' (The poor old fool's a bit gaga,
thought Tom; she's forgotten it's your mother she's talking

about or she'd be too Victorian to do it!) 'And this dashing off to London because Mickie wants it, if you please, so that I can't get to my own grand-daughter's wedding. And then leaving me without a home to come back to, or a soul to wait on me, at my age. Well, of course she's your mother, now I come to think of it!' – the old lady's voice began to die away sleepily – 'so perhaps I shouldn't – Still, I think we must see a great deal of each other when you're better, my dear Flora! I knew how to manage *my* daughters. I kept them in order and married off all six of them, and no nonsense about it.'

'Rather you than I,' muttered Tom as he said good night to his sister from the door of her room.

'I don't know! I think she talks sense!' said Flora, her eyes bright with fever. 'She doesn't seem to be as blind as most people about Mother! What do you suppose she means about a man about the house, Tom?'

'The plumber I should think, you donkey! Shout if you want anything, or if she begins to hunt for "me dear husband's back stud" which she always keeps on her *bidet*! Night night, and wake up with some sense, my poor boob!'

CHAPTER TEN
THE DARK VALLEY

Nous avons perdu la route et la trace des hommes
Parmi les méandres du ténébreux vallon
Vers la Ville inconnue.

SF Merrill

It is never, even in the best of times, an exhilarating process to arrive home after a night journey. Even in the old days of first-class sleepers, when the house was warm and welcoming, and maids ran out to greet her, Rose had found the day which followed long and flat and tiring. There had always been so many trifles to attend to, so much shopping to do, notes to answer, so many people to see and arrears to make up. But on this bitter March morning, after four days packed with emotion, excitement, and the demoralising relapse into the old comforts of life in her hotel, Rose felt like an escaped slave returning to her master as she stood outside the house once more. For the house with all its needs and duties was indeed her tyrant, with dear Mrs Childe as a most efficient overseer, even if she hadn't a whip like Uncle Tom's Lalage, and Stuart who stood there fumbling with his latchkey was like another gaoler with his chains, for it was after all Stuart's food and Stuart's comfort which added so appallingly to the burden of the house!

'If only Mrs Childe has come early,' she sighed to herself, and felt her heart leap with relief as she heard the chink of cups in the pantry on the other side of the hall. And then as she saw Tom's great tousled head, his spectacles glinting in the sunlight, and his old dressing-gown waving in the draught, it leapt with joy, and she felt that the old house had prepared some welcome for her after all.

'Tom! How lovely! Why didn't you tell me you were coming up? Last night was it? Oh, you should have let us know! To think I've missed a night with you safely under our roof!'

'But you've missed a lot more, let me tell you!' said Tom when he had hugged Rose, banged his father's back, and told them both of the change in his immediate future. 'Don't think all the news I have for you is so glorious! Let me break it to you while I get down to this omelette. I've only broken the eggs so far!'

'Six! Oh Tom! All the dairy left at once. Never mind. We'll eat your good news in them, won't we, Stuart?'

'I'll have a bath first I think!' Stuart was also feeling the gates of the prison house closing on him, as he anticipated his return to under-staffed office. 'Just leave my food to keep hot –'

'Well, there'll be squalls ahead for you, Daddy! I must break it that we've a house-party gathered under your roof. You'll find Flora in your room, unless she's changed places with our other guest. In that case it'll be old Grannie Carr-Berwick you'll discover in your bed, like little Goldilocks. Only I expect her locks are by the side of it!'

There was no doubt about the nightmare of her return now, thought Rose, when Tom had told his story. But her holiday had done her enough good for her at least to break into helpless, irrepressible laughter at the recital. Stuart, in view of the appropriation of his room, was indeed unable to share it. He was with difficulty restrained from going off to telephone for Ian Carr-Berwick to remove his unwanted property at once, but Rose protested.

'Oh no, no, let's leave her and Flora to sleep till Tom's gone! I'll have to get trays and carry them up if we wake the two of them, and we must enjoy every minute of Tom!'

It was odd, thought Tom, with the reflective philosophy which his upbringing had led him to apply to home affairs, that Flora couldn't see how family affection was a matter of quality, not quantity. His mother had always poured out on Mickie the love you give to a bright, brittle, beautiful possession which has needed all your care and devotion. To Tom she had always given the grateful devotion of a weaker nature for a stronger, as she would say laughing. She had begun to rely on him when he was a sturdy little boy in her difficult dealings with the other two, and he never questioned her devotion. She might have had the same for Flora, if only the poor fool hadn't so battered and brushed love aside that Rose's dealings with her daughter were always spoilt by a nervousness and anxiety which brought out, of course, the bully in Flora. Today, as often in the past, Tom wondered whether he should not give his mother a straight talk on standing up to Flora, and showing her where she got off. He wondered too whether he should not warn her that that old beldam last night had been trying to make mischief, but he decided against it. Half the trouble in the world was due to meddling, and even Flora couldn't be such a fool as to believe that his poor, tired, pretty mother was indulging in an illicit love affair as well as doing all the housework! He had to break to Rose the catastrophe about Mrs Childe, and he was quite sure that his mother was more upset about that than she or any woman could be about the desertion of any lover.

'Oh no, she won't come back!' She repudiated Tom's re-assurances hopelessly. 'Darling, half the women in Castleburgh have probably tried to snap her up already. Never mind, I can be a slut now, and she wouldn't let me. I'd always meant to be a cheerful slut at this job, and I haven't even been cheerful yet!'

But it was not very easy to feel cheerful when Tom had gone off, taking the laughter of the house with him, and Stuart, disgustedly making use of the top bathroom, and breaking into his dressing-room for the suit and shoes without which, for reasons inexplicable to a wife, he could not go to the office, had woken up the incongruous house-party on the first floor. Linda and Griffen were soon to arrive, to remove the obstruction on the line as Tom said, but meanwhile Rose had to prepare and carry upstairs two trays of breakfast for as difficult a couple of guests as the old house had ever entertained.

Flora's reception was very much what she anticipated. To Rose's loving greetings and attempted embrace, to the anxious inquiries and the tea-tray laid beside her, she gave no acknowledgement but to turn her face to the wall, saying that she had been awake for hours, listening to her mother and Tom laughing downstairs.

'We thought you were asleep!' pleaded Rose. 'And it's so nice to see dear Tom as cheerful as ever. I'm going to ask Dr Maybury to see you, Flora dear. Tom thinks you are quite done in.'

'I won't see the doctor,' was Flora's only reply, and that too was just what Rose expected. But what she had not been prepared for was the sudden outbreak from Mrs Carr-Berwick next door, its vehemence only a little impeded by the lack of her dental plate.

'No wonder the poor girl's ill! Arriving here in such a state and no one to care for her, if I hadn't happened to be on the spot. It's time you and Linda began to take your duties seriously, Rose. In my days people didn't run off after one child and neglect the others. When mine were ill I was glued, literally glued to the house!'

Even the tray which Rose produced was not a real peace-offering, for chocolate was the only drink the old lady could take for breakfast; she did not care for omelet unless it was freshly made. If Rose, like Linda, was unable to get her orange or grape-fruit for breakfast she would just make do with an egg, and perhaps a wing of chicken, for it was not as if she had any appetite in the morning.

Rose was always glad to see Linda, but never, she owned, more rejoiced than when her friend appeared to dress and remove old Mrs Carr-Berwick. For Rose herself, Grannie had only the barest word of thanks, but to Flora, she outdid herself in sympathy and offers of help. And Flora, delighted evidently to find any ally against her mother, responded warmly. It was difficult to believe that even Flora could be prejudiced enough to share Grannie's absurd attitude, but the two certainly parted the best of friends.

When Rose looked back upon the days which followed it seemed to her that she had been blind not to understand the drift of Flora's misery. She should have realised that the girl was suffering from a mental rather than a physical shock. She should have sought her confidence, impossible as such a task always seemed, instead of contenting herself with dainty cooking, aspirins, glasses of hot milk, and hardly-won oranges, and trays of food which Rose had to cook, prepare and carry upstairs herself. It was true that Flora allowed no more intercourse, and fiercely refused medical advice, but Rose should never have satisfied herself, when all symptoms of fever or chill had abated (and indeed sulking in a warm room is a quick cure for influenza), that Flora only continued to lie there because she was angry with her parents. A mother should have realised that even such an absurd ally as old Grannie was just the determining weight in the scales by which her daughter assessed Rose's guilt. She should have guessed that Flora's overbearingness found in the old lady's autocratic injustice just the stimulus she desired in her weak, distraught condition. She should have – but at this point Rose was liable to stop herself, and admit with common sense that she herself had no time to improve on her methods, however much wiser she might have been. For the house, with which she had seemed to be coming to terms before she left home for the wedding, had the upper hand of her now beyond question. Mrs Childe's defection would have been a blow in any case; her disappointment in receiving no answer to the olive branch which she sent off by the first post was of crushing weight, yet she felt that by now she had learnt so much, and accustomed herself to so much of her routine, that she could have managed all right for Stuart and herself. But the care and cooking for an invalid made an impossible difference. After two days Flora's appetite apparently returned, as her plates were always scraped clean, though without any acknowledgement. The burden of preparing lunch as well as an evening meal threw Rose's day out of gear, and meant, it seemed to her, that washing up never ceased. She was willing to sacrifice her rest time in the afternoon, or any other scrap of leisure to her daughter, if Flora would consent to accept them, but any attempt at conversation was snubbed unmercifully. But surely, thought Rose pitifully, if she had really loved her daughter as she loved Mickie she would have found a way! At least she would have managed to make Stuart find his way to Flora's confidence. Sometimes in the past she had almost wilfully emphasised her difficulties with the girl so as to rouse in her husband a healthy spirit of competition in showing his superior tact. But Stuart had no tact in the weariness of his home-coming, his annoyance to find his dressing-room occupied (and for Rose's sake the girl must obviously remain on the first floor), and his dislike of seeing the wife, who had blossomed again into gaiety at the wedding, turned once more into a worse drudge than ever. After the most perfunctory sympathy he informed Flora that if she wasn't better in a day or two he would get the doctor, and see that she was packed off to a nursing home before her mother's back was broken. Surely, surely, Rose thought, she should have recognised that her daughter, lying there sullenly in her room, her dark hair unbrushed, her eyes staring out from her hollowed face, was shut up in that desolate prison of the soul, herself the gaoler, refusing to believe that anyone cared enough for her to visit or aid her, when she herself had locked the door upon them.

It was only as her chill passed off that Flora sounded the depth of misery. As long as she was feverish she could toy with the idea that pneumonia might end her troubles, and go back and back again over the miseries of her past life and the loneliness of her lot. But as her sleepy broodings passed into the depression which follows influenza, the future alone rose up to stare her in the face. Like so many self-centred people she always adopted the worst view of every situation with strange credulity. It did not occur to her that Tommy Hartnell was notoriously inaccurate, and that Miranda's desire to pack her off in a hurry might be a pretext to get rid of a tiresome colleague rather than a fear for her safety. Sometimes she lay shivering when the bell rang, convinced that Military Intelligence were on her track: sometimes she thought of running away, and disappearing from a home where she could find no sympathy, a mother in whom she could not confide, a stepfather who would most certainly turn her out if he knew the truth. But, as Tom said truly, the state of her finances forbade that course till next quarter-day, and by that time she

would certainly be on the register again and called up. And after her previous career, and the glory of her exploits, how could she endure to enter the ranks as a private or rating, or cast in her lot with munition girls?

There was no hope, she told herself, or, rather, there was only one hope. Once, in the strange reckless glory of those days in Eastminster she had insisted on crawling along a half-blocked passage to the rescue of a groaning sufferer. She would never forget how the space grew smaller and smaller, and the walls and floors seemed to be imprisoning her, so that she could move neither forwards nor backwards, and then suddenly she saw an opening and a light, and there, clearing the way for her, was Percy Hosmer with a pick, speaking cool, pleasant words of encouragement, the light gleaming on his spectacles. Now, in this ghastly hole in which she found herself again, she might surely look to him for help. He knew her at her best; he was infinitely tolerant and sagacious; his views on sex were bounded by no foolish conventions. How much she would disclose or keep secret she did not attempt to determine exactly; how much she would expect of him as a saviour she did not quite define. She only knew that he was the one person in the world who still cared for her, for with Flora cared and admired were synonymous terms, and that she could only lighten her load of misery by talking to him again. So therefore she got up one day, when Rose was out, and telephoned to his office, leaving an urgent message for him as he was absent. She did not overlook the disadvantage that he was already acquainted with her mother: that fact still depressed her as it had in the train. But she could surely trust Percy to assess a weak character like Rose at her proper value.

Thus it was that she lay next afternoon with her door open after tea, intent on his bell and his voice in the hall. She must make sure that her inconsiderate mother did not turn away the only visitor she wanted to see! And so, by an unkind turn of fortune's wheel she not only heard the bell and the rustle of Rose's dress in the hall. She heard also with disastrous clearness Rose's sudden exclamation of pleasure and greeting.

'Oh, it's you! I am so glad to see you. I have been longing to have you here again and tell you all my news!'

'I know some of it,' said Major Hosmer in a kind warm voice which Flora had somehow imagined was kept for herself alone. 'I know you've got Flora here. She 'phoned and asked me to come, you see.'

'Did she? Oh, I am so pleased, for she's so lonely and unapproachable, and very unhappy, I feel sure.'

'But in any case,' pursued the Major, as his hat and belt and gas-mask clattered on the oak chest, 'I'd have been round to see you if I hadn't been very busy with a course for some of my youngsters. Of course I want to hear all your news.'

'About Mickie's wedding, you mean? Indeed I've looked forward to telling you. Only I shall be the most dreadful bore, for I've hardly seen Linda – she's been nursing her mother-in-law through 'flu – and all my friends seem ill, or as busy as I am with poor Flora. So you must stop me if you can't bear it!'

Her mother and the Major were in the library now, and Flora, tossing her head back defiantly, got up and crept, in dressing-gown and slippers, halfway down the stairs. She was too much surprised and disgusted by the apparent intimacy of their friendship to object to a trifle like eavesdropping. Of course she recognised how foolishly impetuous and friendly her mother was, and doubtless the kind Major felt bound to humour an old lady, but what right had her mother to presume on Flora's friendship for her American friend by inflicting her silly enthusiasms on him? And it was Mickie, of course, whom she had to discuss first with him; as usual Mickie was first.

'It was the loveliest time,' Rose was saying in her low eager voice. 'I feared it would be rather heartbreaking, and I had made up my mind just to live through it, but Mickie and Iona were so brave and gay and happy that you couldn't feel like that. Linda and I took Iona to our hotel of course – our husbands preferred their clubs naturally – and Mickie came and established himself with us. He said he wasn't going to let any silly old conventions keep him away from Iona. They even turned us out next morning to buy new hats for the wedding – "the only way to make sure you'll neither of you dare to cry!" – while they went for a walk in the Park, and dear little Iona came in late and just hurried into her soft cream satin and lace, as if she were a little girl bustling to a party. She looked so lovely, Major, rather like a happy little Leonardo angel who was trying to be serious – I only felt like crying once when she was making her vows, in her pretty childish voice, and I happened to notice how young and plump and purplish her arms looked – I don't know why that seemed so touching. And once again when the sun caught Mickie's gold curls (which Tom will say he Marcel waves), just like a Charlotte M Yonge novel, only I don't suppose heroes used hair lotion! Oh dear, I'm afraid I'm drivelling –'

('You are indeed,' thought Flora grimly.)

'No indeed,' said the Major kindly. 'You've drawn me a wonderful picture of those two young things in the spring of their youth and love. But I do feel for you very deeply, Mrs Fairlaw, brave as you are, for I can't help guessing at the shadows in your heart.'

'I got a little comfort even for those – I don't know why, but I began remembering a lovely house I used to stay in, with a huge bay window looking over the sea. When I first got there I could hardly sleep for wanting to watch the sun rise, or the moon over the waves. In the middle of the visit I'd enjoy them, but notice them less, and then, when I knew I'd soon have to go away, I felt all the old joy in snatching their beauty every minute. And so I told myself that's what life is like for them, for our children now. They never miss the moon or the sunrise because they may not see so many of them! Oh, I didn't mean to be so foolish!'

('I suppose she's crying now, poor fool,' thought Flora. 'If she knew how Percy hates tears!')

'Just speak out all that's in your mind if it relieves you,' said the Major in his gentlest voice. ('Hopes to get her as a patient, I suppose,' thought Flora indignantly. 'He was bracing enough with me when I broke down over my real sorrows!')

'Oh you are kind! I wonder,' said Rose, feeling indeed considerably surprised at herself, 'why I can tell you things which I shouldn't dream of telling anyone – even Mickie. I did have another little message of comfort, though it seems too trivial to tell you of. Just above me was a very beautiful little window – most of them were hideous – in memory of some boy who died in the last war I think. There was a Christ, young and erect, in the Easter garden, and there was a young, golden-haired St Michael in armour, crushing down the dragon. And it just occurred to me suddenly how wrong we are to think of the saints and heroes in the Bible as old – I do believe it's all the fault of the awful German holy pictures in children's books, and fat German singers in *Parsifal*. Thirty is young when you think of it – it was a young man who ended his life on the Cross – the old people in the story don't come very well out of it, the high priests with white beards and poor St Peter, and one always thinks of Pontius Pilate as middle-aged. But St John was young, I'm sure, and Mary Magdalene, and most of the apostles. We make too much of age, and wisdom, and experience, and all the rest, and so we think that long life is so important. But it's not. It's what you get out of life and make out of life, however short it is, that's the only thing that matters. Oh dear, how can I bore you with my silly thoughts?'

'But you don't. Believe me, I appreciate very much this glimpse into the mystical side of your nature, Mrs Fairlaw.'

'And that's why I'm so terribly grieved about my poor Flora,' said Rose, frowning a little because she always felt foolish if her obvious day-dreams received such a label. 'In a way she's never been young. She's never let herself go or enjoyed life – except perhaps for the time she faced danger so bravely. If only you can find out what is at the root of her misery! If only you could help her to get out of the dreadful prison she's shut herself up into. Do you remember the very first time we met how I told you that I was going to be house-bound, and you laughed at the expression? Well, it's true of poor Flora. She's shut away into herself, and she doesn't even undo the black-out as I do, and try to air and clean her house from attic to basement.'

'A very interesting allegory, Mrs Fairlaw, very interesting.'

'Oh, I know allegories and analogies don't work because of course it's ABC to clean out a house compared with trying to clear up your mind or your heart – and soul too, perhaps. Flora's job is far harder than mine, but she won't be happy till it's done!'

'Nor will you,' said the Major, 'and believe me, that's come to matter to me quite a considerable amount. It's been a great privilege to me, to get to know a mind of as fine a texture as yours. It's struck me very much throughout our acquaintance how you've always been ready to take all the blame in discussing your estrangement with your daughter, and how you've always suppressed any little evidence which might show her at a disadvantage – I know enough of her view of the past to put two and two together, you see. She won't begin to escape from this obsession of her own loneliness and misery – the prison house of which you speak so aptly – until she comes to recognise how cruelly she has misjudged and wronged you.'

'Don't trouble! You won't have the chance!' The Major and Rose looked up from their seats, aghast, to see Flora standing at the door, her black velvet dressing-gown swinging back from her yellow pyjamas, her dark hair drawn back tightly from her sallow face. 'It hadn't occurred to me, when I asked my friend to come to see me, that he would spend his time pulling me to pieces behind my back with my harshest and severest critic, that's to say, with my mother. Though I expect you'd be very glad to make a new woman of me, for her sake as you said, not for mine but hers I notice, it's not a job that can be undertaken by a traitor.'

'Flora, stop!' The Major rose with his arms right up in the air by now. 'You're talking like a child. You know the very great admiration and respect I have for you, but you also know perfectly well that as a psychiatrist I have to view your character from the angle of your friends and relations. I told you that long ago, and since I had the privilege of knowing your mother I have gained real help in understanding your case. Why I failed with you before was just simply due to the want of that unexplored angle. Now I am coming to sit with you to try to straighten out these unhappy affairs you have in your mind. And I have also a message to give you from your friend, Miss Miranda Temple.'

'What message have you that she couldn't write to me?' demanded Flora, temporarily arrested in her wrath.

'She wrote to me because she said she knew you would destroy any letter from her unopened, and I should guess,' added the Major candidly, 'that she was just about right there!'

'I don't want her message!' Flora's heart, which had missed a beat, pounded at her side till it hurt. What message could there be but some cryptic hint that the worst had happened, and that all was over with Guy – or, it might be a warning that her name was to be dragged into his affairs?

'Miranda's failed me, just as you, Mother, always have, and you, Major Hosmer, have failed me now. I wanted to ask for your advice and sympathy and help. I never dreamt that my mother had managed to win you over to her side behind my back, as she has everyone else. I'll go away now and leave you to her beautiful, mystical imaginations. I don't ever want to see you again!'

Rose and the Major sat aghast and speechless as they heard the clatter of Flora's sandals up the stair, and the sound of a banging door and a key turned in the lock.

'Oh go up to her, go up to her quickly! Make her see you and tell her how foolish, how impossibly foolish she is,' gasped Rose.

'I'll go and see, but it would be fatal to show weakness to her or give her the pleasure of snubbing me,' said the Major, his kind round face unnaturally grim. 'I'll see if you like, but – Flora!' his voice came from the top landing a minute later, 'are you going to let me in, and talk this out reasonably or not? You won't? Very well, then, I must wait till you come to your senses and send for me again. You won't ask in vain, as you know!'

'If we only knew what was wrong,' he mused, when he rejoined Rose, who stood pale and trembling, in the library. 'This message for example! – I'll hand it on to you: "We were all wrong about Guy. He's merely got a transfer, and now he's somewhere in the South with his wife and child" – I'm afraid it suggests some unfortunate love affair, but evidently Miss Temple felt the news would bring Flora some relief.'

'I'll write it down and put it on her supper tray,' said Rose more hopefully. 'But – but you see how much I am to blame. It was true that I kept you from her with my chat about Mickie. Oh, she has some justice on her side! And it's terrible for a proud person to know she is being discussed behind her back! I should have been more careful –'

'She should have been too proud to listen at keyholes!' The Major still looked unrelenting, but he was evidently preoccupied. 'I must confess I don't like the look of the case at all – a girl in that mental turmoil shouldn't be left alone. Why not send for your doctor?'

'She won't hear of it and I don't suppose she'd see him! Anyway our own doctor has gone and I've a dreadful feeling that his substitute would just want to take her tonsils out! He always does!'

'Well, when her father comes in I advise you to speak to him strongly, very strongly, Mrs Fairlaw, and make him insist on her unlocking her door and speaking to him –'

'But he isn't coming in tonight. He's fire-watching at his office.'

The Major shook his head and stood for a whole minute lost in thought, while Rose puzzled herself as to the peculiar urgency of his manner. Flora was shut up in her misery and refusing comfort, but so she had been for days.

'Has she any sleeping-draught?' The question was almost shot at her head.

'Only one dose left, I'm afraid, but I'll try to make her take it, if only she'll let me in! I was to have got her some today and some more aspirin, for we've hardly any left. Indeed I might go to the chemist now –'

'I'll call on my way,' said the Major authoritatively. 'You shouldn't leave her alone in the house. And – and – look here! About this fire-fighting –' his face cleared oddly. 'Do you know what to do when you're left alone? I've been giving a lecture on it at your Miss Macfie's hostel, and was horrified to find the general ignorance. Turn off the gas and electricity at the main if you hear guns, or safer still of course when the sirens go! Now, do you know where your meters are?'

'No, because Stuart does all that!'

'Well, I'll show you. It's best to be prepared. And it's a good thing to know anyhow, in case of a bad fuse or gas escape. Always go straight for the main, you see. It'll be down these stairs –' without waiting for her consent he plunged into the darkness of the basement.

'I wish I could stay with you!' The Major still spoke with his unusual curtness when, his voyage of instruction over, he collected his goods in the hall.

'Oh so do I! I'd love to give you dinner again, or let you give it to me, but of course poor Flora would guess and be angrier than ever!'

'Just so, otherwise nothing would induce me to go.' Still the Major hesitated as if he wished to make some pronouncement, and then again changed his mind. 'Well, well, this is the prescription and she's no spare bottle? I don't suppose he'll send it down tonight, but you've got just one dose for her? Nothing else of the sort I suppose about the house?'

'No, indeed! We're very bad customers at our chemist's! Stuart doesn't believe in any drugs, and Mickie used to say I had far too many toilet bottles and far too few medicine bottles for a woman of my age!'

'I see! I see! Well, I'll look up your husband tomorrow, and we must arrange to have Flora's case taken in hand properly. She can't go on like this, for her sake or yours. Keep an eye on her tonight if you can, and get her off to sleep as early as possible after her supper.'

Rose still puzzled over the Major's manner when he had gone off, with such halting steps that she half-expected him to turn back after all. But when she had served a specially tempting supper for Flora and carried it upstairs, with his message carefully pinned to the napkin, she found she was to have no chance of carrying out his orders.

'I don't want any supper!' was Flora's only response to her knock at the locked door.

'Oh yes, Flora dear! I'll leave it, and I expect you'll feel inclined for it later on!'

'No, I shan't want any supper. Take it away,' repeated Flora dully.

'There's the message from your friend on the tray, Flora.'

'That can make no difference to me!'

'Well, my dear, let me come in and make your bed, and get you a hot-water bottle, and give you your sleeping-draught.'

'No! I don't want anything! I shall sleep right enough!'

For a moment Flora's voice and words filled Rose with an odd, uneasy foreboding, but almost at once the telephone rang, and Linda's joyful voice told her of a wonderful letter from Iona. 'Not only wonderful because all her pronouns were right – Mickie must be teaching her – but she says he's got 'flu and won't be allowed on duty again for a week at the very least. Now we can both go to sleep tonight, darling –'

'I always do since I took to running about so much, though I do dream a bit. But it's marvellous. Do read the letter, dearest!' . . . 'And how's Grannie?' she asked perfunctorily when she and Linda had smiled over Iona's report that Mickie was wonderful, and Bindleton was wonderful, and the people in the hotel angels about Mimi, and that there was a chance that Mickie might go on a course soon. . . . What did old ladies of eight-five matter in comparison with that!

'Much better in spite of my nursing, as she says so prettily. She's got Griffen back now, thank Heaven, though I don't suppose Griffen does – thank Heaven I mean! She's talking about going away for a change now, because she feels it her duty to her country to be as well as possible. And do you know, she's making the extraordinary suggestion that Flora should go with her! She seems to have hit it off with her in some extraordinary way. How *is* Flora? Wouldn't it be heavenly if they did go off together!'

'Oh dear, Linda! I've such a lot to tell you about my poor, poor Flora, but I think I won't on the telephone. I am dreadfully worried about her, and what's more I can see Major Hosmer is also. She's angry with him and with me, and it was my fault too. And she won't touch her supper, and I took so much trouble over it!'

'Just you eat it up yourself at once,' said Linda heartlessly. 'I'm sure you need it lots more.'

Rose took Linda's advice, and though she felt better afterwards, and was overjoyed to think of Mickie safely laid aside for a little, she could not rid herself of a sense of guilt and a persistent anxiety about her daughter. Twice she knocked gently on that closed door in vain. There was a connecting door between Stuart's dressing-room, where Flora lay, and her own bedroom, but she dared not try it. It was of no use to annoy the girl more, and at least if she went to bed Flora would know she was at hand if she needed her mother. She would surely call to her, and oh, if only that call would come, thought Rose disconsolately as she lay in bed, reading *The Daughters of Queen Victoria*. It was not a very suitable book, for what indeed would that indomitable little queen and autocrat have thought of a mother and daughter who lay apart, separated in hard fact and in sad allegory by a locked door? That her child, her own daughter, should lie there, torn by jealousy and suffering, however imaginary were her griefs, just a few feet away, barring herself from all the love and consolation which Rose longed to bring, was impossible, intolerable. 'I must open the door,' was Rose's last waking thought.

It was her first waking thought also, and must not the subconscious mind of which Major Hosmer liked so well to talk, have been working busily in her sleep? For treading on its heels, even before she had grasped what was this odd stuffy smell in her room, was the other thought: 'You must turn it off at the main!' She was out of bed, and halfway down the basement stairs, before she had let herself acknowledge what was happening. And even then she forced herself to turn the tap carefully, and raced upstairs, telling herself that, as the gas had been escaping through her key-hole it could not be too late, and that the key of the outer door of her bedroom would, she was almost sure, though it hadn't occurred to her before, fit the lock of the dressing-room as well. With hands so shaking and cold that they hardly seemed to belong to her she put in the key and turned the lock, and it was only as the gust of foul air greeted her that she let the horror of the truth come alive to her. Flora had said she would sleep all right because she had lain there determining never to wake again. She must get help at once – Stuart, the doctor, the Major, she told herself, with the stunned determination to be practical, when a voice as if from far away, and certainly unconscious of its surroundings, muttered: 'Don't strike a match!'

That was the true Flora! Even in her numbed horror the thought came to Rose with a stab of pride. It was the Flora who had risked her life again and again in her work, and was instinctively bent on saving others now. And she was alive still! Conscious still! Rose flung open the window, fumbling with the shutters feverishly, and flung open both doors of the room while her breath seemed to come in ever shorter and shorter gasps. Could she get to the telephone, and whom could she summon? Must the doctor know? Didn't they prosecute would-be suicides? Must Stuart know? When his horror and shame would be so intense? Would even the Major's interest in Flora survive this? All these thoughts flashed oddly through Rose's mind, as, half-suffocated, and wholly worn out by her long days and nights of toil, she fell on the floor in merciful unconsciousness.

CHAPTER ELEVEN
IN GENTLENESS OF HEART

Move along these shades
In gentleness of heart; with gentle hand
Touch – for there is a spirit in the woods.
Wordsworth

'I was afraid I'd killed you. Are you all right?' Those words in Flora's harsh whisper welcomed Rose back to consciousness. Rose's face and neck were wet, and there was a confused scent of eau-de-Cologne and brandy, mingling with the persistent sourness of the gas. Otherwise, as she stared at Stuart's dressing-room in the dawn, at the vast solid gentleman's wardrobe, the rows of boots and shoes, and all the familiar paraphernalia of the dressing-table which, by his conservative traditions, blocked up the window, how could she have believed in the nightmare of the last hour?

'You're ill! You shouldn't be here!' she whispered, trying to get out of bed.

'Oh, keep still,' said Flora in her old gruff voice. 'Even if you drove me to it I didn't mean to hurt you!'

Did gas quicken your consciousness? Or else why should Mickie's remark, long ago, that Flora would be an excellent nurse if Rose were ill, and the Major's insistence on Flora's demand for someone dependent on her, flash across Rose's brain? With a diplomacy for which she had never given herself credit, Rose stifled her instinct to make the least of her discomfort and murmured:

'I – I feel so odd, Flora!' as she closed her eyes. 'I – I'm so cold!'

'I'll put a bottle in your bed – at least the house has hot water now, and I'll put you back at once – in the blankets I think!' Flora was practical and helpful at once.

'It's – it's the windows and doors being open, I suppose,' said Rose, her teeth chattering in good earnest, as she regained her four-poster. 'I suppose, Flora, you – you couldn't bear to come in beside me?'

'Oh yes!' Luckily Flora did not recognise that it was for Flora's sake that her mother made the suggestion. 'We must let out the smell I suppose! Unless I go back and finish it off. It would be better for everyone. Why did you stop me?'

'Why did you risk your life to save people in the blitz, Flora?'

'That was different – I imagine they wanted to live, and anyhow some were children. I haven't got anything left to live for!'

'Have I hurt you as much as that?' whispered Rose, drawing a little nearer to the cold figure, lying flat on its back staring at the rose and parrot chintz, grey and formless in the cold gloom.

'Oh, it's not you altogether!' For a moment Rose feared that Flora would withdraw herself once more, and then suddenly the girl turned her face away and broke into harsh, choking sobs, haunted still by the stale smell of gas.

'Flora! Flora! My little Flora!' Rose dared venture no further.

'Oh well I suppose you want me to tell you all about it,' moaned the girl, and Rose summoned all her tact and wisdom to her aid desperately.

'No,' she replied, 'no! I don't think so. You would hate me tomorrow if you told me now. You'd think I'd forced your confidence. I'd rather, much rather that you saw Major Hosmer alone and told him everything, everything, and got his advice. He's kind and understanding and he's – he's your generation and I'm not. And if you decide that Stuart and I had better not know he'll keep your secret.'

Rose finished her plea doggedly, in spite of the stiffening of the figure by her side, and waited. She hardly knew how she was going to press her point, but the bitterness of Flora's rejoinder stung her to outspokenness.

'To the man you've stolen from me, Mother?' asked her daughter, with a wild note of hatred in her voice.

'Listen, Flora!' Rose raised herself on the pillows and gathered all her forces. 'I might cry over you, or I might laugh at you, but I'll only ask you to listen and to use your reason. You've read psychology and you know something of life. Did you ever really know any authentic case of a middle-aged man falling in love, for I imagine that's what you imply, with an elderly woman? Young men have passions sometimes for older women, I grant you, though I must say I've only met such cases in M Blum's *Mariage*, or novels by middle-aged women, where you'd admit, probably, there was a good deal of wish-fulfilment or whatever the right word is. But to talk of a man of forty or so falling in love with a woman of fifty is just absurd, and you know it!'

'Other people said so!' muttered Flora. 'Tom said they were teasing you about your boyfriend at the wedding. Grannie Carr-Berwick said Cousin Mary had some story that he was always hanging about the house.'

'So he has been, and do you know why? First to tell me how much he admired you, and then to teach me how to cook,' replied Rose with spirit. 'I wonder Mary didn't report that she saw him take my hand in his, because he certainly did when he was teaching me how to make *Sauce Meunière*! Flora, look round the room' – for now the dawn was lighting up the cream panels – 'look at the photo of your father, look at the sketches of you all when you were little. Look at my little old bureau which my mother gave me forty-five years ago at Seriton and holds all your father's letters to me, written in the last war when Major Hosmer was a schoolboy! Think of how quietly and happily I've passed from youth to middle age, and middle age to old age, yes, I am old now, as the days passed in this dear old house –'

'Not happily!' interposed Flora. 'You know you never loved Stuart passionately. It's women like you who have a late awakening.'

'Oh, Flora!' Rose had to restrain her hysterical laughter. For how on the top of that ghastly reality behind her, the fact that her own daughter an hour ago firmly intended to end her life, were you to cope with a remark so fatuous and trite as that? But she must not laugh, and she must not ask Flora, as Mickie would, what smutty novel she had got hold of now. 'Flora, supposing that were all true, and I were the sort of old woman who trails young men after her, is Major Hosmer that sort of man? He's not even young, he's the most level-headed person I've met, though your father finds his technical terms a little trying. He's a sane, healthy, normal man from a sane new country. He grew up, as I expect he told you, with a hero-ine complex, and that was what made him so overwhelmed with admiration for you in the blitz.'

'That was before he met you,' said Flora, her face still averted.

'Oh well, I'll be candid and admit that he thinks you misjudged us. But he doesn't want to prove you wrong, he only wants to put you right. He's a passion for order and beauty and efficiency. He sees me as he sees this dear, shabby, little old house which I manage so very badly, and just wants to tidy things up. He sees you, probably, as some majes-tic, soaring modern building, where foundations perhaps need shoring up, or with pillars that would be better for an iron girder. Which job do you suppose such a man would prefer? Flora, you must talk to him, you must tell him everything, at once.'

'It's odd, you know,' said Flora turning to her mother with an abrupt change of subject. 'I should have thought you'd have screamed and cried, and asked me why I'd done this, and rung up Father and doctors and the police –'

'But I didn't have to, because you spoke as I came in, and no one must know, no one. Though I hope you'll tell Major Hosmer because I can see now he feared it. He cared for you enough to foresee it while I was blind! And what's the use of telling you what I feel about it, or asking you what I should have felt if – if I had been too late? I'm not brave enough to face it yet myself.'

Was it want of courage, Rose wondered, when Flora suddenly and mercifully fell off to sleep? Or was the real truth perhaps that for the last two and a half years, she, like everyone else in the country, had grown so stunned by the repeated, merciless blows of fate that another hit, however personal and surely aimed, could hardly rouse you? Or was it that perpetual work and perpetual preoccupation were reducing, not raising, her to the level of working women who accepted life with such ready tears, followed by equally stoical resignation. 'Yes, our Flora, she was the one who tried to do away with herself, but she's doing fine now in service at Bathgate.' That was how her first cook would have put it. And had her long patient care of her daughter done something, perhaps, to bring Flora a few steps back to her again? She must not, she knew, presume on Flora's concessions to her tonight: she must walk warily indeed in the morning, but at least she would make her point of reconciling Flora, absurd as it sounded, to the Major again.

To Flora lying upstairs all next morning it seemed incredible that no sign or reference to last night's scenes should be made by her mother. Rose, smiling lovingly, brought in a breakfast tray at ten o'clock, and suggested that Flora should move into her bedroom, which was already swept and dusted, as it would be more comfortable for the Major to have the nice arm-chair, and he would be with her early in the afternoon. As Flora had been wavering, as she reviewed her failure last night, through Rose's interference, between a harsh determination to rebuff every overture of her mother's, and an alternate longing to pour out the story of her troubles, she found this bracing neglect not a little disconcerting. But as she listened suspiciously to the sounds about the house, she had to let her rather elementary sense of justice admit that certainly her mother was not avoiding her with trivial excuses. For as there were no maids, and not even Mrs Childe, thought Flora with a strange prick of conscience, it must be her mother who was switching the stairs, using the carpet-sweeper, answering all the tradesmen's bells, putting coal into the drawing-room, cleaning the bathroom, and clinking pots and pans in the kitchen. It did not occur to her that she might get up and help, for still her main thoughts were a battleground between the strange, unreasonable, helpless joy of being still alive, and the bitter regret that all her problems were not, after all, over for ever. But it was useless to pretend, even to herself, that the imminence of death had not given her, as it gives so many stricken people today, a new, irrational hope in life. Percy would be able to help her somehow, she told herself, and though she stiffened all over at the sound of his bell and listened suspiciously for any hint that her mother was betraying her to her friend, she was reassured by the immediate sound of his feet and a knock on her door. Rose indeed had only murmured: 'Lancelot, good at need!' to the Major as she admitted him. She was far too wise to risk Flora's suspicions again, though what Cousin Mary would have made of her greeting she didn't, she told herself with an involuntary chuckle, dare to think.

How much was Flora telling the Major, she wondered as she prepared the tea-trays, and how much was she herself going to tell Stuart? One trouble indeed of what she termed this silly nonsense about the Major was that it forced upon her the odd consciousness of how far she had drifted from Stuart in the years. They had never, of course, she admitted frankly to herself, been very close together. If ever a marriage deserved the term of convenience it had been theirs. It was so long since, without words or regrets, they had passed into relations which would have shocked Havelock Ellis and his disciples profoundly. She could hardly remember now the stages by which they had drifted, naturally it seemed, into platonic relations, if that was what people meant when husband and wife had mutual respect for each other, the common interests of home and family, and fastidious self-restraint and good manners even in the differences created by those family complications. Such a relationship had worked well enough, she saw now, in the artificial conditions of an easy, happy world which had gone for ever, but could it stand the test of their present solitary mode of living? The old social life of the past was over; no one had the servants or food or the heart to attempt hospitality except for the young. Save for the exchange of news with her friends on the telephone Rose might have been living in the heart of the country, and though Stuart still met his friends at the club, she could hardly imagine that their bitter comments on the world

situation or food shortage satisfied his full needs for sympathy. That they shared the same fears for their country and family was obvious, but it was so long since they had indulged in intimate confidences that they seemed to have agreed, without words, to suffer in silence. Only the merest plank of trivial gossip and exchange of news bridged that estranging reserve. Stuart was too shy and taciturn to fathom its depth: she herself was too shy of his surprise and awkwardness if she made the attempt. Even now she had only awakened to the situation because Flora, and even Grannie and Cousin Mary, idiotically suspected her of an imaginary love affair, and because of the far more serious reflection that Stuart was the last person in the world to whom she could naturally confide this dreadful escapade of Flora's. Grannie Carr-Berwick would have had her husband on the carpet at once; Linda would have sought Ian's arms at once; all the wives she knew would have rushed for their husbands' protection; and she could only think, as she deposited a tea-tray outside Flora's door with a cheerful knock, what sort of wife could she be who stood here vaguely picturing herself saying to her husband, for want of any habit of true confidence, 'Oh by the way, Stuart, I forgot to tell you that Flora tried to commit suicide last night!' What a hideous by-product it was of all the misery of war that every soul was shut up so bitterly into its own fortress unless love could assault the defences and make an entry. And then she was startled for the moment out of all such heart-searching by the turning of the handle, and the appearance of the Major in the doorway, saying in a low, strangely moved voice:

'Please come in! Flora wishes to speak to you.'

Rose entered the room, timidly, incredulously. It was to see Flora high on her pillows, her hair falling in the untidy locks which so oddly suggested to her Flora as a little girl with a straight fringe, and with eyes brimming with tears as they had so often in those faraway days. But it was for the first time in her life that she heard her daughter gasp out the words :

'Oh, Mother, Mother, I am so sorry about everything!'

'Now, Flora, that's my brave girl, but you must avoid emotion!' Rose looked up from her yearning embrace quickly, hoping to catch a glance of admiration and love for so strange and heartfelt a penitent in the Major's eyes, but they remained quite inscrutable to her behind his round glasses as he went on: 'Now I think you should let your mother sit down quietly while you tell her your whole story. I think it's her due.'

Of all the incredible things which the war had done to Rose, the strangest was that she could sit here, listening to this wretched tangled tale, without shuddering away from its narrative in horror. It was true, of course, that it seemed so incredible that she could not take it in. Her eyes fell upon an old group at a shooting-party at Seriton which hung here still, in spite of her children's scathing criticisms, just because it was the best portrait she possessed of her own mother. What would that gentle mother, so securely entrenched in inviolable traditions, have felt if she had heard this story? Or Grannie Carr-Berwick, who sat beaming in front of her daughter, complete with fringe and pork-pie hat, whom she had just married off summarily to the dull moustached nonentity beside her. Or Cousin Mary, young and sporting in a tam-o'-shanter, trailing skirt, and tweed cloak? Or all the men of the party, so autocratically jovial and sure of themselves, who would certainly have got busy at once with horsewhips for what they would have called the seducer? And what would they have thought of Rose herself, if they had known that she could spare a thought in this, in all this, as to whether the affection of the Major, whom they would certainly have dismissed as a rank outsider, could survive such a story, and if it could possibly be her own fault that, even before this appalling confession, he had lost some of his admiration for her daughter? And then, even while her brain was swimming with her anxiety to treat her daughter's story with such a right display of love and forgiveness as would not rouse her antagonism, and the horrified thought that she might perhaps have to retail it all to Stuart, the Major spoke again.

'Now that you know, Flora's mind will be eased, I guess, and there is no reason for this unhappy story to go any further. It need be no concern of anyone's but mine in the future, for I have just asked Flora, Mrs Fairlaw, to do me the honour of becoming my wife.'

'But you can't! You can't!' Rose only found her voice when the Major after that got up, saying firmly that Flora must lie down and rest without another word to anyone. Rose was in the hall with him before she even managed to stammer that.

'You must let me come in here for a word with you,' said the Major with his usual quiet self-control. 'I told Flora

I must have a talk with you and she understood. You see, my behaviour must seem to you most unprofessional, shockingly unprofessional, but how was I to help it? We know Flora well enough, you and I, to admit to each other without disloyalty that we must take any story of hers with some modifications. But what was I to do when she declared that this dreadful, this appalling action of hers was due to the fact that she believed she had forfeited my affection . . . poor silly kid,' ended the Major in a wholly unprofessional voice.

'But hasn't she, surely?' stammered Rose. 'After all she told us, after all she's done, I can't believe you want to marry her. It's – it's intolerable that she should look upon you as – as a forlorn hope!'

'Now see here, dear Mrs Fairlaw!' The Major offered her a chair and sat down beside her, his brows knit in concentration. 'What you've got to consider is this, how many meanings there are in this word, love. Let me tell you straight out that I had in my youth as normal and passionate a devotion for a girl as any man can have. She loved me, and agreed to wait till we could afford to marry, and then another man struck in and carried her off, and she died a year later, from his neglect and ill-treatment. Well, I know you'll think this an absurd thing for a commonplace plain man to tell you, but it's a fact that from that moment I felt that ordinary love was over for me, and that I'd vow myself to the service of unhappy women. It was after that that I took up psychology, and a very great help I found it,' he continued thoughtfully. 'It helped me to realise, of course, that I possessed unspoilt the heroine complex which might even yet arouse the feelings I thought were dead for ever. Then I saw your daughter in those days of danger, and I was swept off my feet, right off my feet, by her courage and compelling personality. That feeling remains, and now, since she's got herself into this pack of trouble I've the other feeling for her as well. I want to help her perhaps in something of the way that she sublimated her ordinary *libido* into a belief that she was atoning for the sufferings of Poland. Human nature's pretty disingenuous in these affairs when all's said and done!'

'Then you love her, you do truly love her?' persisted Rose. She had no knowledge of psychology, but this she knew beyond a shadow of doubt, that only someone who loved Flora could ever hope to help her.

'I do, as I've tried to show you, but I'm also going to say this,' the monotonous kind voice went on. 'When I came here and got to know you I began to see things from a new angle. For one thing I saw that Flora had herself to blame more than anyone else for the story of her childhood which had worked on my pity. And for another thing you gave me a new idea of what love could be. No, I'm not so foolish as to say that I fell in love with you – that implies a desire for possession and the hope of a return which were never in my thoughts. But as I've watched your gentle unostentatious courage and self-sacrifice, and the selflessness which turns all your thoughts to those you love, and your gaiety and good-fellowship mixed with those odd beautiful thoughts of yours – well, I've some- times dreamt of what married life could be, if we could ever have met on an equal plane in age and background and everything else. I've told Flora straight out that I don't suppose I shall admire anyone as much as you, and that you'll always have a special place in my thoughts.'

'But – but could she bear it? When I've failed her so?' Rose clung desperately to the one point on which she could venture any comment on this extraordinarily moving speech.

'She's got to have absolute candour now,' said the Major sturdily, 'and I've told her so. Poor child, at the moment her pride is pretty well broken down and I've told her to thank God for that. You see, I had to make her confess that she'd even have tried to marry me to cover up her – her mistake, though I told her too that she was too brave and fine to have carried that through, and I mean it. But she'd got to be broken to pieces, as she is, before we can build her up again, and that I'll do so, and be very, very proud of her some day is my absolute conviction, Mrs Fairlaw. We've all of us a love of creation, you know, and my heart is truly set on creating or recreating the real Flora, as she was meant to be, as she will be!'

'You're wonderful to her, and – and you've been wonderful to me,' was all Rose could find to say as she looked into the kind pitying eyes focused on her behind the spectacles. Had any other man in the world, she wondered, ever founded the affairs of his heart so completely upon his theories; had anyone else ever seen in passionate admiration and complete disillusionment a basis for a successful marriage? Or was all the world perhaps going to learn from men with such theories as his how to order the unruly desires of sinful man, and see love not as a consummation but as creation? 'You're sure that she doesn't love this man – Guy?'

'She only told me that if she'd got my message last night she would have tried to end everything just the same, rather than see him again!'

'I see! But still – I can't feel sure, to put it plainly, that she's not taking an unfair advantage of your goodness.'

'That's for me to decide,' rejoined the Major. 'And I'm glad to think it's doing something for you as well. You'll always remain an ideal to me, you see.'

A silence fell between them which Rose was too bewildered to break. She feared to examine the gossamer web of high emotions and idealised love lest, if it broke at her touch, it might reveal some wholly unexpected thorn or furze bush below. She dared not even try to come down from the high pedestal on which he had placed her, for that, she realised by a sudden inspiration, was the last thing he wished. For she saw him now not only as a sympathetic companion or a beneficent helper, but also one of a great line of visitors and descendants from the New World, looking with a certain nostalgia at the Old World, loving, while yet they might almost despise, a certain hereditary sense of values, a fragrance of times past, a set of outmoded virtues as intangible as the mist floating round a forgotten island of the Hebrides, or the dusky bloom of little Georgian streets in a London twilight. He longed to cure Flora of her faults, but just at the moment he longed to help Rose in her helplessness and unhappiness. He saw Flora as a figure of Victory, waving her standard on the battlements, could he restore her to her true personality. But he saw Rose as a fainting captive in some ancient dungeon, lonely and misunderstood, needing his help. And such was the chivalry of the New World, greater surely than any of the Crusaders of old, that he half-forgot the fact that she was many years older than he, married, settled inalienably in her life, and dreamt in some dim way of her rescue. And so strange and wonderful seemed that flame to one who had been married for years to an undemonstrative husband, who, locked away in his own fortress, never sought to enter hers, that for one mad moment Rose wondered what life would be with such a companion and friend, so intimate a spiritual ally. And then next moment she shook herself mentally. Was it not enough to have the privilege of this delicate understanding with so rare and simple a soul without letting their friendship be clouded by any touch of sentiment that could only be a transient puzzled emotion, of which they must afterwards be ashamed?

'Yes, you are a romantic indeed,' she said, 'and I love you for it. It makes you want to help me, and you do, for what could be more wonderful than to think of Flora, transformed by your love and becoming the person she was meant to be? She was never meant to be shut up in this little old house in a conventional city in the Old World. You and she will go forward together in a newer world, as youth should, but your memories of us, house-bound here, will always inspire me. For you see you have made me understand the work I have to do, and the fact that I speak of it to you shows how much confidence I have in you. I have my own job, to find out how to make life endurable for my husband, for like Flora he is by nature inclined to shut himself up in his own sorrows and perplexities.'

'That's very true!' To her infinite relief Rose saw that her urgent if disjointed remarks had succeeded in their object, and the Major was wholly himself again. 'I'm glad you say that. For your husband is a very lonely and unhappy man, I fear. Oh, not through his own fault or yours for a moment, but as so many men of his generation must be. They risked everything and endured hell for four years in the last war, only to see their work wasted and their sons committed to the same fate. And their pride is touched at our losses in the East till they feel it unendurable. Women see the loss of life and agony and horror; men see the end of their country's majesty overseas. He can't speak of it, you said once, so he suffers the more. He needs all your help and inspiration, and I know you'll find the way to give it. We've each got our tasks, Mrs Fairlaw: no one wants to take the easy way out nowadays.'

There was enough of a question in his voice, though it must be a question for which there was no answer, to make her raise her eyes to his and say bravely:

'I think it's you who have given ideals to me. I shall always look upon you as' – she took the plunge bravely – 'as a sort of son, a son who has grown up to be my father confessor, and now you'll be my son-in-law as well.'

Then, secure of herself again, Rose looked into his eyes, and for a moment they clasped each other's hands, like travellers meeting and parting at a cross-roads, whose ways must lie in opposite directions. Once more she longed to ask him if he was sure of happiness in the way he was to tread with Flora, and if that shadowy pilgrim, True Love, was to accompany them, but she forbore. She could rely on the pride

and devotion in his tone when he first spoke of her daughter, and on the magnetic charm of Flora's beauty and youth. What lit this strange conversation was only a passing gleam of twilight, a strange, fairy-like glimpse of what might have been, had their lots been cast together in time and place. It would pass with the hour, with the moment, and she had retained the precious jewel of his friendship. 'And this, I imagine,' she told herself, 'is what any affair between decent middle-aged people would come to!' And when she came to look back on it, how it had helped, by its demand for sense and clear thinking, to deaden for a little the awful shock of Flora's adventure.

'Now we must be practical,' she said, as the horror of last night came back to overwhelm her again. 'What shall I do with my poor Flora now? I want to keep her near me, but I'm afraid, so afraid, that she may only dwell on all this with me as I've had to know, and that it may estrange her to feel I know everything. People don't give their confidences most happily always to those whom they see every day, do they?'

'No indeed!' The Major too was himself again now. 'I'd say the best thing you could do would be to let her go off with old Mrs Carr-Berwick for a change of air. She told me it was suggested, and she's taken an odd fancy to the old dame. I fancy that she finds someone as limited, yet so autocratic, a sort of change, you know, and it'll do her a heap of good to be with someone as utterly selfish and exacting for a little. We're all of us the better for seeing a caricature of ourselves now and again! And I've told her I'll come down and visit her now and then, and indeed I think I'll get a true welcome!'

It was on this note that they parted, and if there was, perhaps, an odd little stab in Rose's heart as she watched the Major walk away briskly up the drive, it vanished when Flora called her upstairs. For all her fears that Flora was using her friend as a way of escape, and failing to recognise the rare quality concealed beneath a drab exterior, vanished as her daughter said with glowing eyes, 'Oh, Mother, Mother, isn't it wonderful? It's like coming out of a long dreadful nightmare! I never, never knew how I loved him.'

Flora might compose herself, but Rose could not. Tonight, with so great a weight of strange events on her mind, it seemed intolerable to go down to the little kitchen and prepare dinner for Stuart and Flora. She was late anyhow, and in her preoccupation everything seemed to go wrong. How did cooks manage to send up soup unburnt when their own particular Romes were burning, or persuade a soufflé to rise when their hearts were in their boots? They would, of course, have had the relief of immediate self-expression; they would greet their husbands on the doorstep with the story of 'our Flora', whereas she had promised her daughter to let her tell as much or as little of her exploits as she wished to Stuart herself. And as Stuart refused to go and visit the invalid till he had dined, Rose was obliged to maintain a reasonable appearance of calm and cheerfulness while she served the meal and waited on Flora. It was not till she was left to wash up, while Stuart went upstairs for his interview, that she could even begin to sort out her conclusions on the extraordinary story of the day.

If anyone had told her three years ago of her thoughts, as she stood at the sink, trying, without much success, to keep her hands out of the greasy water! It was, she supposed, as she had decided before, the repeated shocks of the last two dreadful years which accounted for her comparative apathy now. Or was it merely that she could not yet realise the truth that in the space of a few weeks Flora had gone off to live with a married man, attempted suicide, and engaged herself to marry a man who knew the whole story and was prepared to love and forgive? What would she have thought, three years ago, of Percy's extraordinary attitude, to life, to morals, to Flora, and to herself? Did he represent a new generation of newer, clearer, purer morality, or one which was certainly, in Grannie Carr-Berwick's eyes, going straight to the dogs? The old world, she supposed, was in the melting-pot, and well did she know, from her experiments at the stove, how impossible it was to tell what the mixture you were boiling up would be like when all the froth and bubbles had died down. Anyhow it would be a new world with new values. She herself, and most of her contemporaries, might find them alien. She had inherited sanctions and traditions from Christianity and ethics alike which made it difficult to accept the Major's standards, though she was ready to confess that his views were far more distinguished by the Christian virtues of faith, hope, and charity than her own. All that we older people can do is to stand back, and let them find their own way without any interference from us, she was telling herself, when she heard Stuart's steps coming down to the library.

'Well, I'm damned!' Rose shut the door hastily upon Stuart. He had evidently made no effort to get loose from his old moorings and had no self-questioning as to the validity of his own views.

'Oh hush, Stuart!' Rose put down the coffee tray anxiously. 'You weren't harsh to her?'

'Harsh! I couldn't say a word! She just went on nineteen to the dozen, and I could only sit there and gape. Is this appalling story true? I can't believe it! Why didn't you ring me up?' as Rose nodded her head miserably. 'Why, it was a case for the doctors or police, not for you! Good Heavens! To attempt such a thing, such a crime and in my house! And if you'll believe me, she told it me as calmly as if she were describing a picnic!'

'A picnic with a thunderstorm at the end,' said Rose. 'That's what's so incredible. She doesn't seem to have any of our values at all.'

'Nor this precious Major of hers! Rose, it can't be true that the odd little chap really wants to marry her after all this? I mean, I recognised after he put up all that stuff, the other night, about Mary being raped on a desert island that his views of life weren't normal, hardly even sane! But even so, to take another man's leavings!'

'Don't, Stuart.' Rose shivered and yet she smiled at that reference to Mary too. It couldn't be real life which she and Stuart were discussing, but some mad novel or play!

'If the chap's only doing it because he's afraid she'll go for a gas oven again, we should get him out of it and have her certified! I shall tell him so straight!'

'Oh, but it's not like that, Stuart! I'm sure he does love her. He admired her enormously when he first met her, he fell in love with her strength, and now he pities her for her weakness. I think, you see, he never sees people just as they are but as they might be. He wants to make a perfect thing of Flora, instead of falling in love with imaginary perfection, as our generation used to do!'

'Well, he's a long way to go!' said Stuart with bristling eyebrows. 'It's all very metaphysical and beautiful, I dare say, but the man might as well put up the banns with a magdalen home out of pity as far as I can see. That's not the sort of pity a man wants to feel for his wife.'

'We can't begin to get inside his mind, Stuart, at least I can't. We've got our own standards, social and Christian standards, and we'll keep them till we die, but we can't expect the generation growing up in this mad, dreadful world to accept our sanctions in ethics or taste, can we? Ours were a map to guide us through pleasant, peaceful plains. They've got to find some sort of track for themselves through a jungle.'

'Well, the Major's met with a tigress anyhow, already!' said Stuart, smiling reluctantly. 'But do you really mean you don't believe in any absolute standards of morality, Rose? I can't believe it of you!'

'I believe them for myself of course. But I do feel our old world has gone for ever, don't you, and our particular point of view with it. That's where Christianity scores – its standards don't change in essentials, though even they may change in interpretation, I suppose. I only mean that we can't impose our standards on others or judge them by ours any more. They have just to find their own road and make their way along it as best they can.'

'Even if it leads them to suicide, or infidelity, or a hopeless mess of their lives?' demanded Stuart. It was a long time, Rose recognised oddly, since they had indulged in so intimate a discussion on any subject, and already Stuart's eyes were turning a little longingly to *The Times* and his pipe.

'What can we do but leave them to do what they think best?' asked Rose helplessly. And after all that was, indeed, the last possible word on the subject.

CHAPTER TWELVE
A TRACK OF LIGHT

. . . And cut a path into the heaven of glory,
Leaving a track of light for men to wonder at.
Shakespeare *Richard II*

Those who have to endure life in wars and revolutions are
like people who stand out on a rock at sea watching mighty
waves break on a reef. After the great shock of ice-green
water has risen, and gathered itself to boil over in a cloud of
foam, they wait, breathless in the tumult, till the angry white
clouds subside into a mazy floating embroidery of green and
white, watching to see which old landmarks of seaweed, rocks,
and shimmering sand will appear again. Even though they
know the next wave will come soon, so soon, and may well be
far greater and more overwhelming than the last, there is a
moment's peace, a moment's still beauty, and they can, if they
must, try to struggle back to a safer position.

Such a respite came in Rose's life for a few weeks when
Flora had departed, relieved of her worst fears and engrossed
by her new happiness, to the only hotel on the west coast

of Scotland which would guarantee Mrs Carr-Berwick such necessities as a fire in her bedroom and hot meat twice a day. Flora herself went indeed unwillingly: Rose had anxious moments about the fate of such an ill-assorted couple in their exile, and worried herself seriously over the rights and wrongs of letting the old lady take charge of anyone with Flora's record. But the Major carried all triumphantly before him, having won Stuart to his side by insisting that Rose could not go on working as she had done for the last fortnight. It had indeed taken Stuart some time to get reconciled to the idea that his proud, beautiful stepdaughter was seriously contemplating matrimony with the odd, drab little Major, but it was much easier to approve of this unorthodox acquaintance of his wife's now that he declared: 'So that's what the fellow was up to all the time! Mary would have it that you were the attraction, Rose!' And although nothing would ever reconcile him to the Major's neat, prim, yet horrifyingly outspoken comments on the sex-life of his family and acquaintance, his psychological jargon, or his accent, Stuart was slowly influenced by the Major's sympathy and invariable unselfishness into declaring that he wasn't sure that Flora hadn't done a very good thing for herself. It was all the easier to believe it when Flora had gone off with the old lady, amidst a mountain of luggage in Ian's car ('Leaving me no more petrol for the month,' as he lamented). For with all her new hopes and resolutions Flora was Flora still, and storms of temper and criticism still raged, though with less fury and far less subsequent sulkiness, in the Laws House. 'A good hard life in the West after the war will do her all the good in the world,' Stuart

told his wife, as he witnessed Flora's tempestuous and bullying efforts to help Rose about the house, and though Rose
feared sometimes that it would take years of the Major's skill
and patience to train Flora in his own neat ways, yet she could
agree with truth that Flora was the stuff of which pioneer
women are made.

And now in the lull which followed, when the terrible
wave of Flora's visit had ebbed away, Rose discovered to her
delight and surprise that she was beginning to get the better
of the house at last. She had been very nearly worsted in the
struggle, it was true, but now that she had no more nursing,
no more trays for an invalid, no hurried shopping for medi-
cines or some delicacy for lunch, she found that she could get
through her housework passably, even if it was not up to Mrs
Childe's standards, and so far prepare dinner in the morning
that she could hope at last for that most precious commodity,
a little time to herself. It was true, of course, that she was still
handicapped against other working women by the size of the
house, and by the fact that her evenings had to be given to
writing letters of a number and quality which would not be
contemplated by a Mrs Childe, but as the rigours of a Scottish
spring relented suddenly into a short halcyon week of thin,
clear, April sunshine, Rose discovered that there were half-
hours now when she could sit dreaming in the drawing-room
window, as she had never done in old days, when she was
organising centre of a leisured home. It was as if from sheer
exhaustion that her mind refused to realise the terrible news
from the Far East and the slaughter and the agony in Europe,
as if even the dark shadows of fear for her loved ones and her

country were somehow held at bay for a brief space. She did not venture indeed into memories of the past, for there danger lay, but suddenly, as the blackbirds sang in the garden, and the spiced scent of flowering currant rose in the air, she found herself taking down well-loved volumes of poetry to find comfort in the magic of words. Everyone shared that magic in youth, but she was lucky in that it had survived into her later years. It was like water in a thirsty desert to pull down an assortment of her best-loved books, and let the poems, or mere snatches of lines, come rippling back into her tired brain, like a singing stream over little pebbles. The boys used to laugh at her for her love of anthologies, but she defended herself by pointing out that one poem by an author suggested another at once to your mind, so that you did not have to get down whole volumes of major poets for thoughts and joys 'which sleep but cannot die, folded within their own eternity.' Everything seemed beautiful and allusive on such days: even the best-known poets bore infinite repetition. And this she told herself was one of the joys which no enemy nor time could take wholly away. Just as surely as women must for ever go on cleaning houses and cooking dinners, the majesty of poets and philosophers would be there, ready to open for them the ivory gates into the dream world. Or was the world of beauty the true world, of which pots and pans were only the tiresome abstraction? *'Fugiendum est igitur ad carissimam domum* (or was it *patriam?*) *et ibi pater et ibi omnia.'* So she mused idly while before her eyes night flew to the rooky wood; charmed magic casements opened on cloud-capped palaces; Wordsworth's mighty waters rolling evermore merged into the surge and thunder of the *Odyssey*; Traherne's orient and immortal wheat stretched down to Sabrina's glassy, cool, translucent wave; the Scholar-Gipsy, and the youth to fortune and to fame unknown, brushed the dews away, to greet the sun upon the upland lawn, till they rested beneath the dark red-fruited yew-tree's shade; and the chorus of *Electra* cried for some cavern for their hiding till they found it in the land of Luthany, the region Elenore.

'Mums has the most ill-regulated mind,' Tom would say severely. 'She can't order the chimney-sweepers without seeing them as golden lads and lasses, and if it's her honour at golf, which doesn't often happen I will say, she walks to the tee murmuring that her honour rooted in dishonour stood; and I don't believe she ever lets the bath-water out without hearing Tennyson's brook, or pays the dairy without mentioning that she on honey dew hath fed, and drunk the milk of Paradise!'

Rose smiled at the thought as on one such afternoon she took out the book which she considered peculiarly her own. For so few people wandered into the Earthly Paradise now, with the dreamer of dreams born out of his due time: she had shared with Emily Dickinson the carriage which held but just themselves and Immortality, before most people had heard of her. And Crashaw and Francis Thompson were friends to her, not just the same snippets in anthologies. And here, inside the cover of Flecker's poems were odd lines from any odd reading which she had loved. What was this?

> The girth severed, the saddle swung,
>   And he went down,

He never more sung winter songs
   In his high town,
In that High Town that Faerie is. . . .

Rose shivered and told herself she must be careful. She must keep to the world of faerie. She must not lose her saddle and fall into the Woods of Westermaine, where dark fears and real terrors lurked for her. 'Very old are the woods!' . . . 'We'll to the woods no more!' So two of her best-loved poets warned her. She was not seeking for courage and consolation in the great treasury of the poets today. All she wanted now was to be free for a little while of the beauty and vision of their world. It was perhaps as well that at this point her quest was interrupted by the appearance of Cousin Mary standing at the front door.

Mary had looked in for tea between two committees, so Rose had, shamefacedly, to take her up to the drawing-room, where a very meagre tray stood in the midst of a generous pile of books. And Mary had obviously no illusions about the need for a little mental refreshment in a dark, ugly world.

'Sitting here idling over books in the sunshine with So Much to be Done!' was her way of looking at it, and Rose, convicted at once of selfishness and uselessness, attempted no defence. 'What are all these? *Anthology of Modern Verse*? Modern gibberish I call it! *Modern French Verse*? Well really! When you think what the French are – cowards and atheists!'

'I think you should read this *Mater Dolorosa* by Berger, Mary!' Rose allowed herself to apologise. 'It tells how the Mother of Jesus went out into the woods alone, heartbroken, on the night of Good Friday; there she found another woman in still greater agony. It was the mother of Judas, and in pity Mary bent and kissed her, and so she expiated:

En vertu d'un mystère infini
L'autre baiser donné sur le Gethsémani.

That's not the thought of an atheist. It's a thought which might make peace possible again all over the world,' she added dreamily.

'Now, Rose, my dear, that's the sort of cryptic thing you like to say which really makes people think you a pro-Nazi,' said Mary vigorously. 'I shall never forget how you shocked my invaluable Mrs Baines at our working-party, when she said it was the duty of Christian countries to exterminate the Germans, just as Moses exterminated the Amalekites, and you thought it necessary to say he wasn't a Christian.'

'Well, but he couldn't have been,' put in Rose impenitently.

'My dear, it's not the point! The point is,' said Mary with more energy than logical sequence, 'that if you've time to sit here dreaming you've time to go out and take up some form of war work again. I should fancy, and I'm ashamed to say it, that you're the only woman in Castleburgh who isn't aiding the war effort. How should we get on if everyone shut themselves up in their homes as you do?'

There was no defence. Mary was perfectly right. In one moment Rose recognised that the edifice of imagination she had built about herself as a world's worker was shattered.

She had some time to spare, now that she had served her apprenticeship, and what Mary had said long ago was true. It was not doing work for your country to keep a house clean and one man fed. At the first opportunity she was relapsing again, she saw clearly now, into that class of idle, leisurely drones whose day in the world was done. What right had she to sit here opening magic casements for herself when half the world was behind prison bars?

'You're quite right, Mary,' she said humbly. 'I'm dreadfully selfish. Do you know of any job I could take on?'

'Well, my dear, I see that you can't manage a whole-time job, and that you're not as young as you were.' In spite of Mary's urgency she did not seem, as she rubbed her nose vigorously, to have any clear call for Rose's services. 'Why not go back to our Comforts Working Party?'

'Oh, Mary, couldn't you think of something where I didn't have to talk!' As the cry came from Rose's heart she realised again how kind, after all, her house had been to her during the last few months. For wasn't any drudgery, weren't even greasy pans, better than sitting listening to the chat of the other workers all afternoon? It had been bad enough in November, but she could picture them now! – the lady whose nephew had written from Singapore prophesying just what happened; the friend whose friend's friend had written a detailed gloating account of atrocities in Hong Kong; the old lady who wanted to know, in a minatory voice, why our secret service didn't know that Japan had been preparing for war and *stop* it. And then someone would come in and murmur in a subdued voice: 'No, Mrs Cardew isn't coming, poor thing.

Haven't you heard about her son in Libya?' And Rose would sit there knitting, knowing that some day another voice would say: 'What! haven't you heard about the poor Fairlaws?' . . .

'I should have thought some interchange of ideas would be excellent for you,' said Mary. 'You told me you never read war books, and if I were you, sitting here idly, I should be reading *The Times*, which I see you haven't opened yet!'

'Cowards have to shut their eyes and imaginations if they're to go on at all,' said Rose briefly, 'and I know I'm a coward. Things like this out of the anthology you despise so much, Mary, help me to be brave:

And if our blood alone
Can ease the iron earth,
Take it! It is well worth
To ease a Saviour's birth.

That gives me courage: the papers don't. But don't scold me for being a coward. Tell me a war work instead! I'm still on the list of the ABC Canteen and the XYZ Society, you know, and I've never heard a word. There's not a great demand for ageing, incompetent women, is there?'

'Well, I'll tell you something you could do!' Mary's poor nose was given a rest at last. 'You know that every Monday for years I've had the cripple children from the Orphanage, and read to them and given them tea. I don't like to give them up, but it means that I can't get to my depot that afternoon, and the laziness and incompetence of the women there sets me back for the whole week. Summers is quite willing to manage the tea – only twenty to thirty come – but she wouldn't hear of reading to them from three to four, and they do enjoy it so much. Could you manage that for me till I find you some real war work? It is, of course, a real work,' she ended with no mock modesty, 'as it frees me!'

Rose assented to the plan with enthusiasm. It seemed incredible that Mary should let her off with anything so simple, even so enjoyable, as reading aloud to children you were sorry for. 'And it would be better not to make much in the way of plans till Flora's married, for though she insists that she won't have a trousseau or a fuss of any kind, weddings do always mean work, don't they?'

'How are they getting on at Doone?' asked Mary, who had the grace to look a little shamefaced when Flora's engagement was mentioned.

'Far, far from well, I fear,' sighed Rose. 'Linda and I compare letters from Grannie about Flora's monstrous selfishness in going out alone in the mornings with Flora's complaints that Grannie is selfish enough to expect her to potter after her about the stuffy lounge all day. In fact Stuart says that they'll probably cut short their stay by going to the registrar's office, Flora with Percy, and Grannie with a courtly old doctor who has told her that her blood-pressure is that of a girl of eighteen! I really do expect Flora to do something of the kind. And Mickie writes that he's expecting to go on some course shortly, and Tom is to get down on leave quite soon, so altogether,' said Rose inconsequently, 'I ought to do some war work.'

With that sop to her conscience Rose spent the next few afternoons with her books, and at work in her garden. She was almost as shamefaced over the latter as the former, for her garden was only a joke among her friends. It was only a piece of ground a few yards square, spreading from the angle made by the two wings of the house to the wall which shut it off from the pavement, bounded by the paved path to the front entrance on one side, and that to the back premises on the other. Stuart had calculated once that his wife's expenditure on soil, manure, and seed catalogues would keep her in orchids for the house all the year round, but then, as Rose retorted, she didn't care for orchids. And she did love her garden patch and had her own ideas about it. She would not listen to experts who told her she must make it a sunk garden with crazy paving and rock plants, for if you live in a town grass alone is sure to give you some colour all the year round, however unmanicured the turf may be. She refused in the same way to give it symmetry, and more sense of space, by one scheme of flowers or shrubs in the borders which flanked the grass. They might look better, but it was more fun to have every kind of plant you liked mixed anyhow together; even if you only had room for six madonna lilies and a foot of sweet-peas and two standard roses you had the joy of growing them and smelling them just the same, and every day provided you with a new thrill. 'Just another anthology,' Tom called it and so it was. She had, however, so little heart for her dear patch in the war that she had left it to itself, for even Mary could hardly feel that it would be patriotic to dig it up for vegetables which wouldn't keep the family for a week. But now, in this odd lull she looked affectionately at her neglected borders, where the daffodils were coming up triumphantly and a forsythia gilded the cream-harled walls, and decided that here too, as in her books, was a beauty independent of fate and time which should surely be preserved in the world. ('Now don't quote "*il faut cultiver*" at me,' Tom would say; it's hard luck on Voltaire that he only exists in the English imagination now as a kindly old nursery gardener!) Her lilies were coming up, curling back their leaves bravely: the plants of delphiniums and lupins had survived the snow. She could not ransack catalogues this year for such rarer joys as lobelia cardinalis or salvias or anchusa. It was enough to buy packets of such accommodating seeds as love-in-a-mist and godetia, candytuft and Virginia stock, and the kindly nasturtium which never despises back-gardens. Nothing, to be candid, would ever make it the sort of garden you could write a book about.

'Though you're just the sort of person to do it,' Mickie would assure her with loving mockery. 'Full of whimsical thoughts and loathsome-grot quotations, and long-winded Latin names of flowers.'

'Except,' Tom demurred, 'that there's always a break in the middle of those gardening books Mums is so fond of, when the owner decides to add a meadow or stream to his shagheap, and put it down under artichokes or irises. And she can't do that without knocking down a bit of the house!'

'And she couldn't tell how the neighbours love her, and are always dropping in to see her *diptherium furiosum* or her *pterodactyl animans*, and tell her all their delicate love affairs, because she goes Trappist when she once gets down to the antirrhinums,' added Mickie.

Rose smiled over their conversation as she dug and riddled earth, and slit her seed-packets in this false, shining spring once more. It had ended, she remembered, by their agreeing that the book would, in strict accuracy, have to be entitled *Two Inches and a Slug*, so that she could not expect large royalties. But however much of a joke it was, it did satisfy, she supposed, every older woman's longing for some creative work, however trivial and absurd it might seem to be, and wasn't that what the dear little Major urged upon her? She could not feel that she had even achieved any such creative work for Stuart as the Major had suggested in that conversation about creative love. It was much easier to dig and hoe a garden than to dig into Stuart's reserve, or rake away the stones and obstructions of years! But at least her husband was a little happier, she hoped sighing, in a home that was managed rather more efficiently, and a wife who was no longer so utterly fatigued that she had to keep silence or nag at him in the evening. He had, she noticed, returned to his book of the Family since Flora had gone, and that surely was a sign that, like herself, he felt partly relieved from a burden, and that, in spite of the silence from Libya and Russia, and the ceaseless advance of the Japanese, a certain optimism had come to him, however unreasonably, with the spring. So Rose thought on the very day when the next and greatest wave rose and fell with a deafening roar, and in the turmoil and seething foam of her anguish all her old life seemed blotted out for ever.

She was standing in the stone porch, looking at her six treasured hyacinths, and waiting for Stuart to return from his weekly night of fire-watching, when the telegraph boy arrived. As Flora preferred this means of communication to the written word, even if it were only to express her boredom, Rose had grown less cold and sick at the sight of the cheerful lad, balancing his bicycle against the lamp outside, before he clicked the gate and came down the path. Then suddenly the signature 'Iona' stared at her, in the bright sunshine, and she knew the rest.

It is of not much use to write or to read about moments like that.

'No answer, thank you!' Although in one moment the five words: 'Mickie reported killed in action' had pierced the fabric of her heart and life as surely as any bomb could do its work on the insentient world, the shell of her ordinary life and voice remained. She watched the boy walk off – one of his heels wanted mending she noticed, and waited where she was, because she saw the butcher's boy coming down the path.

'Mr Gorse has sent you a nice rabbit, 'm,' he said with such pride that Rose, the faraway Rose, even managed to smile and thank him as she took the repulsive parcel. It was not of course conceivable that ordinary daily life and meals would go on again, ever again, but she had no voice or words of course to explain that. She even told herself mechanically that she had better go and put it to soak in salt and water when suddenly the vision assailed her of the little animal in life: she saw its absurd scurrying back paws, its dancing white scut, its bright nervous little eyes, and before her own came a sudden vision of Mickie, sitting very fair and plump in the nursery window-seat, in his blue jersey, reading aloud to Tom:

'And so the Flopsy Bunnies reached home safely after all,' he would always end that tale of Peter Rabbit, and then they played a game of running in and out of the odd connecting doors of the house, ending up at her arm-chair as home and safety. . . .

She sat down in the porch, because at that a horrible tingling agony began to thaw the numbness in her brain. She must go indoors, she supposed, and think how she was to show this bit of paper to Stuart – it would be worse after that, because then she would know it was true. Only she must wait because the baker's cart was here now, on its bi-weekly rounds, and as the boy had seen her she must take her order.

'Bread, 'm,' said the boy, and she still sat there in the porch, with the sunlight falling now on the long brown loaf in her hand. She did not realise that she was looking at it until into her mind came unbidden other words – 'which is broken for you' – and she knew now that the thought of a broken body could not be held at bay much longer. What was it, she grasped eagerly at yet another disconnected thought that might protect her for a few minutes longer, what was it which she had read somewhere about those words? That the literal meaning didn't fit the countless processions of solemn worship to the raised Host down the centuries, the bells and incense and the pealing choirs – rather it implied, said this hostile critic, a gesture of tossing something away over your shoulder, flinging that morsel of life away, as if it were of no value. It had impressed her then, because she felt that in truth it gave a higher, sublimer value to that Immortal Consecration. Was there somewhere, very far away now, some link between that symbol of eternity, and all the beautiful bodies of youth, broken and tossed carelessly away by the cruelty of man? –

We that have seen man broken
We know man is divine . . .

She found herself repeating the words stupidly, as if they might be a charm to keep her from the vision which was taking clearer shape now, that must break and tear her heart to fragments. But not yet, she told herself, bending forward instinctively as if to protect herself, for the gate was opening again and Stuart was here.

He knew already. She could tell that beyond question as she saw his face, neither pale nor drawn but changed, strangely, irrevocably, into the lines of old age. As he looked now he would look when he was eighty, as he would look when he lay dead. Ian must have rung him up, she told herself, before he and Linda went off to join Iona, and to see him so changed was to impress upon her the reality of her own anguish too. It was waiting to drown her, yet now again she must struggle to the surface, to try to help her husband some-how, to find some voice of sympathy which would pierce his stark loneliness. And then, just as the past with all its senseless misunderstandings swept over her, she found words at last:

'Oh, Stuart,' she whispered hoarsely. 'Your boy, your boy!'

Even in that moment she could see by his glance that Stuart understood. Here and now she was flinging aside the link which had bound her and Mickie so closely, and offering Stuart the tribute of his first and rightful claim on his own son.

'Yours as well as mine,' he replied gruffly, standing beside her in the porch. Did he share her feeling that to enter the house was to enter for ever the grave of all their happiness and hopes?

'Yours and Lilias' and mine,' she said, speaking wildly to herself rather than to him. 'She and he are so young and beautiful that they will know each other in the courts of Heaven –'

'Shall we go in?' said Stuart, and she recalled herself. Such wandering words would not help her husband.

'Yes, I suppose so. Only Stuart, do you remember the first time we all came here together? Do you remember how we all came in two cars, and Bobs wasn't in his – in Mickie's – so he cried and cried.'

'Don't, Rose!' Stuart stared over her shoulder at the door. 'I remember Bobs, ofcourse, your Cairn, but as for the rest –'

'Let me just remind you, Stuart! Mickie found Bobs, here, just here by this step, looking as if the house belonged to him already, and he and Mickie fell on each other with relief, and you said – I can hear you now – "My dear boy, what a fuss! We were only separated on the journey for a little time after all!" You must help me to feel that now, Stuart, for – for –'

It was no use to struggle against the wave any longer. It was sweeping her away out of any sight of familiar thoughts and comfort. Only the rock was left visible, and to that she must cling for Stuart's sake till he left the house.

'You must have some breakfast,' she said, 'something to drink anyway –' as he shook his head with loathing. 'Come and help me to get it –'

'I think I'll just go off to the office.' Stuart followed her obediently to the kitchen where he took a cup of coffee mechanically, and was even persuaded to eat a little when she asked him to cut some bread and butter. At least he had not shut himself up alone as he would have in other days: at least they seemed to be clinging together in the desolation of the tide about them.

'I think I'll go to the office now. Ian's away, you see – he 'phoned me that he and Linda were going straight off to poor little Iona. So there'll be no one there today and it's a busy time. Do you – do you mind?'

'Oh no. You'll come back in the evening and that will be something to look forward to.'

'Do you mean that?' Stuart's face worked as he looked at her, and across Rose's grief came the knowledge that she could only bring any help to her husband, as she had to Flora, by showing her need of him.

'Indeed I do!' she said. 'Think what we've both shared all these years! We need never think of our silly little mistakes long ago, unless some day we can bear to laugh at them. But think of the happiness and pride we've shared together, just you and I!'

So Stuart went off to the office, after halting suggestions that she should lie down or get Cousin Mary to come and sit with her. Rose could just refrain from the horror which either scheme inspired, and then she was left alone at last, to make her own way to Gethsemane, and try to find, among the massive trunks and cruel, overhanging branches of the dark, threatening trees, another Sufferer who had passed that way alone.

At a quarter to three she left the house, locking the door carefully behind her. It was the afternoon on which, she remembered suddenly, she had promised to read to Mary's class of cripple children, and she would rather keep the engagement than face the alternative of explaining the reason for her absence to Mary. 'Nothing can hurt me now,' she had quoted laughing to the Major a few weeks ago, and it was far truer now. She could not, indeed, bring herself to take *The Cuckoo Clock*, which she had laid out for them. Mickie had loved it so much when he was ill, and she could not be sure of her voice if she recalled that little figure in the bed. She picked up Hans Anderson's *Tales* instead, because no one had cared for them but Flora. 'He's always trying to make you feel sad,' Mickie had protested indignantly over the little Mermaid and the Snow Queen. Next week she would make a careful choice, but today she would just concentrate on keeping her voice clear and her mind a blank.

But neither determination was very easy to realise. She had expected to feel pity and sympathy for the helpless incapacitated children, but she was horrified to discover that instead a slow ugly distaste arose in her as she chatted to individuals before she took up the book. Some looked quite happy, some were not grotesquely malformed, and they were all polite, but today it seemed suddenly so monstrous that every kind of skill and artifice was employed to keep these wrecks of humanity alive, while the world was pouring out its young and healthy and beautiful by the million to death. Could she feel it any compensation that he had died for such as these? Or must she stifle that ugly rebellion by telling herself that after all death itself was better for him than a life maimed or deformed such as these, if he had just escaped from that falling plane which was to haunt her thoughts now eternally by day or night? To suppress such thoughts became impossible, unless she read on swiftly and mechanically, careless of the tales she chose, or the effect on her audience. Half-past three, she saw by the clock, when she seemed to have been reading for ever, twenty to four, a quarter to four, and then at last as the minute-hand dragged on, past the five minutes till the goal seemed to be in sight and the story, of which she knew neither words nor plot, was coming to an end, 'and so, you see, little Hans,' the words at last caught her attention, 'even the saddest stories have a happy ending after all –' Then for a moment the Snow Queen's icicles seemed to melt in Rose's heart, and she looked round the room with a warmth of love and pity in her heart. For, after all, wasn't she at one with these maimed children and all the pitiful wrecks of humanity, in heart or body, all over the world? And if you could see, however dimly and far away, that those bleeding, broken bodies were part of the sacrifice made with so divine and contemptuous a gesture, you might come at last to see the reality beyond – '*Fugiendum est igitur ad carisimam domum*' . . . her mind reiterated as she read again, by request of the bright-eyed shrivelled little creature by her side – 'and so, you see, little Hans, even the saddest stories have a happy ending after all.'

But the day was not over for her, even though the story of her life seemed over for ever now. Even as she opened the garden gate she realised that somehow the house didn't look quite like itself. She knew its moods and ways by now so well that she could not be mistaken! So that she was horrified rather than surprised when a tall figure suddenly and violently wriggled its way out of the library window – that open window was the explanation of her feeling that the house looked odd – and Flora flung herself suddenly upon her mother's neck crying:

'I had to come to you, my poor darling Mummy! I had to come to help and comfort you!'

It was only at that moment that Rose understood something of what was meant by maternal sacrifice. Women could deny themselves little things for their children gladly: they could see the agony of war and death, by a supreme effort, as a part of the Great Sacrifice. But never before had she realised that she might be called upon to stifle all the nervous dread and bitter disappointment, the scoldings and slights of years, not just to herself but to the son just torn out of her life, and accept, somehow or other, Flora's offer of love and sympathy. She had come home almost gladly, in the thought that now at last she would be alone with her memories, and that out of them and her longing to comfort him, she might find some way to aid her husband. And now instead of that dim twilight, where she might find some vision of peace, was Flora, busy, as Mickie himself would say, with her fireworks all over the place. For a moment she felt herself stiffening in Flora's violent grasp; for a moment the words: 'You never loved him!'

almost escaped her lips, and then it seemed as if the old home, lemon-yellow against the unfathomable light of the clear sunset, rebuked her. It had stood there for so long, offering its shelter and protection to so many generations: so many mothers and daughters must have kissed beneath this very porch. So many ghosts must linger here, as Mickie's dear spirit might linger now, to tell her that love was all that mattered, love here and now whatever the past had been or the future might bring.

'It was very dear of you to come, Flora!' she said in a stifled whisper.

'I knew you'd need me!' said Flora complacently. It was so odd to Rose that though her heart was aching so intolerably and her whole mind was set on being nice to Flora, her immediate preoccupation was to escape this bearlike hug which was driving a button straight into her neck.

'Come indoors, dearest,' she said, fearful of offence. 'How did you get here so soon? I see you got in through the window! Had I left it open?'

'Yes, I suppose so,' said Flora, impatient of everyday detail. 'I came off at once, just as I was, with no luggage or anything, just to be with you.'

'You did leave a message for Grannie, I hope! Did she know?'

'She got a telegram from Ian and told me straight out!' Flora dropped on to the sofa in the library, shuddering.

'Oh, Mother, I don't know how to bear it! He never knew that I really loved him!'

Certainly Mickie had no reason to know it. Even as Flora

spoke Rose had a vision of the little boy in his kilt, growing stiff and white and taut as his elder sister came into the nursery. For if the authorities could curb Flora's propensity for bullying they could not keep her from teasing her brothers, and she had always been an adept in malicious little pinpricks. And then Rose rebuked herself for the odd flush of rage which had assailed her, and remembered how Flora had become a mere joke to her brothers. Once out of the nursery they had united to tease and irritate her when she was tiresome – only a few weeks ago Rose had reproached herself for allowing it. Even death must not evade justice, and now if ever she must be fair to her daughter.

'Families don't talk about their love for each other, do they?' she said steadily. 'Mickie was very proud of all you did in the blitz, dearest. "Flora's a great girl," he said, I remember.'

'He was so generous – so beautiful and so brave,' mourned Flora. 'Percy's made me see it all so clearly lately. But he can't know now I was sorry, now he can never know. And poor Father! Like me he's got to bear the reproach of slighting our darling as well as grief at losing him!'

If this outpouring were the result of Percy's treatment, Rose could only wish, like the beggar in the Arabian story who released a jinn from a bottle, that someone would put the stopper on again for ever. It was with the utmost relief, not only for the distraction it caused but in view of his simplicity and sincerity, that Rose saw her husband come up the garden path. He might indeed feel truly today that she had need of him.

'What! Flora!' Stuart began, but he was soon cut short.

'Oh, please don't put me through another catechism. I've explained to Mummie that I had to rush to help and comfort her. And you too, Daddy, though you never loved him as she did!'

'Come upstairs, Flora dear, and we'll get your room ready,' Rose intervened. She could only venture on one glance at Stuart to implore pardon for Flora, but she felt he understood.

'Does Mrs Carr-Berwick know where you are?' demanded Stuart abruptly.

'I think I left a message! Oh, my dears, don't bother over these tiresome details. I came because my heart told me to! Of course if I'm in the way –'

But Rose had gently shepherded Flora to the stairs before Stuart could reply, as seemed but too probable, with a simple affirmative to the last suggestion.

There was always a great deal of Flora about the house, Tom had said. This evening her hat and gas-mask and gloves covered the hall chest, her suitcase was in the library, her fur coat on the landing, her voice and step and a scent of bath salts and steam all over the top landing. Yet when Rose escaped and knocked cautiously on her husband's door she realised that Flora had in truth helped them this evening in a way she had certainly never dreamt of. For even in their bitter sense of loss, there was something conspiratorial and what the boys would call matey in their meeting, at last, for the moment alone.

'Oh, Stuart, I'm so sorry! I'd far rather be alone with you, but she means well and we must try not to hurt her!'

'She'd better hold her tongue about – about Mickie,' said
Stuart. 'Tell her I can't stand all that – and how on earth she can
have the face to talk!'

'I know! One can't begin to understand. Just try to think
she means well! But I do mind so dreadfully for you, my poor
old boy.'

'Oh, it's all the same anyway – no, that's not true. I'd
looked forward,' said Stuart with a great effort, 'to being alone
with you.'

'Oh, Stuart, really!' cried Rose, her self-control failing her
at last. 'In spite of everything?'

'In spite of what?' asked Stuart in his most matter-of-fact
voice again, turning to his dressing-table. Flora might, on a
sudden impulse, come rushing out of the tower of her reserve,
as she had appeared out of the library window, but never,
never would that be Stuart's way. If for a moment Rose had
hoped that they might lay aside the reserve of years and that
she might ask his forgiveness for all the unacknowledged
failures of the past, and that together they might cross hands
over that slow invisible current, and step out together on a
safe bridge of confidence, she knew at once that her hope was
vain. It was not in her husband's nature to recognise, or if he
recognised to admit, such intangible, sluggish depth below
their conventional relationship of trust and friendship. She
must suffer from Flora's outspokenness and steel herself to
endure while her daughter's rough hands dragged out and
dissected the past, the past which should surely have been
sacred just for one day to her and her boy. And she must steel
herself to realise that the only way to closer friendship with

her husband lay in denying herself the luxury of any words of reconciliation or love, or any reference to the faults of the past.

'Oh just my mistakes and – my inefficiency,' she replied vaguely. 'But it comforts me to feel you were glad to get back, for I do need you so very badly, Stuart, now and always.'

That was as far as she dare go tonight. The doors and windows of Flora's house were flung wide open now, but Stuart still looked out through only a mere crack in his door. But it was open and with that she must be content. And Flora would soon go off, banging doors and gates, to her new life, so they must bear with her this evening, and endure her fits of sobbing sympathy, her self-accusations, and her tempestuous efforts to cook and care for them. Part of her time at least was spent in conversations on the telephone, with her fiancé to begin with, and then with Grannie Carr-Berwick. Mercifully it transpired that Grannie's hotel would be a convenient base in the west for meeting the Major, so she proposed to return to the tyrant in two or three days – 'when my mother can spare me!'

So the evening wore on till Rose was alone at last, and could steal up to Mickie's room, to gaze from his windows at the stars so very far away, in the silent scented darkness of the spring night.

CHAPTER THIRTEEN
REBUILDING

They walk in the city
Which they have builded,
The City of God
From evil shielded.
Robert Bridges

There is no greater mistake in wartime than to try to look forward into the future. That optimists were disappointed and pessimists justified seemed to Rose to sum up the history of the last two years, except that optimists and pessimists had been equally wrong in their forecasts as to where the blows of the enemy would fail or succeed. To Rose in her great grief it seemed strange that even Stuart should share a certain spirit of optimism at the beginning of May 1942 when one by one the strange fairylands of the East were stripped from us, Malta lay a scarred wounded body in the Mediterranean, and all the might of Germany was mustering against Russia. It was best, she decided, to think as little, hope as little, fear as little as possible. And yet inconsistently, though life seemed over for her, in her private life she found she must set some little goal before her or she could not go on at all.

'When Iona comes back' was one little hill on the horizon. At times it might only seem a Calvary; and yet there must be some comfort in having near her again the girl whom Mickie had loved, who had given him such happiness. But Iona lingered on at Bindleton, in Linda's charge, loath to leave the officers and wives who had known and loved her husband and to break the last link with the short weeks of her married life. 'When Flora is married' was another and a wholly desirable goal. For it seemed doubtful, in view of Flora's relations with Grannie, whether the Major's feverish search for rooms would be successful before the strange couple came to blows. After that there would be Tom's leave to look forward to, Rose told herself, with the sick apprehension that only too soon it would be embarkation leave. And after that? There would still be Stuart to help and comfort, it was true, but apart from that there would be nothing but daily, wearisome drudgery in the house till some unimaginable dream of peace, too late to save her sons. It was wicked, she told herself, to see that vista as so wearisome and monotonous. She ought to feel glad and thankful that so dear a home was left to her. And in the end she might have saved herself the pain of such anticipations and such self-exhortations, for her house was not left to her after all.

It was only a chance bomb, jettisoned at random by some heedless boy, which fell on one misty evening in May on the Laws House. 'Little damage and no casualties' was the official report locally of so minor a catastrophe in the public estimation.

There were no casualties because the house was empty. 'And to think if we'd stayed on with her we'd just have been murdered in our beds – and that!' said Jessie to Catrine. 'It just shows you what service is!' The family were absent, because the Major had managed to find his rooms in Achraig, and Flora decided to join him and be married in the little West Coast town at once.

'I won't be married in Castleburgh,' she had said. 'It would be much more fuss for you, and I should almost have to ask that hateful old Grannie!' Such details as had escaped of that great duel between the two Old Men of the Sea filled both families with unholy mirth, and Rose often wondered if Grannie declared, as Flora did frequently, that she would never be selfish again now that she knew how damnable a selfish person could be. If it seemed perhaps a little selfish to drag all her family, and Tom on a day's leave as well, over to the west of Scotland to assist at her wedding Flora never discovered it. For the truth was obvious that but for this arrangement her parents must almost inevitably have lost their lives in the catastrophe.

'It was psychic my bringing you all here, simply psychic,' said the bride in an awed voice, when the news arrived very inopportunely at the luncheon to which they all sat down after the wedding ceremony in the pleasant little old straggling hotel.

'A bit of luck, certainly,' said Stuart, but that mask of age and despair had settled upon his features again. Was he really glad, Rose wondered, or was he tempted to feel, like her, that if even now they had been at Laws, they might be lying down in 'that sleep which knows no waking', the dream which had so often seemed so desirable in the utter exhaustion of the last three months? 'Why, we might be stuck trapped and pinned down in the basement at this moment,' he added reflectively, however, showing that his thoughts were made of sterner stuff.

'It's so strange that I should have saved your lives when I have so often made you all so unhappy!' said Flora in the same awed voice, her face as pale as the cream jersey suit she wore, her eyes dark with horror and many memories.

'Pity you didn't save the house while you were about it,' put in Tom irreverently, 'you being such a prophet and all. And as a matter of fact, wasn't it Percy here who fixed the date?'

'It's real sad to think of that historic and delightful little residence being lost,' said the Major. 'Though I'll say I shall always feel that it was Flora who, under Providence, saved your lives.' A look of such perfect love and trust passed between the newly married couple that even now Rose's heart gave a little leap of joy. Every shadow had departed now from her fear of their future, and that queer interview with the Major seemed only a dream.

'Oh, people matter so much more than things,' she said a little incoherently, thinking with joy that her daughter had reached a safe haven at last; 'Does Ian say if it has all been absolutely destroyed, though?' Through her mind raced oddly a review of things which were lost to her for ever: 'Not sensible things,' as she told Linda afterwards. 'The album with snapshots of the children was worst because it couldn't be replaced – and Mickie's school and college groups, but I remember thinking I could replace them, and then such silly things like my books or things I've hoarded like soap and hairpins and face-cream, before I even began to realise that I'd never see my dear drawing-room again. It's odd that you can hardly feel more about total loss than about losing your bag in the train!'

'The police are allowing no one inside the garden walls yet,' replied Stuart. 'Those are still standing, oddly enough. The men wouldn't even let Ian in as my representative. It seems to have been an HE which exploded harmlessly in the flower-beds.'

'Hurrah! Mum's garden vindicated at last!' said Tom triumphantly, though his face was rather white. 'You won't have to dig it up there for years and years after such a turn-up.'

'Ian gathers that the new wing was utterly destroyed; most of the building was simply flung down on to the drying-green below. Ian says you can still see the exterior of the old house from the road, though he imagines it must be a complete wreck inside anyhow. Look here, it seems as if we could get through to Castleburgh if we leave by this 3.15. It's the train you've got to get for Glasgow anyhow, Tom, so we can go together. But I'm sorry you shouldn't have a peaceful night here, Rose, unless you'd like to stay behind?'

But Rose was equally possessed with the certainty that she must hurry back, even if there was nothing left to hurry back to.

Never, she thought, had she passed a stranger hour than that in the little unknown town, when Flora and the Major had driven off, their radiance hardly dimmed by their sympathy, and she strolled with Tom, their packing done, down to the pier of the fishing village. Mist hung over the pale desolate hills behind them and the grey loch beneath. The sluggish yellow seaweed heaved in the faint rise and fall of the tide. On the grey high road and by the grey loch there was nothing to show which way the seasons flew. Here they seemed to stand in an isolated moment of life, devoid of past or future alike, connected by no ties of this visible world at all.

'Poor snails without our shells,' she said, remembering her old thoughts.

'Poor Mums, house-bound no longer,' laughed Tom. 'Have you lost a tyrant or a friend?'

'How can I tell? Half of me feels like that Traherne thing – do you remember:

It was my David's tower
  Where all my armour lies,
The fountain of my power
  My bliss, my sacrifice.

No, that's exaggerating, but it was our home after all, even if it bullied me. It's your father I mind for most –'

'I don't suppose he minds so much now that he hasn't Mickie to leave it to,' said Tom.

'But there's you, Tom!' whispered Rose, with a two-edged sword in her heart at that thought.

'Oh well, perhaps! Anyway, perhaps it's time old things were cleared off out of the way. You know Mickie and I never cared awfully for old houses and cathedrals and such – I didn't know many fellows who did, to tell the truth. Just as well not to be too keen on architecture nowadays, though I must say the people with a taste for ruins have it all their own way just now. Hullo, there's Daddy!' Tom stopped and gave an appalling whistle as he saw his father coming down towards the desolate pier. 'Here we are, busy trying to console each other, Papa.'

'Least said, soonest mended,' suggested Stuart with raised eyebrows.

'Oh no, I'm sure the Major would say Mums should talk it all out at once, and you too, Papa. I expect he thinks you're hopping with inhibitions! I can't say I can think of any consolation really, except that the lighter one travels nowadays the better.'

'Well, one's got to have a roof over one's head,' suggested Stuart. It was a relief to see that he could speak out to his son.

'But perhaps ours was too big,' suggested Rose. 'I've thought sometimes lately that we should all have got on better if we couldn't all have got away, as it were, into our own houses. Think how you used to shut yourself up in your room to keep your books and collections safe from Flora, Tom. And think how Flora shut herself up in her room to sulk. And I'd sit in the drawing-room – ' but there Rose's voice failed her, for in the holidays she had not often sat there alone. For Mickie was always hovering about the radiogram, and even when his friends came in they would laugh at her and tell her not to be silly when she got up to go away to leave them alone. 'We might all have quarrelled more but we should have saved ourselves so many, many misunderstandings – ' She paused, fearing lest Stuart might feel she addressed herself too particularly to him. 'Now in old days when the house was just the tower,' she added hastily, 'the people in it couldn't have been so room-bound.'

'I should think not,' said her husband sardonically, 'as there was never less than ten in a family.'

'Hellish it must have been,' agreed Tom.

'Well, think of it another way. We're looking west, aren't we, now, right across the seas?' (And Rose stilled the voice in her heart which spoke of the Islands of the Blest which men had dreamt of from those shores long ago.) 'When Flora gets to America after the war she won't shut herself up in an old house full of old traditions and little rooms. She'll settle in some tiny place, all open to the sun and air and friends –'

'I don't imagine Percy will have a practice on a ranch,' protested Stuart with his usual common sense.

'More likely a furnished apartment as shut in as damn-all,' agreed Tom, 'way back in Nine Hundredth Avenue.'

'Oh dear, you're both of you very good for me,' laughed Rose.

'You're very good for us too,' said Stuart unexpectedly. 'You're taking this very bravely, you know, Rose.'

'I expect because it all seems so unreal,' admitted Rose, 'with just us three shut off in this unknown misty place, with no particular background or future. And it's true enough' – her voice changed – 'that possessions don't seem to matter much now.'

'That's what Mickie always said,' agreed Tom, flinging a stone idly into the water, 'that we all make too much fuss about possessions.'

'Did he? Oh dear!' Rose sighed as Stuart turned and

walked up sharply to the end of the pier, 'If only Daddy could bear to speak of Mickie! I'm afraid it was the way Flora would talk so – so dramatically of him!'

'He'd have hated all that sort of Flora's bunk,' Tom said easily, 'but Daddy's wrong too, I think. You see, Mums, if we're going to send all the chaps who get bumped off in this war into Coventry, we'll have precious few left to talk about. It hurts a bit at first, of course, and I was afraid it would hurt you too much, but it's what Mickie would like himself. He'd hate to be nothing to us but a stained-glass window, and I bet Iona will feel the same!'

'But, Tom, how do you think of him now, if you don't mind my asking you? No, I shouldn't have said that!'

'Oh, I don't mind. I often had it out with him. You can try to get all idea of time out of your head. That's a bit difficult but that's my line, or you can think of him as still having a job of work to do if you're inclined that way. There's no reason to deprive yourself of the great Perhaps in a world where the certainties are so ruddy awful. I say, Mums, it's a pity I wasn't a parson and then I could have made a better thing of this for you!'

But Rose pressed his hand to show that she did not want him different in any way. She recognised that every generation must have its own approaches to reality, and that her citadel of prayers and thoughts would seem meaningless to Tom. She did not suppose that she would ever reach even the same indefinite exchange of views with Stuart. Perhaps everyday men and women could never, she thought, share their spiritual visions easily together. It might be that the abstract logic and reasoning of a masculine mind was so far above the simpler faith of women, or was it perhaps that women, who dealt so persistently with satisfying the simplest needs of life, and in their own bodies nourished and brought forth life, were really in closer touch with spiritual truths? After all, it was in an occupied country, ground down beneath the heel of a world-wide empire, that women hurried, before men, to an empty tomb, and that a woman first looked up from a rock-bound tomb to see Life vindicated for ever. 'He said unto Martha . . .' she reminded herself, as Stuart called to them to come back to the hotel to collect their luggage. There was the bill to pay and the train to catch, and farewells to Tom to be said when they reached Glasgow. The strange misty hour of truce was over indeed, but out of it she and Stuart emerged, she realised, far closer together than before. They were bereft of the past by the loss of their son: the future seemed to them vanished with the last sight of Tom and the destruction of their home. But at least they clung together, poor shivering survivors of the wreck, as Stuart, settling down opposite to her in the corner of the railway carriage, said:

'Rose, I can't tell you how I admire your courage!'

'About the house? Perhaps it's only because it still doesn't seem true! It only comes in waves when – when I remember such silly things. Did I tell you, for instance, that Mrs Childe turned up to call on me two days ago? She'd seen our news in April and was sorry, and then when she saw the announcement of Flora's wedding in the papers she gave her lady notice, because she was glad to come back and show me my way about, if once that madam of a daughter of mine was out of the house! She didn't even ask if I wanted her – she just said she was sure the house needed her! I expect she turned up with an attaché case this morning, and I'm quite sure, Stuart, that she got past the wardens and had a good look-see. In fact I've no doubt, if they'd left her alone, that she'd have begun to rebuild the house! It's you who are brave, Stuart, you've lost so much, everything!'

'Not you!' said Stuart unexpectedly, with little apparent effort. 'It makes one think a bit, what might have happened last night. Suppose I'd been left alone, I mean, if you'd been killed – and by the way, I've promised the Major to have the doctor for you as soon as we get back, Rose. He doesn't think you're looking at all well!'

Rose repressed a smile. Stuart, a stoic over health himself, was always reluctant to admit that any of his family looked unwell. It took a bomb, evidently, to make him admit that his wife might be anaemic.

'I expect I need a rest, and I shall have only too much time for it now. I do feel dreadfully like someone who's been grumbling over a tiresome invalid and repents now she's dead. Oh, Stuart, it's all so far worse for you. Are you worrying dreadfully about your book?'

'Oh, that doesn't matter!' Stuart retreated into himself at once. 'After all, Tom isn't interested in it –'

But Mickie had been, was the thought in both their minds. He had often annoyed Stuart by his references to the *Book of Fossils* or the *Chronicles of the Kings of Fairlaw*, but he encouraged Stuart to read extracts from the pompous or humdrum diaries.

'I don't know whether to tell you now or not! Yes, I think I must! If the tower is still standing there's just a hope for your book! I didn't dare to confess it before – indeed that's why I didn't care to tell you about Mrs Childe's visit, you'd have been so horrified. She was so scandalised by the look of the library – and you know I'm still not much of a hand with a sweeper – that she insisted on what she called a good clear-up so that she could give it "a good thorough" today. She got down to it at once, so I went to the rescue of your papers. And I cleared all your manuscripts and most of the books on the floor, and put them in that oak chest in the dining-room. It has a lead lining, you know, so if anything's escaped that would have –'

And at that Rose stopped in surprise. For Stuart crossed to her seat and put his arm round her as he said, in a voice which showed how much the loss of the occupation of years had meant to him, 'Rose, you're the most wonderful wife any man ever had!'

Rose had dreaded her first sight of the house, and she had dreaded an interview with the doctor who had such a bad reputation for dragging out tonsils. But the two cancelled each other in reality, for the doctor ordered her to rest in a nursing home for a week (not without dark hints that there might be a trace of poisoning in her throat) and it was only, lying comfortably in bed, that she heard from Stuart the fate of their home. And though she begged to know the worst, the worst was not as bad as she had feared after all.

'It's been an odd business,' said Stuart. 'The bomb fell in your flower-beds as you know, and the blast had blown the whole new wing to bits. The outside wall of the turret adjoining it has been badly knocked about, but the rest of the old house stood up to it in the most extraordinary way. Of course there's not a pane of glass left and part of the roof has gone, and the interior is what Tom would call a shambles, but as far as I can make out from the outside the doors and mantelpieces, and even some of the furniture, are intact. There was still a vase of flowers by the fireplace and Lilias' portrait was absolutely untouched.' It was, Rose recognised, with pride and surprise, the first time that he had ever spoken of the portrait to her.

'That old chest,' Stuart went on, 'is absolutely intact, so I'll be able to do something with my book after all. Though I don't mean to shut myself up with it again in the same unsociable way, Rose dear! It seems they can shore up the turret without too much expenditure of labour, and Mrs Childe, who was on the scene of the disaster as you foretold, declared that when once they've cleared off the glass and plaster she'll have a cosy little home ready for you in no time. I fear she's specially pleased that your pantry has gone, and that you'll have to use what she calls that good kitchener in the basement. But as her husband has got a job in Lanark she means to come and establish herself with us altogether, I gather – "For though your lady means well," she told me, "nothing will ever make her really handy about a house".'

'Oh dear, what a defeat!' laughed Rose, her spirits rising incredibly at the prospect of having a home again after all, and a husband who was amused by and sympathetic with domestic details. 'But I must own that victory is sometimes to the vanquished! She'll give me plenty to do, but not too much, and the Fairlaws will live a feudal life in their fortress again!'

She could laugh with Stuart in the safe refuge of her nursing home, but it was no use to pretend that she did not dread the first sight of the house. And she hardly knew whether to be glad or sorry when she found that Stuart had arranged for Iona to come in their car and take her for the first time. 'She's nothing to do, poor child, Ian says,' explained Stuart, 'and she simply jumped at the idea of it when she got back yesterday. She was coming to see you anyhow.'

'It's marvellous that there's so much left!' That was her daughter-in-law's characteristic comment as Rose, trembling a little, pushed open the temporary gate in the faithful garden walls.

'Yes, the tower doesn't look so very different,' agreed Rose with careful composure, as they picked their way on a bridge of planks across a yawning chasm of earth, rubble, glass, and splinters. They had timed their visit for the workmen's dinner-hour, so the place was deserted. But after one glance into the porch Rose turned away from the indescribable havoc and mess within. She must not think of herself. She must not let Iona begin to imagine how this wreck of her home brought suddenly to her imagination the wreck of all the young beautiful bodies in the world. But she felt that Iona's calm childish eyes were fixed upon her and she looked up with a passable effort at a smile.

'I shouldn't have let you come till it was tidier,' she said. Iona was very pale and the dark lines under her eyes told of her wakeful lonely nights and many tears, but her smile was as cheerful as ever as she replied:

'Oh, but it's marvellous to think that Mickie's room is left, though I suppose we can't scramble up to it very well today. You were glad it was the new part that went, weren't you?'

'Yes indeed. I've thought once or twice that it was just fitting all that part should disappear, the Victorian comfort and complacent luxury, you know. What's left is just a sort of symbol of Scottish toughness and endurance and courage, isn't it? – the things you need to build any new world on.'

'That's just what Mickie would have said!' Iona had paid Rose the highest compliment she knew. 'He wasn't a bit keen on possessions, was he? But he'd like to think dear old simple things were left. Aunt Rose, let's camp out on this workmen's trestle. I do want to talk to you!'

The earthy deal board stood just outside the porch in the sunshine. For the moment they were sheltered from the cold east wind which had shrivelled the spring across Europe for six long weeks. It was tossing the radiant lances of a great elm-tree in a churchyard on the far side of the lane, but the roots had withstood the shock and blast, thought Rose. And there was some beauty, some spring left even in this desolate wreck of her garden, she discovered suddenly. For there by the wall one tiny spray of japonica still clung, its buds still opening cheerfully to the sun.

'Look, there are some flowers after all,' she said, as Iona put her warm, plump, childish hand on her arm.

'Yes, and there's a thrush looking round for some odds and ends for its nest,' said Iona, though it was a wholly matter-of-fact look which she gave to the wary, bright-eyed bird, which was hoping for something out of the wreckage for its own home. 'Isn't it a darling? And rather brave if you come to think of it. Aunt Rose, did Mummy tell you?'

'What, dearest? I haven't seen her yet, you know!' Rose's heart missed a beat as she turned to look at her son's wife.

'Didn't she? That was rather noble of her. I didn't know there was honour among mothers. Well, I expect you've guessed now!'

'Yes, I expect I have!' Rose restrained herself carefully from tears or comments. 'Iona – you know –'

'Yes, of course I do, darling! I partly stayed on down there till we were quite sure nothing was going wrong. You see, it does make all the difference, doesn't it?'

'Yes, all the difference,' answered Rose, staring as steadily as she could at the rosy buds on the ruined house.

'You see at first I couldn't believe that Mickie had really gone for always,' said Iona. 'Now I can feel he's only gone for a little and is coming back. He'd have thought it all a great joke, being a father I mean,' she added reflectively. 'I expect he and Aunt Lilias are awfully pleased about it. I always think of her as a sort of twin sister of yours, you know!'

'You think she knows?' asked Rose, not daring to ask the more direct question.

'Why, of course they do! People must know things in Heaven, nice things anyhow,' said dear simple Iona. 'That's why I try not to be too unhappy in case Mickie should know and mind. And we often used to talk about what fun it would be to have a baby, so I know just what he thinks about it.'

'I'd love to know what kind of things, if it's not too curious,' said Rose humbly.

'Oh, sometimes he'd say our children wouldn't have nearly such a good time as he had, but then we'd agree that after all they'll never grow up expecting life to be a sort of Eton and Harrow. That's why I liked what you said about this house so much. Mickie said we must get rid of the frills and keep the real stuff, which is the same thing, isn't it?'

'You're very brave, Iona, braver than I can be, I'm afraid, about a world that's destroyed and gone for ever.'

'Mickie said it was rather bogus anyhow,' replied Iona. 'Do you know, I read all through the christening service last night and it seemed to me to belong a lot more to a baby who'd got to grow up tough than one in a lace veil who was entered for Eton already. Though as a matter of fact, Mummy has a lovely veil,' ended Iona, descending from her unusual flight of eloquence with a laugh.

As if from very far away bells began to ring in Rose's heart as she and Iona began to exchange more domestic questions and answers about what Grannie Carr-Berwick would certainly refer to, they agreed, as the Great Event or the Little Stranger. But through it all and through her tremulous sense of happiness Rose's memories flew back to her own feelings so many years ago when she, like Iona, had looked forward to a baby in the last war. She too had felt that something of her husband would come back to life with her child: she too had talked to her Tim of that child's future. But such fears of bombs or invasion or even of defeat as must surely haunt even Iona's serenity at times were almost absent. Nor did she and

Tim ever really envisage any difference in the world in which their child would grow up. It would be a better one with no more wars, of course, but for the child they planned just such a career and home as those they had known, surroundings as beautiful and a life as secure and guarded as that they had enjoyed before the war. She had indulged herself in happy tremulous thoughts of motherhood, of course – she had seen herself travelling to Bethlehem and her babe as one born in a manger. But in her vision, she knew now, the manger was draped with embroidery, and nurses as well as guardian angels hung over it in adoration. Iona's baby would indeed probably come into the world in such surroundings, unless indeed the worst happened. Iona would be a young adoring mother with leisure to worship and deck her baby. But in the back of her mind would always be the other certainty of the future, the need of preparation, and the acceptance of a world without luxury or privilege.

'About Christmas, I hope,' Iona was saying and Rose's thoughts flew back to her first Christmas with her baby. Then her vision of the Epiphany had been of a train of gold-crowned, majestic oriental monarchs, laying rich gifts at the cradle as they cried: 'News, news of the Trinity, and Mary, and Joseph far over the sea!' while minstrels and maids stood forth on the floor. Now her thoughts were straying to the stark, shivering picture of a modern poet:

> . . . were we led all that way for
> Birth or Death? this Birth was
> hard and bitter agony for us, like Death, our death.

And then she blamed herself bitterly for her cowardice and selfishness. What matter if the world of the privileged and idle and cultured passed away? Its death would never cloud the lives of Mickie's child or his generation, because it would be impossible for them to imagine.

'I always thought it would be lovely to have a baby at Christmas,' she said.

'Lovely,' agreed Iona. 'It won't seem so cheeky somehow to hope then that he's going to help to make a new world some day.'

The workmen were coming in by the gate with a cheerful clatter, and at those last words Iona got up and held out her hand to help Rose to her feet, straight and smiling in the sunlight.

'Good morning, missie,' said the old foreman, smiling, as most people smiled at Iona. 'This is no' a sight for you! You should have waited to come till we'd got it all sorted. It'll be a home for you yet, though it'll never be the same place again.'

'Oh, I don't know,' said Iona. The thrush had flown away with a promising bit of fluff for its nest in its yellow beak, and her eyes were following it a little wistfully. 'Things can't always be the same, can they, and I expect we shall all love it when it's built up again.'

AFTERWORD

Winifred Peck was born in 1882, the third child of a clergy-man, Edmund Knox, who subsequently became suffragan bishop of Birmingham, and then bishop of Manchester. She was the second daughter of a family of six. All of them (except for Ethel, the eldest, who was deaf and rather slow) were exceptionally brilliant and scholarly, but the four boys, although they had tender hearts, could not express their feelings readily, sometimes not at all, so that they risked seeming cold or even indifferent. To Winnie this was never a problem. *Enter Winnie and kisses everybody* is a stage direction in one of her brothers' schoolroom dramas. At home she was the peace-maker, work-ing, at the age of eighteen, on her first book (a life of St Louis from which she earned £30) but ready, if necessary, to hurry downstairs and soothe away an argument, often theological, between the bishop and his sons. It was partly to get away from these disputes that, in the autumn of 1911, she married James Peck, a hard-working, honourable, Scottish civil servant. They had three sons, of whom the second died of TB during the war. The lost son, and the daughter she never had, are recurrent figures in Winnie's later novels.

House-Bound appeared in October 1942. When the Second World War broke out, James and Winnie were living in Edinburgh (the Castleburgh of the book). So, too, are Rose and Stuart Fairlaw – in Laws House, an ancient stone-built tower in the Old Town, to which has been added an elegant Victorian wing. During the years while their children had been at school, Rose and Stuart 'had been free of nine or ten rooms in the upper earth, while three women shared the exiguous darkness of the basement.' These three women had done all the work of the house between them, so that there was no need for the mistress to know so much about it as to wash up a teaspoon. Now, for the first time, Rose is facing life not only with fewer servants, but with no servants at all.

Winnie herself, up to the outbreak of the Second World War, had never contemplated such a thing. For their summer holidays, her father and stepmother had rented a series of country vicarages, but they always took the servants with them. Once, when there was a hitch in the arrangements, Ethel and Winnie dressed up as parlourmaids to serve lunch; their brother Eddie told the guests that unfortunately they were deaf and dumb. Winnie seemed to remember that this had caused her to drop the soup, but that otherwise the girls had carried on steadily to the very end, thus 'saving appearances'.

Saving appearances – as though they were more worth saving than reality – became the very heart of the matter. The mistress of the house (as in the twenties and thirties she was still called in *Mrs Beeton's Book of Household Management*) had to maintain a gallant, or perhaps ludicrous, fiction. She had to pretend that bells were answered, fires lit, potatoes peeled 'below stairs' without the least anxiety or strain, all the time knowing that if the system were to break down even for a single day she would hardly be able to manage, for she had never been expected or learned to do so. There was a feeling of the middle classes at bay. Manufacturers offered assistance – gas cookers, carpet-sweepers, custard powder – but there was a curiously sinister undertone in the phrase 'labour-saving devices'. In time, clothes and dishes would be taught to wash themselves, but that was not yet.

House-Bound opens at the end of 1941, in Mrs Loman's domestic agency in Castleburgh, crowded with indignant employers. They have come in vain: the former applicants have been called up, or have taken better-paid jobs in munitions. Loss, destruction, heartbreak, will come later, but for the moment the citizens of Castleburgh are faced with what seems to them a nightmare, an unendurable inconvenience. 'You must send someone round tonight without fail! You'll not be expecting me to manage my house myself!' And Mrs Loman, stung, replies, 'I don't know why not! Millions of women do just that!'

It is greatly to Rose's credit that with these words the revelation comes to her that she could undertake the work of the house by herself. But, surely, not at her age and in her position in life? 'Millions do.'

By 1942 Winnie had been writing fiction for more than twenty years, and knew exactly how to create a family whose links are close, but not quite what might be expected. Rose Fairlaw lost her young husband in the First World War, and has made a second, more sedate marriage with Stuart. She can't manage her own daughter, the dark, disagreeable, haughty (but pitiable) Flora. However, she cares passionately for Mickie, Stuart's delicate son by his first wife.

Rose and Stuart's own son is, fortunately, a cheerful, bespectacled philosopher. It might seem that all of them will have to face the prospect of looking after themselves, but that is not so. The whole burden falls on Rose. It never occurs to Stuart, for instance, from the beginning of the story to the end, to polish his own shoes. Mickie insists, so he says, on having a real lady, who's never done a hand's turn, for a mother. Stuart protests that 'people like you, leisured people, keep culture and beauty alive in the world.' But Rose has been struck by a vision of herself as belonging to an 'utterly useless and helpless' class of women. The war has made that painfully clear. Stuart is totally unbending. 'I can't have you opening the door to tradespeople!' Rose, on the other hand, is heroically unprepared to lower any of her former standards. She will do as millions do, but she will also do what they don't.

Laws, of course, is a household of the 1940s, without electric heating (someone has to get up early to light the range), without a washing machine or a dishwasher. The housework is done to be done again next morning, and cooking means hours of effort to produce something which is gone in three minutes. There are brass stair-rods, which must be polished, and endless ringing at the back door, which must be answered. There must be flowers on the table, 'for it had not yet occurred to [Rose] that you might eat and sit in a room which had had no benefit of brush or duster.' The last words of Virginia

Woolf's diary for 8 March 1941 are: 'Occupation is essential. And now with some pleasure I find that its seven; & must cook dinner. Haddock & sausage meat. I think it is true that one gains a certain hold on sausage & haddock by writing them down.' Rose has no such compensation. Life, day by day, develops into a wearing struggle between herself and the house. 'It was with new eyes that she scanned her home now, wondering if she could subdue it to her own control, or if it would get the better of her unmercifully.'

What unnerves her is the endless day-in, day-outishness of her new life.

'. . . everything in a house reminds you of something else you've got to do. You start up from the hall, and remember you must carry the laundry up, and when you're halfway you see you didn't dust the chest on the half-landing. And two steps higher up you remember you left the apples stewing and must run down to take them off. And that reminds you that you must tele- phone to the greengrocer, and while you're doing that you remember you ought to fill up the salt-cellars, and when you take them to the dining-room you see the flowers are dead, or you didn't finish polishing the floor that morning . . . And of course... none of these things are of any sort of use to the world at all, and yet I suppose they've got to be done!'

Rose is soon at the point of collapse. But with a fine stroke of irony the employment agency, relenting, sends her a daily help, Mrs Childe. 'In a revolution Mrs Childe would rise to any heights, while Rose herself would sink to any depth.' For a shilling an hour she undertakes to train Rose, who up to now hasn't been sure whether you wash vegetables with soap, into a passable 'upper-servant'. The work is now done thoroughly, but it takes Rose the whole of her day, and leaves her, she feels, irremediably dirty and tired.

'Believe me . . . the days of feudal domestic service are over. Now, tell me, Mrs Fairlaw! How do you propose to re-organise your house?' Major Percy Hosmer, from Cleveland, Ohio, breaks into the story, representing the new energy and shock of the arrival of American troops in Britain. The Major is a comic creation on a grand scale and we look forward to his appearances, but he is also a powerful solver of problems, appearing at moments of most need, a partly magical figure, like the Admirable Crichton, able to adapt to any conditions while remaining always himself. In this capacity he finds the answer to all Rose's immediate difficulties, producing a perfect fried sole and even doing the washing up, but also facing the crucial question of Flora.

He has met her before (Winnie allows herself this coincidence, which we accept readily because of the Major's oddness). This was when he had been stationed at Eastminster, where Flora had been working with a Red Cross unit and had shown gallantry, even heroism, in the Blitz but then, presumably as the result of a breakdown, had become his patient. Percy Hosmer has been trained, he tells Rose, as a psychiatrist (though he is referred to later as a psychoanalyst). About the whole question of the study of psychology Winnie, though

deeply interested, had her doubts. 'Of the work which psychiatrists are doing for defective, nervous, delinquent and
subnormal infants it would be impossible to speak too highly,'
she wrote in her autobiographical volume *A Little Learning*.
However, the average parent is left simply with the belief that
repression and discipline are bad for the young, 'as indeed
they often used to be'. But movies, comic strips, cereal packets,
the whole overwhelming tide of amusement, deprives children
of one powerful and beneficial influence – the need to develop
their own games, which requires, above all, imagination. In
the Manchester playroom no one ever dreamed that the
'young people' needed any amusement beyond being
together, 'and indeed', Winnie recollected, 'they did not'.

Flora, on the other hand, had cost vast sums at a school in
Sussex, learning bee-keeping and Greek dancing, javelin-
throwing and the care of pigs, and 'all those other activities
vaguely classed as forms of self-expression.' As the Major puts
it, 'she did give me the privilege of hearing the story of her
inner life, and sad hearing it was too', although so distorted
as to be barely recognisable. Rose, as Flora's neglectful and
even uncaring mother, had come out as the villain of the
piece. Perhaps Winnie herself did not realise how much she
disliked Flora.

In contrast to Flora, of course, is Iona, 'dear simple Iona',
whose courage is of a different kind. Courage, which always
gets Percy Hosmer 'right down where I live', is something to be
studied in *House-Bound*, taking as it does such varying,
sometimes grotesque, forms. Impossible not to feel some kind
of unwilling admiration, for instance, for Grannie Don't Chah

See, who sweeps off to her afternoon rest saying that she has the sense to keep herself well for the sake of the country, or for the indefatigable organiser of Women's War Effort, Cousin Mary. Rose and Linda correctly think of Grannie Don't Chah See as a relic of feudalism, and Cousin Mary – always right, which is what makes her such a trial – as belonging to the transition stage of women, 'when they had to be rather uppish and self-consequent to be noticed at all.' But it is something, after all, to represent a historical period. Linda and Rose, it's true, have to bear agonising loss. Grannie and Cousin Mary do not. Nor do they have to do their own housework, but we can see that neither of them would easily accept defeat.

In the 'Martha' chapter, Winnie modulates from comedy to what was most serious to her. In the Gospels, in John XI, it is to Martha (the same Martha that Luke describes as too busy with 'much serving' to sit and listen like her sister Mary) that Christ makes his gracious promise: I am the Resurrection and the Life. Winnie makes Rose hear, or at least comprehend, this text for the first time at a memorial service to which – except to please Stuart – she had not wanted to go. The words seem to stab her spirit awake. 'It was not the saintly Mary or the mystic disciple . . . who had been thought worthy of those words which still arrest mourners of every creed, or no creed at all.' This is the justification, or perhaps the sanctification, of the laundry and the brass-polishing. It dawns on Rose, a Mary by temperament, that all service ranks the same with God.

Many readers might find these passages sentimental in treatment, but Winnie was in no way afraid of sentimentality.

In *A Little Learning*, which is about her education at Wycombe Abbey and Lady Margaret Hall, she speaks of 'that emotional, semi-mystical and literary sublimation which is, of all others, I think, safest and happiest for a girl in the formative years of life.' 'Safest' seems debatable, but Winnie would not have said it if she did not mean it.

Nor would she have allowed herself these speculations if they hadn't been corrected, at every stage of her life, by a sharp sense of the natural and the probable. Consider the married life of Rose and Stuart. After a short escape to London she comes back to Castleburgh to find Stuart 'fumbling with his latchkey . . . like another gaoler with his chains, for it was after all Stuart's food and Stuart's comfort which added so appallingly to the burden of the house.' Stuart, with his solid law practice, his calm but useful war work, his set ways (home at seven for his bath and drink, retreat to his study after dinner to smoke his pipe and sort out yet more papers for his achingly dull history of the Fairlaw family), his fixed opinions, his raised eyebrows – what kind of a partner has he been to the dreaming Rose? Mightn't a novelist be expected, after the losses and disasters they share, to bring them closer together?

> 'I'd looked forward,' said Stuart with a great effort, 'to
>   being alone with you.'
> 'Oh, Stuart, really!' cried Rose, her self-control failing her
> at last. 'In spite of everything?'
> 'In spite of what?' asked Stuart.

Confession and reconciliation are luxuries which Rose is not allowed. In any case, Stuart has no idea what she is talking

about. But change must come. The idea of *not* being house-
bound, of living free, has its symbolic value of which Winnie,
without over-insistence, keeps us in mind. Human beings, it
seems to Rose, are confined by invisible locks and bolts within
their own memories and the inhibitions with which they
have grown up. We can't deliver ourselves. How are we all to
get out?

For that, Rose will need the courage which, in spite of some
despairing moments, she has shown from the first. 'What
young people have now is what we never had, freedom in our
own homes,' Winnie wrote in *Home for the Holidays*, 'though
how sadly true is the old picture of its price as perpetual vigi-
lance. But any over-worked mother should, I think, comfort
herself with the knowledge that her children are not going
to worry if home and housekeeping have not the exquisite
finish we once knew.' There is nostalgia here, Winnie would
never have denied that. But there is also the confidence
to leave the past where it belongs and to make a reasonable
job of the future.

Penelope Fitzgerald,
Highgate, 1999